Photograph by Hannah Jackson

Marc Gee has written over eleven stage plays which have been performed at The Edinburgh Festival and Everyman Theatre, Liverpool to name a few. In 2001 one of his plays Al's Lads was made into a full-length feature film and premiered by BAFTA at The Cannes Film Festival. Presently the film has been sold to over twenty two countries world wide. Marc has lectured in theatre, film and writing novels at various institutions throughout the country, such as book clubs, prisons, universities, colleges, the BBC, literary festivals, primary and secondary schools. This is his second novel.

Marc's third novel will be published in 2011 and is titled, *'Have you heard about Alex Sinner?'*

BY THE SAME AUTHOR

Plays
UC – DAI – LOI
Al's Lads
We Three Kings
Pablo
Fredonia
The Swim Home
Bunty the Bouncer
Strange Ways
Knock Em Dead
Just a Simple Man
HMS THETIS

Film
Al's Lads

Novels
Autumn Kill

DECLARATION OF GUILT

Marc Gee

Copyright © 2011 Marc Gee

The moral right of the author has been asserted.

Apart from any fair dealing for the purposes of research or private study, or criticism or review, as permitted under the Copyright, Designs and Patents Act 1988, this publication may only be reproduced, stored or transmitted, in any form or by any means, with the prior permission in writing of the publishers, or in the case of reprographic reproduction in accordance with the terms of licences issued by the Copyright Licensing Agency. Enquiries concerning reproduction outside those terms should be sent to the publishers.

Matador
5 Weir Road
Kibworth Beauchamp
Leicester LE8 0LQ, UK
Tel: (+44) 116 279 2299
Fax: (+44) 116 279 2277
Email: books@troubador.co.uk
Web: www.troubador.co.uk/matador

ISBN 978 1848766 297

British Library Cataloguing in Publication Data.
A catalogue record for this book is available from the British Library.

Typeset in 11pt Times New Roman by Troubador Publishing Ltd, Leicester, UK
Printed and bound in the UK by TJ International Ltd, Padstow, Cornwall

Matador is an imprint of Troubador Publishing Ltd

*For my dear
Mother and Father.*

FOREWORD

In Marc Gee's second novel, *Declaration of Guilt*, I found the raw talent developed further from the fine standard first seen in *Autumn Kill*. My encounter of Marc Gee's first novel was through a recommendation while undertaking my doctoral studies in Criminology. The insight I received complimented my academic research giving a more balanced and wider picture than that developed by academic tomes.

Marc Gee has certainly stepped up a notch in his story telling. The smooth transition from past to the present in *Declaration of Guilt*, and the pull of 'cell 43' is a sly touch.
A gripping pathological genre of classic fiction.

Dr Cushla M Allison, Criminal Profiler.

"Whoever undertakes to set himself up as a judge of Truth and Knowledge is shipwrecked by the laughter of the gods…"
Albert Einstein.

KLAUDIA MATYJAS
AGED 30
POLISH
NOVEMBER 1946

CHAPTER ONE
And so it began on that winter's night in November 1946.

Opposite the giant brick walls of Wawel Castle a dishevelled young man found refuge in the shadows of a dreary café. Warming himself with a bowl of stew and slices of stale bread he sat in a shadowy corner; his thin gaunt features partially lit by candlelight. In the past couple of weeks that he had been in Krakow he had eaten very little. Gorging the food, glancing from side to side, he had learnt to be vigilant and was self conscious of who might be watching. Poland, like the rest of Europe, was struggling to recover from the war. Suspicion was wide spread; tuberculosis rife and the blood of its people still fresh on its pavements. It was a dangerous place.

Washing the last of the stew down with black coffee and a shot of vodka, he had worked everything out to the finest detail and worked out his strategy on the back of a napkin; street map; time; logistics and transport, there could be no slip ups when planning the perfect murder.

Klaudia Matyjas had waited-on hundreds of men; young

and old, since the end of the war. The young man sitting alone in the corner of the café was just another hungry face to her. She had no idea of the evil that was taking place under her nose. Mesmerised by her pale, thin face and the tattooed numbers running up her arm he watched her fragile frame glide from table to table, collecting dishes, glasses and giving the odd slap to a man who fancied his chances. From the inside of his leather satchel he removed a tobacco tin containing thin sticks of charcoal and a small sketch pad. Tearing a piece of paper from the pad, he started to sketch intensely. Occasionally rubbing the tip of his index fingers across the rough surface of the paper, he took another shot of vodka, his hand slowly taking on a life of its own as the portrait of the waitress came to life in front of him.

Then the blackness of the night drew in. One by one the candles were pinched out by the café's owner. "Move your arses you night owls. My bed is calling." Unnoticed the young man left discreetly. Pulling up the collar of his coat around his neck he shivered in the doorway of the café. Across the street a skirmish broke out between two bundled-up men. As their fists swung into each other a bottle smashed. More blood. It was nothing new. Looking over his shoulder his brown eyes peered through the frosted glass of the café door as he watched the waitress struggle with a tray of dirty dishes through the swing door of the kitchen.

Stepping into the street, a blustery wind twisted around the young man, swirling icy snow around his boots. Head first into the cutting wind he walked across the frozen pavements of the city, oblivious to the burning embers of cigarettes in the dark doorways. For the past two weeks he had paid a scrupulous landlady for a room of squalor on the east side of Krakow. She asked no questions and that was how he liked it. Money talked for a silent tongue as well as food in Krakow. That night, as he listened to the groans of the prostitute through the thin wall of his room, he concocted his plan and worked out his next step. The next step that would change his life forever.

The following morning he trudged through the thick snow under the shadow of the majestic St Mary's Basilica. Across the medieval Market Square, which once held public executions, he paused briefly to look at the nativity statues before leaving the busy square. Continuing down the cobbled road of Brodsky, he passed a line of women each selling a single loaf of bread, their bodies and faces drained of strength. Turning left onto the main street of Stradomska he passed numerous wooden shutters concealing the odd smoky cafe once frequented by boisterous German soldiers and shops selling curiosities left over from the occupation. Strolling through the Jewish district of Kazimierz, the paint peeled facades of the crumbling buildings were a stark reminder of the poverty that still gripped the city. After devouring a small loaf, which he bought from a street vendor, he headed towards the glare of the frozen River Wista. It was a prehistoric reminder. Suddenly feeling light headed he stopped to regain his breath. Feeling weak after walking for over an hour in the snow he considered taking a tram but decided to continue and found himself on Pitsudskiego Bridge. Looking across the river towards the south bank he made out the industrial area of Podgoze which during the war had been the Jewish ghetto where over sixty five thousand Jews had been incarcerated.

Crossing the bridge he looked down at the frozen river, its glare blinding. Wandering around aimlessly, he kept going, the slog of the deep snow seeping the strength from his legs. Podgoze was littered with derelict buildings. An ideal place; discreet; deserted. Apart from the odd, bent over figure, there was no sign of life. Committing the area to memory he blindly followed a brick wall and came across an abandoned building.

Throwing his shoulder against the rotting wooden gate he forced it open and slipped inside. A snow covered courtyard opened up before him. At the far end a brick storeroom with dilapidated wooden doors. As he walked he slipped on the cobbles underfoot. His heart raced. His breathing heavy.

Inside the storeroom the air smelt of rotting earth and dried blood. Feeling a cold gust of wind on his neck he looked up and saw that part of the roof had collapsed. Open to the elements he watched for a few seconds as the heavy, grey clouds hung in the sky. Around the walls, thick iron rings were embedded into the rust coloured bricks. Running along the base of the wall was a stone trench leading to an iron grid. He surmised that the building had once held cattle. A slaughterhouse maybe? Poignant, the young man grinned, something he hadn't done for a long, long time. Maybe, this was the place he had been looking for; just maybe.

His eyes investigated further as a few feathers floated down from the pigeons scratching across the broken roof above him. Then his eyes gleamed. At the far end of the room was an identical wooden post with an iron ring fixed at the top. In the minutes that passed he had stood motionless. His mind returned to the previous week, and to Auschwitz. As a visitor to the death camp he had walked in the shadow of his hero as well as the electric fence. But it was being told about the execution of the Polish prisoners that held his imagination. Over 7,000 Polish prisoners of war were held captive in Auschwitz, the majority being tortured beyond imagination. Tagging on to a small group from Israel who had travelled from the Middle East as homage to their murdered relatives, they were given a tour of the camp by one of the survivors, a proud but haggard man in his forties, whose eyes bled with nightmares. His words were brittle, choked, the visitors weighed down with guilt. Their tears flowing like the tears of their own flesh and blood.

Led inside one of the brick buildings the group made their way down the stone steps to the torture bunker and took a sharp intake of breath. A line of iron doors ran either side of a long dark tunnel. Inside, one of the cells had been bricked into tiny compartments with a small, iron door at the base. Explaining the horror, the guide described how the Polish prisoners were made to strip then crawl on their hands and knees through the door. With no room to move, sit or lay down the prisoners had little choice but to stand upright through the blackness of the night. Stagnant air filtered through a tiny hole in the brickwork as they stood in their own vomit, urine and faeces. The following day these men were then expected to work an eleven hour day. An early death was imminent. As the allies marched through Europe, the Nazis fast-tracked the trials of the emaciated Polish prisoners. Above the atrocities of the cells was a room where the Nazis held a kangaroo court. Standing in front of a wooden desk the Nazis would pass judgment on the Polish soldiers. Their hearings took less then a minute. Sentenced to death, their bodies shook with terror as the thunder of bullets rained into their comrades bodies outside. Through the boarded up windows which hid the executions, death was only a few feet away where certain soldiers were to be subjected to another humiliating death.

The young artist was transformed.

The previous evening the waitress who had served the young man had taken pity on the hungry face by discreetly giving him a plate of dumplings out of view of the owner of the café. Food was scarce, a valuable commodity.

Lying in wait he followed her as she left the café. After turning a few corners and walking a number of streets, she became conscious of the crunching footsteps in the snow behind her.

Swinging round with a venomous look, her slight hands clenched into tight fists. "Why are you following me?"

"I'm sorry. I didn't mean to scare you."

"What do you want?"

"I wanted to give you this." From the inside of his satchel he presented her with her charcoal portrait. His hand shook. "I did it of you in the café last night. I hope you don't mind?"

"Why are you following me?"

"I'm not; I thought you might get into trouble if you were seen taking it from me."

Looking at the portrait she felt flattered but weary. Focusing her stare back at him her voice remained hard. "I have no money for this. Is that what you want?"

"I don't want any money."

"What do you want then – sex I suppose?"

The words stumbled out of his thin lips. "No, it was the last thing on my mind."

"Liar, all men want sex."

"I'm not a liar." Embarrassed, he could feel the cheeks of his face starting to flush.

"What do you want then?"

"Nothing."

"Nothing is nothing! Everyone wants something."

"It was for the dumplings."

For the first time her face transformed with laughter lines. "You want me to believe it was for a plate of dumplings that even the cat wouldn't eat."

"It's the truth."

"There is no truth left in this city, the Nazis took it with them when they left. You're not from Krakow?"

"No."

"Where are you staying?"

"Across the river." He was lying.

"It is too cold to talk out here. I have vodka if you want to come?"

Avoiding her eyes with his as if not to give the wrong impression she set off; headlong into the snow drift and the hushed streets.

It wasn't what he had planned, but he was only too happy to follow.

At the end of a small park a line of houses were stacked upon each other. Stamping the snow from their boots on the front step of the house they entered. Inside it was darker than dark. A wooden staircase circled its way up through the decaying building. As he followed, the stairs creaked, the smell of damp laundry patting his face. Reaching the second floor their shadows merged into one. Taking hold of his hand she guided him along the landing. From behind doors he heard coughing; a baby crying; a heated exchange. She said something, he didn't hear; his heart louder than her voice, words replaced with the sound of a key turning in the lock. Pushing open her door the waitress struck a match to an oil lamp. A honey yellow glow crept out onto the landing and cut lines across his face.

"Are you going to stand out there all night or are you going to come inside."

Stepping inside the room he closed the door behind him. Gradually his eyes adjusted to the drabness. He made out a makeshift bed rolled out on the bare floorboards, a chamber pot and the only furniture in the room, a wooden stool and a small chest of drawers which rested in the dark corner. It was a damp and miserable place.

"It's up to you whether you take your coat off. I usually get into bed then take a layer of clothing off at a time." Standing with his back to door he was paralysed with the thought of sex and murder. Slipping out a bottle of vodka from under her coat like a magician she poured the vodka and handed the glass to the youth. "Thank you for my sketch. I look pretty in it." She drank the vodka in one and poured herself another.

"You are pretty."

"I used to be."

She had few possessions and was a saint as he played the martyr. Her black, circled eyes enveloping him as he stood lost. She crept under the blankets. Knocking back the spirit, he then removed his coat and knelt down as a lingering cold gripped the room. Sliding underneath, they pulled the blankets up around their necks. Pouring another shot of vodka they drank and held onto their glasses for warmth. The youngster looked at her perfect, white profile. It was as if her face had been carved out of ivory. Painstakingly words were replaced by loneliness and desire. Holding his face in the palms of her hands she pulled him towards her. Kissing for the first time, the grey smoke of their breath became one as it floated over their faces. Her lips were rough on his but they tasted sweet and strong from the vodka. Unbuttoning their clothes, they afforded a sad smile as they fumbled in the cold. Both craved affection. Cocooned with warmth their hands slipped around each other's waists. Her body was older than his and smelt of fruit, his of a thousand mile journey. She was like a skeleton. Under her skin he could feel her ribs as she rolled on top of him and straddled him with her long legs, the fringe of her short black hair dropping down over her face. Writhing in ecstasy, her nails dug into his chest. They kissed again. Moving his hands from the sweep of her back he swept them up across the ripples of her rib cage to the nipples of her petite breasts. Whisking his hands up to her shoulders he clasped them onto the back of her neck and pulled her down towards him. She could feel him shaking and knew he was inexperienced. Taking control she touched his lips tenderly with her fingertips and smiled down at him; tears dropping from her black eyes onto the cheeks of his baby face.

One final kiss my love. His virginity lost. Her hope momentarily restored.

As dawn crept through the tiny window of the room the body of Klaudia Matyjas lay in the arms of the young artist like a broken puppet. All day he had sat cross-legged on the wooden floor; his body covered in dry sweat. Shaking and silent, he had become obsessed with the tattooed numbers on the arm of the woman. Those numbers had driven him into the desires of darkness. Through the window he watched the flakes of snow with a dry throat and a throbbing head from the night's vodka. It had been the second time he had been drunk. Not only with the vodka but with lust and pent-up hate that boiled inside him. Before the room once again disappeared into the darkness of the night he inscribed into her arm his own trade-mark.

In the early hours of the morning as the snow turned to drizzle the murderer sneaked out of the run-down building, dragging the woman's body behind him. Wrapped in one of the blankets which they had made love under the previous night, he lay the body onto a stolen wooden cart and scurried off like a rat into the warm morning sunshine.

Transporting the body through the streets of Krakow, the wheels of the cart rattled with the burden of the load. Pushing; heaving; his hands were frozen to the wooden handles of the cart and at any time he thought his fingers would snap in two. A person struggling with a cart in Krakow was nothing new. Nobody gave him a second's glance. Crossing the bridge over the River Wista, one of the cart's wheels became trapped in the tram lines. Panicking, a bare leg flopped out from under the blanket. Quickly covering up the body, two American soldiers appeared from nowhere and helped him release the wheel. They never asked questions. He didn't ask any.

"There you go buddy." Nodding a thank you and aware of the threat of danger he pushed the cart away.

As the sun cast an orange glow across Krakow the weary figure pushing the cart made it to the disused building. Dropping to his knees with exhaustion he looked down at his hands. His crippled fingers were sore and blistered and resembled the legs of two dead crabs which have been flipped onto their backs and left to bake in the summer's sun. Cupping them together, he brought his hands up to his mouth and blew. Looking at the bulge under the blanket, he could feel himself trembling. Laughing nervously; tormented tears filled his eyes. Now the fun would start. Although his hands would take a little longer to thaw out, the blood of a killer ran through his veins.

Removing the blanket from the body, he reflected on the night before. The couple never knew each other's names.

And so it began, on that cold winter night in Krakow on 23rd of November, 1946.

HEATHER WILSON
AGED 15
ENGLISH
OCTOBER 1946

CHAPTER TWO

The drunks who propped-up the bar of 'The Blazing Stump' in the East End of London were a mixture of granite-faced Dockers; prostitutes past their sell-by-date, and lost souls who had survived Hitler's Luftwaffe and The Blitz. Stale sweat mixed with black-market perfume cut through the haze of cigarette smoke which floated around the walls and scratched the surface of the sawdust floor, that over the years had seen its fair share of spit, broken glass and spilt blood. In the shadow of the docks, rows of bricked warehouses and flour mills ran either side of the ale house. Opposite, silhouetted against a full moon and black sky, stood the giant cranes of the shipyards. 'The Stump' was the natives home-from-home. They were people of the night and on this Friday night it was no different from the hundreds of other Friday nights when they had got drunk, threw a few punches, or hitched up their skirts down a back alley for a few extra shilling.

Through the pub window a flickering street light cut lines across Len Hutton's craggy face. Heavy-set, he sat alone on a bar stool sipping his pint, his eighth of the night. Watching the alcohol take hold around him he pulled on a Woodbine and coughed a chesty cough, a smoker's cough. Approaching sixty, he'd seen it all. An ex-merchant seaman, with a button nose, receding grey hair swept back over his head and nestled on the shoulders of his leather jacket. Crooked yellow-teeth, stained from years of nicotine, matched his yellow shirt and his baby-blue eyes could convey a thousand sea-faring stories. From fist-fights in Hong Kong through to feeding basking sharks in the Straits of Gibraltar. As the calluses on his large hands wrapped around his pint, something caught his attention out the corner of his eye. Swivelling around on his bar stool he leant forward and wiped the condensation from the pub window with the palm of his hand. Squinting through the blackness of the glass he struggled to focus through the reflections on the window and the glare of the streetlight. Outside in the shadowy cobbled street he saw a streak of light, it looked unnatural; surreal. Then the realisation of what it was hit him like a thunderbolt – as the hairs stood up on the back of his neck his eyes widened, a look of horror sweeping across his face. "Jesus!" Springing to his feet, the pint slipped from his grasp sending an explosion of beer and shattering glass across the wooden floor. Crunching the smashed glass under the soles of his leather boots he barged through the drunks, spilling beer in his wake. Someone shouted "fight!"

Usually, but not this time.

Crashing through the double doors of the pub Len was hit by the smell of the sea and a vision that would haunt him forever. A few hard-hitters looking for a piece of the action staggered after him and froze in disbelief. What seemed like a young teenage girl was engulfed in flames. Staggering across the road one of her shoes skidded across the polished cobbles; her high-pitched screams cutting through the air like a knife. More drunks fell out of the pub and watched as Len ripped off his jacket and stepped towards the human fireball. A trail of flames clung to the girl as she spun around in circles before smashing into a warehouse door. Crashing to the ground, her skull smacked the curb with a tortuous crack. Dropping his leather jacket over the burning girl, Len fell to his knees and started beating his hands on the epileptic body as it bounced violently up and down. A woman screamed. The smell of paraffin and burnt flesh poisoning the air. The palms of Len's hands started to burn as he frantically thrashed his jacket from the girl's head to her back, then down to her thighs and legs. After what seemed a lifetime the flames were eventually smothered. Len choked, his face smudged with black smoke, his eyebrows and eyelashes singed by the intensity of the fire. Defeated, his hands shook as he benevolently placed the jacket over the girl's head. Some of the women turned away, horrified by the sight of the girl's body and her screams which had now died along with her young life.

Exhausted, Len climbed to his feet and looked down on the body as it twitched for the last time. The palms of his hands were arid and strands of hair were entangled in his burnt fingers. Feeling dizzy, he could hear his chest wheezing as the air fought against the smoke in his lungs. Len was suddenly nudged to one side as the beer bellied Landlord tipped a bucket of water over the blackened, charcoaled figure. He was too late. The water brought hissing and a cloud of steam up into the cold night air. All that was recognisable was the girl's shoe resting in the gutter. A small black lace-up, and the hem of her smouldering flowery dress. The shrill of a policeman's whistle zipped into the ears of the huddled crowd. A baby-faced copper with short blond hair and acne, barged his way through the silent onlookers. "Police! Out of the way there. Let me through!" Looking down on the corpse, he whisked his hand across his mouth and nose as the smell of death drifted upwards. Turning white, his stomach churned. Spinning on the heels of his polished boots, he pushed his way back through the spectators. Falling against the pub door, his legs buckled as he curled forward and retched up his guts. He wasn't the only one. Overhead, the pub sign of 'The Blazing Stump' swung and creaked as a cutting wind blew. Paint peeled, the sign showed an old sea-dog slumped drunk in an armchair, a pewter mug of ale spilling out of his hand. His wooden stump in flames in the hearth of the open fire. Ironic.

A comforting hand patted the back of the policeman's shoulder as the heavy voice of the Landlord came from behind him. "You alright son?"

Wiping his mouth with the back of his hand the policeman slowly recovered. His eyes bloodshot and watery. Turning to a scruffy kid wearing a peak cap that shadowed his eyes, the Landlord spoke in an unyielding voice. "Go to the station as quick as your legs will take you lad and ask for the Desk Sergeant. Tell him what's happened here." The kid ran off, the tail of his coat flapping after him. His clumpy boots thumping across the cobbles.

"Come with me." The Landlord escorted the ashen-faced policeman into the deserted pub; macabrely a couple of drunken stevedores, oblivious to anything, were still slumped at the bar singing an out-of-key sea shanty. As the Landlord stepped behind the bar the policeman felt beads of sweat trickling down his brow. Running his hand across his forehead he caught his reflection in the mirror at the back of the bar and noticed a splatter of vomit across the shiny, silver buttons of his police tunic. As he brushed his hand down the front of his uniform, a shot of brandy was slid across the bar in his direction; he nodded a *thank you* at the Landlord's fat, ruddy face and knocked the spirit back in one. The brandy was harsh and caused him to take a sharp intake of breath. One-by-one the drunks filed back into the pub. Sober, mortified, lifeless eyes. Some of the women sobbing uncontrollably. Catching Len's gaze, the policeman turned his back as embarrassment turned into pent-up emotion which shuddered through his body. Gulping hard on the acid at the back of his throat he gripped the bar for support and found himself sobbing uncontrollably.

Into the blackness of the night Heather Wilson's family received a knock on the door. It was the Devil's knock. Within seconds, a sister, a brother and a mother's lives would be destroyed as the detective related the news about the grim discovery of their loved one. Asked to identify body, the girl's father stood over the charred corpse. His red eyes bled, scratched with tears. He could only recognise his beautiful daughter from the bottom of her flowery dress and a single ringlet of hair; matted and charred.

Breaking down he turned to the detective at the same time trying to find his voice. "Have you got him?"

"Yes sir. He was arrested this morning."

"Will the bastard hang?"

"He'll swing; we'll make sure he does."

GEORGE HARRIS
AGED 27
ENGLISH
OCTOBER 1977

CHAPTER THREE

1977
Thirty one years later.

This was no ordinary day for James Jacob. It was going to be a memorable day. Known as Jake to his close friends, he didn't know it, but it was the day that was going to change his life forever. Focusing his brown eyes on the digital clock he took in the time. 7a.m. The last time he had looked it had been 6.45 a.m. It had been a restless night. He had to get a move on. For a few priceless seconds of love he watched as Carol rolled over and continued sleeping next to him. Purring like a cat, her auburn, shoulder length hair was draped across her naked shoulders. The previous afternoon they had made love. Unknown to both of them it would be a long time before they shared another tender moment. Outside, the breeze had been joined by heavy rain which bounced off the open window. Somewhere he heard a milk float, a car firing up. In the distance the shudder of road works. Closing the window he felt uneasy; jittery.

In the stillness of the bedroom he dressed quietly. Slipping on a pair of threadbare jeans and a white t-shirt, he quietly left the bedroom and made his way down stairs into the kitchen. Barefoot, the soles of his feet felt the cold as he walked across the black and white tiles which spread across the kitchen floor like a giant chess board. Catching the spicy aroma of last night's Indian take-away lingering in the air, Jake looked out of the window onto an unkempt garden. Contemplating the job he was about to do, what the risk meant, and the consequences that could follow, his heart started to race. Not a good sign. Outside a mist hovered over the lawn and wove its way through the children's swing which swayed deftly in a cold breeze. Pulling on a pair of socks and leather boots he caught his reflection in the blackness of the kitchen window and once again contemplated what lay ahead. A moment of dilemma; his face without expression. Regardless of the shiver that ran through his body he could feel himself starting to sweat as he checked the time on the wall clock. Not once but twice. Move.

Running his fingers through his short black hair he looked at an open book resting on the table, entitled 'The Life of Henry the Eighth'; the page was ready to be turned. Carol loved her history; visiting museums, art galleries and the couple's love of travelling as back-packing students had taken them far and wide. On the wall was his favourite snap taken of the two of them standing under the Eiffel Tower the previous summer, a summer long forgotten, a summer where they had rekindled their honeymoon almost fifteen years previously. His eyes were then drawn across the room to the far wall and to the Vetriano print of 'The Singing Butler'. Sighing heavily, his shoulders drooped. How he would love to swap his life for that couple dancing on the beach.

"By the grace of God, hopefully one day she'll understand."
The time. Move.
As daylight crept into the house Jake pulled on a pair of black leather gloves and punched the knuckles of his right fist into the palm of his left hand sending a loud smack across the kitchen.

Opening the fridge door he reached in and took out a carton of fresh orange juice. Catching a sight of a magpie through the window he watched it fly upwards before perching on a nearby rooftop.

'One for sorrow'.

Becoming unnerved for few moments he waited as its mate suddenly joined him.

'Two for joy'.

Blowing a sigh of relief he took a large gulp of the orange juice and wiped his mouth with the back of his glove. The leather felt like sandpaper scratching across his lips. Slinging on a leather jacket he picked up his crash helmet and stepped outside.

The heavy rain had been replaced by drizzle and the cold breeze was taking hold amongst the branches of the bare trees. The chains from the swing made an eerie clanging noise making him turn in his tracks. For a split second at the top of the garden he thought he saw a baby sitting on the lawn. Then the child was gone. An icy chill shot down his spine. If it was a message from somewhere he didn't understand what it meant and he put it down to his mind playing tricks.

Making his way round the side of the house Jake removed a rain-soaked tarpaulin from his Kawasaki motorbike. Pulling on his helmet he swung his long legs over the bike and turned the key in the ignition. Kick-starting the bike; it sparked into life, spluttering grey smoke out of the exhaust. Pulling out onto the driveway Jake stopped and secured the helmet's chin strap. As drops of rain fell onto his visor he glanced up at the black clouds and spotted Carol at their bedroom window. Brushing the hair off her face she smiled. It was the best smile in the world. She mouthed, *"I love you."*

Jake fought against the demons inside him and rode off.

The main road into the city centre of Oxford was heavy with

rush-hour traffic. As Jake rode into a heavy downpour he stopped at a red light and glanced to his right at the enormous brick walls of Brainforth Prison and he questioned the providence that might await him. As the rain bounced and battered against the visor of his crash helmet Jake struggled to see the way ahead and he could feel the rain seeping into the thighs of his jeans.

A red light.

Turning left at an intersection, he nipped down a side street, a short-cut.

Another red light.

Subconsciously, the adrenalin thumping in his heart told him he was running late. Every light seemed to be against him. Telling himself to relax he joined another main road and pulled up at another set of traffic lights. Waiting for them to turn green he muttered to himself. "Come on, come on." After what seemed a lifetime, red turned to amber, then to green. Swinging the bike left at a junction Jake spotted Harris and flashed his head light. Smoking a cigarette Harris was sheltering under the branches of a large oak. From a distance he cut a sloppy figure in his leather jacket, but close-up he was well over six foot with short blond hair. Spotting Jake he stubbed out the cigarette under the sole of his black boot and slipped on his crash helmet.

As the rain continued to pound, the bike pulled up. Quickly securing a sports bag onto to the back of the bike, Harris jumped on, like a cowboy straddling a horse.

"You're late."

"Blame the traffic."

"I thought you might have got cold feet?"

Jake didn't answer.

"Are you're still up for it?"

"I'm up for it."

But there was no conviction in Jake's voice. As if he wasn't nervous enough. Without looking Jake moved the bike away from the kerb into the stream of traffic. A white van blasted its horn up his backside. Harris turned and threw-up two fingers at the irate driver as the bike swerved into the middle lane. Rejoining the flow of traffic Jake heaved a heavy sigh of relief.

Concentrate, concentrate.

"Just relax Jake; everyone's nervous on their first job."

Easier said than done.

At last the deluge stopped but the nerves kept on coming. Pulling-up on the High Street Harris climbed off the bike as Jake slid down the zip of his leather jacket. Instantly he felt relief as damp sweat was released from around his chest. Unzipping the sports bag Harris checked the contents before looking up and down the street. Pulling up the cuff of his jacket he checked the time on his wrist watch. "Two minutes to opening time, give or take a few seconds." Hyperventilating, Jake's breath steamed-up the inside of his visor. Harris flicked him on the arm. "Are you alright?"

Lifting his visor Jake's voice held a nervous tension. "Yes."

"You don't look alright. You look white as a sheet. You need to relax."

"I'm alright. I just want to get it over with." Clocking Harris ogling a couple of office girls walking past; Jake gave him a dig in the ribs. "Hey, keep your mind on the job."

"Just relax."

If he tells me to relax again I'll kill him.

Across the wet pavement both men eyed the entrance to the Building Society. As the lights flickered on inside, a business woman wearing a trouser suit pulled up the shutter and unlocked the main door. She had the smile of someone who had worked behind a counter for a number of years. Little did she know what was coming. As the staff moved around inside the Building

Society Jake glimpsed a sawn-off shotgun inside of the sports bag. "You said no guns!"

"Keep your voice down Jake. I told you to relax. You do your job and I'll do mine."

Jake pulled Harris back by the arm, his grip was strong. "You said no guns."

"I lied."

There was a steeliness in Harris's eyes as he brushed Jake off and strode towards the Building Society.

Inside three young women were still waking up to the forthcoming week. Sipping cups of coffee the cashiers chatted happily about their weekends with their families, oblivious to the fact that within seconds they were in for a rude awakening. Like an illusionist Harris marched through the glass doors and all in one movement removed the sawn-off shotgun from the inside of the sports bag.

Pointing the shotgun in the direction of the two cashiers Harris shouted from inside his helmet. "Do as I say and nobody will get hurt!" One of the girls, a slim brunette with the name-tag Mary pinned to her suit lapel screamed, the mug of coffee slipping through her slight fingers. Like lightning Harris hurdled over the counter.

"Stay where you are!" Mary dropped to the floor. Hysterical, she started cowering under the counter, her fingers ragging at her hair. "Please don't shoot, please, please I have two children."

"Shut up!"

Trembling, the other woman's eyes were wide with trepidation, but although she was living a nightmare she remained composed. "What do you want me to do?"

Wearing the name-tag Amanda, she calmly placed her coffee on the counter and raised her hands up into the air.

Throwing the sports bag into Amanda's lap Harris growled

through his crash helmet. "Empty the tills and put the money in the bag; hurry!"

"Please don't hurt us, you'll get the money." Amanda stared down both barrels, her long black hair strewn across her round face and sweaty forehead.

"Quicker, quicker!"

"Ok, ok, please don't shoot."

"If an alarm goes off you'll get it!"

"Please no!"

Emptying the tills Amanda's hands trembled as she stuffed the money into the bag. The colour had drained from her face; as her green eyes flashed from the shotgun to the tills then back to the money. Missing the bag, a fistful of bank notes scattered across the floor.

"You stupid bitch, pick it up, hurry!"

"Ok, ok, I'm sorry, I'm sorry."

"Quicker, quicker." Falling to her knees, Amanda snatched the money off the floor like a starving animal foraging for food as the spilt coffee seeped up through her long, skirt. Filling the bag Amanda shook uncontrollably, tears heaving through the anguish; her whole body was on meltdown.

A telephone rang.

Taking a glance around the room Harris's eyes shot to the front door then back down to Amanda who was pushing the bag of money towards his feet.

"That's all there is." Clasping her hands over the back of her head she curled herself up into a ball; the jagged pieces of the smashed coffee mug cutting through her stockings into her knees. At the back of the counter a door suddenly opened. Grabbing the sports bag Harris swung the sports bag over his shoulder and pointed the shotgun towards the door. The manageress walked in, her head buried inside a paper folder.

"Will somebody answer the phone please?" Looking up, her

face dropped as she was met by a black leather clad monster holding a sawn-off shotgun to her chest. Slowly her eyes rolled back inside her head. Legs folding beneath her, she fainted, crashing backwards, the back of her head smacking the wall, before slumping forward over Mary's back. A shriek from Mary pierced the tension as the strong smell of urine drifted up inside the crash helmet sending a wave of acid up into Harris's throat. Through the steamy visor, Harris looked down at the three women quivering with fright.

Harris's voice was unchangeable, strong. "Stay where you are. Don't move or come after me, set off the alarm and you'll get it. Understand!" Then like a phantom he leapt back over the counter and barged out through the glass doors.

It took less than two minutes.

Sprinting across the pavement an alarm blasted out. Jumping onto the back seat of the bike Harris screamed down Jake's ear.

"Go, go, go!"

Roaring off, the bike left scorch marks in the tarmac. Weaving in and out of the traffic Harris struggled to put the shotgun back into the sports bag as he held onto the money for dear life. Turning off the High Street they found themselves stuck in heavy traffic.

"Shit! What should we do?"

"Take it easy Jake. Turn right, down here!"

As police sirens filled the air the bike shot down a cobbled mews. Lined with cars the bike swerved clipping a few wing mirrors. A despatch rider coming at them in the opposite direction hit his horn. Swerving to avoid him, the bike took a sharp left. Finding themselves on a busy main road Jake spotted two policemen running towards them. Panicking he swung around in a circle, nearly tipping the bike over. Regaining the balance of the bike Jake brought it under control then turned another corner.

Heading in the wrong direction down a one-way street;

Harris screamed something inside his helmet. As the traffic hurtled towards them the bike veered to avoid an articulated lorry.

The noise of the shotgun was deafening.

Mounting the pavement the bike instantly bounced back onto the road. Crashing over onto its side the bike and the two men skidded along the tarmac. Sparks flew up from the exhaust like fireworks; the road burning and cutting up the bodies of the two men as they rolled over and over and over. Jake's helmet smashed against the kerb, his body eventually sliding into the gutter with a sudden jolt. Silence.

Through his cracked visor Jake saw rain clouds circling overhead in slow motion. A split second before the bike had flipped into the air demolishing the window of a clothes shop. Crashing through the window the debris and glass had exploded into the street. The screech of car brakes came from all directions as the smell of burning rubber and petrol impregnated the air.

Disorientated; his vision became hazy, his head dizzy. Realising he was lying in the gutter pain shot through his body from every angle. Recovering slowly, Jake gingerly lifted himself to his feet. One of his legs was badly cut, blood was pouring from a rip in the knee of his jeans and his right arm felt like it had been ripped off. Shoppers started to mill around as drivers climbed out of the cars to inspect the carnage. Deafness. Inside his helmet was a vacuum of silence. Then his hearing returned. Looking around he spotted Harris; his crumpled body was lying in the middle of the road like a discarded rag doll.

Limping and holding his arm, he staggered towards Harris across the broken glass and crouched down beside him. It was if he were in a silent movie; living a silent nightmare. Inside his body the pain intensified with every second. His ribs; his back; his shoulder and arm; warm blood pouring out of his leg; congealing into his jeans.

Harris lay motionless. A few yards away the smoking shotgun and the bag of money. Sweat covered his face. Help; Jake needed a face in the crowd. Police sirens. A voice cried out for an ambulance.

"Harris! Harris!"

Slipping off Harris's crash helmet, a trickle of blood dribbled from his nose. His face was ashen, ghostly and lifeless. Jake's eyes shot across at the bag of money, then back at Harris. Lifting-off his own helmet Jake revealed his sharp features to the crowd of onlookers for the first time. Wiping the sweat out of his eyes he pinched Harris's nose and lifted up his chin. Opening his mouth he took in a deep breath then placed his mouth on Harris's and started giving him the kiss of life. Everything around him was a blur, the agonising pain in his arm having crept up to his shoulder. A voice came from behind, "An ambulance is on its way." Excruciating pain went through Jake's insides as he blew more air into Harris's mouth.

"I'm a nurse!" Dropping to her knees a young woman placed both her hands on his Harris's chest and started pumping frantically. "Talk to him."

"Come on Harris, come on." Resting the side of his head on Harris's chest, the nurse listened and hoped for a heartbeat; nothing. Out the corner of his eye Jake clocked two pairs of polished, black boots. The siren of the ambulance; the screech of brakes, then running and voices. As the nurse continued to pump, two policemen gripped Jake's arms and unceremoniously dragged him to his feet. A shriek of agony shot from deep inside his body.

"Serves you right lad." Escorted away by the policemen Jake could taste the blood and vomit inside his mouth. A trail of blood following him. Looking back over his shoulder, Jake watched the nurse frantically working on Harris. Then he saw her stop. Exhausted, she looked up at the two ambulance men and shook her head. The scene was chaotic, the destruction of a bomb blast. Limping through the crowd Jake held onto his arm wincing with pain. There was no sympathy in the shocked faces that stared back at him. If looks could kill. Harris was dead; he was dead, the money lost forever. Twenty minutes earlier he had rode past the walls of the infamous Brainforth Prison. Nicknamed 'The Hanging Prison', it now housed category-A prisoners.

That's where he was going to spend the next decade of his life.

CHAPTER FOUR

Sweat ran round the inside of Jake's shirt collar. All day he'd been sweating. In court, when the Judge passed sentence, in the hospital when he had to face his ill mother and in a side room of the court when Carol had sat with her head in her hands. It had been sweat mixed with bitter tears.

Locked inside the grey walls of the prison van Jake sat slumped forward staring down at his handcuffs. Contemplating the next ten years behind prison bars anxiety stirred his guilt. With any relationship there came responsibility. With responsibility there came fear of failure. Jake was an excellent motorbike mechanic but when he was made redundant it was like a kick in the teeth. When a small garage became available to buy Jake's aspirations of running his own business became a reality. It was now or never. He had talked about it so often he was beginning to sound boring. But there was a problem; a big problem. Jake was in debt, seriously in debt. His Uncle Billy, a pensioner and father figure, was a small time gambler, the horses, the dogs, that's about as big as it got, but one night he had found himself in one card game too many and had lost a fortune. An unpaid gambling debt had put him in a precarious position with a local gangster. Pay up or else. So Jake footed the bill and took on the remaining debt. Re-mortgaging his house, he paid most of Billy's debt but not all of it. When he lost his job it was if he was cursed. The unpaid mortgage had put a strain on his relationship with Carol and it was taking its toll. The first repossession letter had already dropped through the letterbox.

Then Jake met Harris with the steady voice. "It's an easy job, no risk; all you have to do is ride a bike, a piece of cake, what could be so easy? If the worst comes to the worst, I'll tell the police I held a gun to your head and forced you to do it. Think of that money, all that lovely cash. It will set you up for life, it will get you that garage and it will keep your house and your life, think of your family. What are you a man or a mouse?"

Shattered dreams, Jake was an idiot.

Pulling his head backwards Jake thrust forward head-butting the back of the metal door. A shudder reverberated around the metal walls of the van as his mind twisted in turmoil.

"What's going on in there?" The prison officer had seen and heard it all before. He knew what to expect when the realisation kicked-in for a newly convicted prisoner who was being taken to prison for the first time. Sitting up front an officer looked through the grill into the back of the van. "Take it easy lad. Are you alright?" Jake didn't answer. The day had been long and arduous. Granted a compassionate visit to see his mother in hospital, he felt like a man being taken to the gallows. Recovering from a broken hip, his mother had slipped on an icy Boxing Day and had been laid-up in a hospital bed for months. Jake doubted whether she would ever come out. At the age of seventy five her bones crumbled like chalk dust from osteoporosis. Her hair was snowy white, her face heavily lined from all the years she'd laughed at Tommy Cooper's jokes, cried at family weddings and sang along to Frank Sinatra records. Jake had never known his father and the only time he was brought into the conversation she brushed him under the carpet. His aunt once said "He was a scallywag. Rotten to the core." His mother's husband who disappeared one rainy night like the rat he was and who never returned. "Good riddance to bad rubbish" she said. Jake had held his mother's fragile hand across the covers of the hospital bed at the same time trying to conceal the handcuffs. On more than one occasion he thought she spotted them her puzzled look unnerving him for few seconds, but he couldn't be sure. If she had spotted the cuffs she wouldn't have said anything. That was his mother; she always accepted him for who he was, good, bad, or indifferent.

Standing in the corridor of the hospital two policemen kept watch. In the short hour they had together Jake and his mum laughed at the same things and reminisced about the same things. His mother was his best friend. She had brought him up as a single parent and taught him to be strong, honest, and to respect his own convictions and to be morally responsible. Now he had let her down, her only son; her only child, following in the footsteps of her lost husband. How he had to learn to live with the guilt and the shame. Her body was fading away, her eyes watery and bleary but she still held a candle to life. When Jake left her bedside he shook uncontrollably, but she remained strong, as always, right till the last second she gave him the thumbs up. "Take it Nelson Eddy – nice and steady son." That was his mother. That was Ruth Jacob.

Carol, on the other hand, was a broken figure. After Jake was sentenced they had ten minutes together in a side room at the back of the court. Those minutes had been the longest minutes in their history. Sitting opposite each other, their hands trembled as they held them across a wooden table. No words were spoken. The only sound was from their tears hitting the table top. Through the only door leading into the room they listened to muffled voices and the passing footsteps of the establishment. She knew they were desperate for money but she had no idea that he would resort to armed robbery. As for the gambling debt, Jake had told her not to worry; "leave it to Uncle Billy, he knows what to do."

That's why he had become a petrol head; Uncle Billy's love of motorbikes had run through his blood since he was a kid. His patched-up bike would be enough to pay of the gambling debt. As for the imminent repossession of their house that was different story.

The monosyllabic Judge had shown little leniency when passing judgment and handing out a sentence of ten years. From the old school, Judge Kingsland had an ice cold demeanour and he had the reputation of punishing villainy as far as the law would let him. If you got him, you got it. Harris had died from a broken neck; the hold-up of the building society with a sawn-off-shotgun had traumatised three respectable women. Someone had to be held accountable. In Jake's defence his Barrister had pleaded with the court saying that through desperation Jake was only an accomplice. If that plea didn't work, nothing would. But the three prime witnesses, the women who worked as cashiers in the Building Society couldn't distinguish whether Jake was the gunman or not. Both Jake and Harris were approximately the same height and build. Both had worn black leather jackets, black helmets, faded jeans and black leather boots. Refusing to stand in the witness box under the advice of his barrister, Jake was powerless to appeal against his custodial sentence. Jake and Carol were broken in more ways than one.

As the prison van rattled from side-to-side it suddenly stopped. With its engine running Jake heard children laughing. It sounded like the children were in a school playground. The sound of innocence. A shaft of sunlight filtered through one of the van's blacked-out windows. Closing his eyes, Jake tried to catch the warmth of the sun on his face. Suddenly Jake's scream slowly turned into an agonising shriek. Reeling forward he once again smacked his forehead against the back of the metal door. Feeling neither pain nor hearing the officer's growl from behind the grill, a small trickle of blood ran down his forehead between his eyebrows, then down his nose. It felt warm as it dripped off the end of his nose like a leaky tap. Bloody drip after bloody drip rolled over his prominent Adams apple. Sliding down the front of his neck the blood eventually found its way under his shirt collar, mixing with the stale sweat that slept on the numbness of his body. It meant nothing, nor did he care.

His leg throbbed; some days were better than others. After the hold-up Jake had undergone major surgery. His leg was smashed to pieces and he had lost a lot of blood, which had resulted in him walking with a slight limp. When the van jolted to a stop it was only minor relief to the pain. Snapping out of his trance Jake tried to pick-up the voices outside. Running his fingers through his short black hair, the handcuffs caught the underside of his nose. A wince of pain shot across his face as he investigated the cut below his hairline. His fingers followed the trail of dried blood down his face and neck. It had stopped, encrusting the inside of his shirt collar. Another voice outside, a shout, he thought he caught his name. Then someone cracked a joke, laughing, it could have been at his expense, something he would never know.

A loud mechanical rumble vibrated through the van. Jerking forward the vehicle drove a few yards before coming to an abrupt halt. As the engine died Jake heard more voices, laughing, and the jangle of keys. Suddenly the back doors swung open. Blinded by the sharp daylight Jake brought his handcuffed hands up over his eyes. More keys turning inside a lock. Footsteps on metal, then a shadow as a burly officer stood over Jake, his heavy set frame silhouetted before him.

"We're here Jacob. What have you done to yourself?" Then he shouted his voice like a gunshot. "For the record the prisoner, James Jacob has a self inflicted wound to his forehead. He will need to see the prison doctor."

Another voice came from the outside. "Observation recorded and logged. Suggest Rule 43 for the prisoner's first night inside."

Silence.

Feeling a hand grip his bicep Jake was led out of the van. Sensing stiffness in his legs Jake felt another hand grip his other arm. A cold breeze swept across his face. Something felt good at last. Two prison officers stood waiting; two other officers holding open the double doors of the van. Just in case. Looking over his right shoulder Jake watched as the electronic, barred gate closed behind him. Looking up all he saw were bricks. No blue sky; no clouds; just millions and millions of rust-coloured bricks.

Jake could smell it. Jake could taste it. Welcome to Brainforth Prison.

CHAPTER FIVE

After being searched, two prison officers ushered Jake through a number of security gates into a large office. A squat, female prison officer with bright-red hair sat behind a desk. Behind her stood another woman in a pinstriped suit. She looked directly at Jake and introduced herself in a roundabout manner. "My name is Fiona Cassidy I am the Deputy Governor of Brainforth." She wore little makeup, if any, and had a grey expression, although her hands showed a slight tan. Looking over her glasses the officer sitting behind the desk tucked a loose strand of red hair behind her ears and took a patient breath. Her tight lips spoke down into a large ledger and on more than one occasion Jake asked her to repeat the question which brought an expression of frustration and annoyance across her square face. All that was missing was the interrogator's lamp shining into his eyes. Name? Age? Weight? Height? Then the more interesting questions. Did he take drugs? Did he have any sexual transmitted diseases? Another form followed another form, then another. Eventually he was led through a door to his right where he waited in a large, glass-walled room with three other prisoners. One, the youngest, looked like he was about to pass-out at any second. His skin was white; his arms were shaking like they were being hit by waves of electric shocks. The other two prisoners craved a smoke and held expressionless faces. Then they were told to strip. After a shower and more questions and form filling, Jake was issued with a prison uniform. Ready for prison life; apart from his own pillow; regulation blanket; sheet and plastic mug which had been donated by Her Majesty's Prison Service, he was given a selection of toiletries in a plastic bag and a pamphlet on prison rules and regulations. Wearing a blue shirt and smelling of cheap soap which made him sneeze; his short wet hair was combed back off his face, a small plaster sitting neatly across his hairline.

"No need for a doctor," some officer had said, his fat face holding a blue bulbous nose. "There'll be plenty of time for doctors in here, if he wants one." If he was trying to be funny, he wasn't, if he was trying to unnerve Jake, it was a job well done. What little air Jake took into his lungs already smelt of prisoners body odour and yesterday's food which hung along the prison landings. It was something he'd have to get used to and quick.

Waiting at another security gate Jake realised it would only be a matter of seconds before he was paraded in front of the other inmates. Dropping his chin he straightened-up and puffed out his chest. One sign of weakness in this place and it could mean a knife in the guts or a dick up the arse. If you had it coming or if you didn't, someone, somewhere, would find a way of getting to you. All they had to do was watch and wait; after all, at the end of the day, they had all the time in the world. Inside Brainforth there were rules making more rules. For Jake, B – Wing slept; waiting.

C – Wing was for first time offenders. Prisoners who would be released into society within two years.

A – Wing was for murderers; rapists; paedophiles and lifers

who wouldn't see the outside world again.

B – Wing was for violent criminals. Prisoners convicted of grievous bodily harm or armed robbery. Jake was deemed to be in that category.

On the other side of a security gate another officer waited. He was a tall, lean, aged around sixty. His shoulders held the muscles from his youth which snugly fitted inside his spotless uniform. He had looked after himself. A jovial demeanour, Jake was to learn as the months rolled over that you let your guard down at your peril with Conrad Miller.

"James Jacob" said the officer passing him over to Conrad like a birthday present.

Conrad threw his hands on his hips and smiled. "My name is Mr Conrad. It's my job to make your stay here as enjoyable as possible." Jake acknowledged Conrad with a fake smile, whilst noticing the one pip on his epaulets, denoting Conrad as a senior officer.

Un-cuffing the new prisoner Conrad weighed up Jake before speaking. "Over the years Jake I've dealt with thousands of prisoners on their first day inside. Some have the attitude, some the swagger; some are know-it-alls, the ones with the glint in their eyes; the hard-knocks; the ones with a chip on their shoulder as large as a rock, and the ones who are terrified. Either way, you'll learn to keep on the right side of me and all the other officers inside Brainforth. Do you understand?"

Jake nodded.

"I want to hear you say I understand."

"I understand."

"Good, you'll be just fine and dandy."

Reaching B – Wing Jake followed Conrad's rolling gait along the third floor landing. Avoiding eye contact with the prisoners he passed or who stood in their cell doorways, Jake could already feel the eyes of Brainforth upon him. Some of the prisoners were looking for a new piece of arse; a new opportunity. Some of them didn't give a damn as to who he was; lethargic at being behind locked up for days on end. Years on end. Through the wire mesh that hung through the well of the prison Jake made out a pool table on the ground floor. Like a spider's web the mesh hung like a safety net under a trapeze in the Big Top ready to catch anyone who had the inclination to throw themselves off the top landing, or on more than one occasion, to be thrown off.

Then out of the gloom the sound of sweet music. As they walked music from the Orient drifted towards them along the landing. Conrad stopped outside an open cell door. "Home sweet home Jacob. Any questions?"

"No." Jake's response was muted.

Across the landing Jake caught sight of two prisoners ogling him. One was squat, with a round face, the other tall, muscular with a long face. Resembling Don Quixote and Pancho, the smaller of the two wore a pink dressing gown and held a compact mirror in one hand. Applying red lipstick to his pert lips, his overpowering make-up disguised his true age. He could have been anything from twenty to fifty. Leaning to the right, his head rested on the other man's arm like a lamb suckling up to its mother. Using him like a human crutch the heavier of the two stroked his long face with his spindly fingers, his biceps bursting out the arms of his white t-shirt. Catching Jake's look across the landing they both blew him a kiss. Kit Kat and Fruit Shot were Brainforth legends. Ignoring them both with a slight shake of the head Jake turned his back on his two new admirers and took his first step inside his cell. Conrad raised his eyebrows and gave him a knowing smirk; *he'll come around, eventually.* "Ok, I'll see you tomorrow; we'll sort out a work detail for you.

An officer will let you out for exercise later. Good luck." Stepping inside the cell, Jake felt the shudder of door being slammed shut and locked behind him.

His eyes widened. The oriental music came from a small, battered cassette recorder. On a steel table fixed to the wall the cassette recorder sat alongside a small potted plant with velvet, purple petals; a folded-up chess board and a wooden box holding chess pieces. On the stone floor in the far corner of the cell a stack of books, ranging from Oliver Twist to Just William, nestled against the open-topped toilet and wash basin. The bunk bed against the left side of the wall filled most of the cell and the only daylight filtered through a small, four barred window. Standing at the end of the cell facing the window was a man performing the gentle movements of Tai-Chi. From behind he looked around forty but it was hard to tell. Barefooted, his short cropped hair held flecks of grey and his slight frame looked athletic rather than muscular. Jake pulled-up the only chair in the cell. As the legs of the chair scraped across the stone floor Jake anticipated the man's concentration would be disturbed; it wasn't. Sitting down with his back to the cell door Jake folded his arms, stretched out his scarred leg and watched the hypnotic movements of the prisoner's arms as it sent distorted shadows bouncing from one brick wall to the other.

After five minutes Jake stood-up and placed his kit on top of the unmade bunk. As his new cell-mate continued to sway in-time to the music Jake took a sideways glance around the dingy cell as the reality of where he was to spend the next ten years of his life suddenly hit him. Slowly he felt a lump lodging itself deep inside his throat and he felt nauseous. The music which had seemed pleasant at first now started to irritate him. Clawing his fingers into the mattress of his bed he felt as if his brain was about to explode. All around him the brick walls seemed to have closed-in on him. Beyond the realms of claustrophobia; he found himself sweating profusely; he coughed and spoke, surprisingly calmly. "Any chance you can turn that music off friend?"

The prisoner ignored the request, or he pretended not to hear.

"Did you hear me?"

Lost in meditation the prisoner continued moving to the music. Jake could feel his chest tightening and his anger mounting. Stepping forward he pushed the button down on the cassette recorder killing the music instantly. "I asked you turn off the music!"

The man swung around on the balls of his bare feet revealing his sharp, angry features for the first time. "Who the bloody hell are you! I was listening to that!"

"You couldn't hear me."

"Well this is my cell as well. Not just yours. I was here first!"

The prisoner slouched down on the lower bunk and shuffled his bony feet into a pair of tartan slippers. Jake gave him a look. *What have we got here?*

Running his fingers through his thinning hair the prisoner slipped on a pair of round glasses and took in a deep intake of air through his nose. Without looking up he stared at the stone floor, and then spoke with an air of sarcasm. "Don't tell me, you're in here for armed robbery or is it GBH?"

"Murder." Making up his bed, Jake wasn't interested in small talk.

"Murder, that's original. Who did you murder?"

"Everyone, old ladies, children, dogs." Jake afforded a smile to himself.

Shrugging his shoulders, the prisoner sighed and picked up a newspaper and pencil off his bed. Rearranging his glasses he started filling in the crossword. "Armed robbery. You look the sort."

A frowned, angry expression shot across Jake's face as he looked down on the prisoner. "You know nothing about me."

"On the contrary I know you better than you know yourself."

Turning his anger, Jake laughed. It was an obvious ploy the prisoner made to wind-up new inmates.

"Now you are trying to work me out inside your head."

"It wouldn't take much working out."

"A good sense of humour. That's another thing I know about you."

"As I said, you know nothing about me."

"I know you once smoked from the fading nicotine on the inside of your index finger and thumb. Do you know the only tobacco allowed in the Houses of Parliament is snuff?" Giving Jake a sly glance up over the top of his glasses he continued. "And from the tattoo of Carol across the inside of your arm, I would say you're married?" Jake caught the prisoner wearing a smug grin. Before he could respond he blurted out another remark. "Churchill's mother had a tattoo."

Shaking his head in disbelief Jake turned his back on the prisoner and continued making-up his bed. The prisoner was either mad, or just simply eccentric. Or possibly both. Who cares it was too early to tell. Emotionally tired, the last thing he wanted was a confrontation. Resigning himself to the fact that things could be worse Jake counted his blessings. He could have been shacked-up with someone who wanted a scrap or a prisoner who took a shine to him; like those two across the landing. One of his mother's favourite saying came to him; *be thankful for small mercies.*

"What are you like at crosswords?" A plaster held the arms and the lens of the prisoner's glasses together; they looked twenty to thirty years old; national health glasses. Chewing the end of his pencil the prisoner was engrossed in the newspaper, frown lines joining the lines running down his temples. "I'm stuck on this one, ten-across, England's 1966 World Cup Captain?"

Scoffing, Jake threw his hands on his hips. "Are you being serious? Everyone knows that."

"Well I don't Mr Smarty Arse, otherwise I wouldn't have asked you."

"It's Bobby Moore."

A puzzled expression swam across the prisoner's eggshell complexion as he filled in the crossword.

"B-o-b-b-y – M-o-o-r-e." His face beamed. "It fits. Well done."

Jake rolled his eyes; his mind had been made up for him, he was inside with a lunatic.

"Ok the next one."

"I'm tired."

"Just one more?"

"I said I'm tired!"

"Ok don't snap my head off – you want to take up meditation, it will help you relax. Stress can be a killer."

"And so am I, don't forget."

"I know the answer to this one anyway. Harley Davidson."

Jake couldn't resist. "What was the question?"

Dropping the newspaper onto the bed the prisoner sprung to his feet. Thrusting his arms out one at a time; his fists coming an inch from Jake's face. Taking a precautionary step backwards Jake's eyes narrowed, his right fist tightening. *One inch closer and you're going to get it mate!"*

"Cut that out." Jake's voice was stern, controlled.

Oblivious to the warning the prisoner continued punching; an unnerving grin forming slowly across his face; testing, testing. Punch after punch continued to flash in front of Jake's eyes. Feeling the air brushing his face Jake stepped back again. "Stop that now!" Then another thrust and another; the punches were getting nearer and nearer, inching their way to a right handed uppercut that would in seconds land firmly on the prisoner's jaw.

Like a sparring partner the prisoner's grunts were followed by a loud sniff. "This movement is called, *punching the tiger with eyes*." Bringing his fist up to his waist Jake drew his arm backwards ready to strike. Then, just in time the prisoner stopped. His chest wheezing; his arms dropped to his sides. Beads of sweat had formed across his face as he returned to the bottom bunk his shoulders hunched forward as if nothing had happened. Resting both of his hands on his knees, the prisoner sucked air into his lungs. As his chest pounded he looked up and gave Jake a look of satisfaction. "As I said that exercise was called, *punching the tiger with eyes*."

"Was it grasshopper?" Tension release, Jake's fist became loose. "I know what Tai Chi is. It's a breathing exercise."

The prisoner found his breath. "It's like it. It's called Qigong."

Taking his eyes from the prisoner to the back of the cell door Jake questioned what might have been. For a spit second when the fists flew an inch from his face he thought about striking back; giving the prisoner a good smack. Something to set a precedence; to make his mark, like a dog pissing up a tree; make him see who was boss. That would have been a good way to start your first day inside; GBH mixed with armed robbery. That could be another couple of years on top of his ten. It was a lucky escape.

Lifting himself up onto the top of the bunk Jake kicked off his trainers which dropped to the floor with a couple of thuds. Falling onto the bed the mattress felt hard, thin, the pillow starched and musty. Placing both arms behind his head he looked up. His eyes swept the ceiling. A ceiling that after ten years would become as familiar as every brick that lined the cell walls. Like every crack of paint inside Brainforth they would become as recognisable as the lines on his face. Closing his eyes for the first time that day his thoughts flashed to Carol. Her face came to him for a few isolated seconds as he tried to trap her inside his thoughts.

"Do you want me to tell you the myth that is connected to Qigong and how it originated?"

Jake sighed. "No."

"It's a good story, you'll like it. It starts with a Chinese warrior riding into a war-torn village on horseback."

Once again Jake's words bounced back off the prisoner.

"Everywhere he turned, all he saw was burning buildings and bloody carnage; corpses were lying everywhere. There was no sign of life but just as he was about to leave the village he heard a baby crying. Dismounting, he drew his sword and walked tentatively and on his guard through the village towards the baby's howl. Death mixed with the smouldering, burnt-out houses, floated through the air. Then, behind the back of a well, he found the baby cradled in the arms of his dead mother...."

Jakes' eyes remained closed, but he was listening.

"....The warrior was faced with a dilemma. What should he do? Take the baby with him, where it could have become the victim of another battle, or leave it in the village and hope that someone would find the child and adopt him. After much soul searching he chose the latter."

Taking a sly glance the prisoner caught the side of Jake's face. Although he tried to play the tough guy he could see he was listening so he continued with the vigour of a seasoned storyteller. "But there was another problem buzzards circled overhead and he could hear the sound of wolves howling in the surrounding hills. Dropping a rock down a well he heard an echo as the rock hit the bottom. The well was dry. Placing the baby in the water bucket the warrior lowered it down into the darkness of the well; his eyes filling with tears. Hearing the bucket hitting the bottom of the well he secured the rope and prayed that the baby would somehow survive and that someone would hear it crying and save him. After blessing the baby and praying to the Gods the warrior mounted his horse and rode off to continue the war.

A month later the warrior returned to the deserted village after surviving another great battle and expected to bury the child. But to his amazement he heard the baby crying at the bottom of the well. Snatching the rope he pulled up the bucket and found the baby alive in the bucket. This is the great part Jake; you see the baby was covered in frogs. Amazingly the baby had survived by copying the breathing of the frogs and taking water from them; hence the mythical story and the breathing legend of Qigong. The 'qi' meaning breathing and the 'gong' meaning meditation, spirit. Join them together Qigong." Jumping to his feet the prisoner theatrically looked at Jake expecting him to explode into applause at his storytelling.

Pausing for some sort of enthusiastic response, it slowly dawned on him that it wasn't forthcoming. Dropping his shoulders he took umbrage, his voice becoming deflated at the same time. "Ah well, that wasted fifteen minutes. Only nine years, eleven months and four million minutes and thirty six seconds to go."

Jake rolled onto his side propping himself up on his elbow, he glared at the prisoner. "Is this what it's going to be like for the next ten years, me listening to you dribbling on?"

"Don't listen to me then."

"It's hard not to, you crackpot."

"Sarcasm is the lowest form of wit and madness is a matter of opinion Jake. Who says where all not mad in our own little way."

"You speak for yourself."

Standing at the window the prisoner closed his eyes and caught the little warmth from the sun which filtered through the bars of the cell. Turning, he picked up the plant off the table and admired the purple petals with the caressing touch and love of a horticulturist. "Do you like plants?"

No answer, the silence being broken by shouting from the exercise yard. Looking through tired, surrendering eyes, Jake sighed deeply.

"This is an amaryllis, all the way from South America. They come in all shapes and sizes. Some have pink petals; some white; some orange some are even striped. It's also named the Hippeastrum which comes from the Greek 'Equas' – a horse rider. Its other name is 'Red Lion' which coincidently is the most common name for a pub in this country."

"Remind me to have you on my Cludo team."

"What's Cludo?"

"It's a game about 'murder'."

Placing the plant carefully down onto the table the prisoner looked at the cell door. "Open."

At that precise moment the cell door opened and an officer popped his head into the cell. "You have an hours exercise."

The prisoner grinned at Jake. "Fancy a bit of fresh air?"

You've got to be joking?

In the small confined space of the exercise yard Jake found himself alone. His mind was locked in anxiety and self pity, a victim of circumstances he wasn't the only one inside Brainforth. Cry your eyes out.

It was late afternoon and the last of sunshine was disappearing over the prison wall. Shadows cut through the ten foot wire fence which encased a five-a-side pitch and a basketball court. Leaning on one of the small goalposts Jake shielded his eyes from the sun and squinted up at the small blanket of blue sky which was trapped inside the surrounding walls of the

Victorian prison. Jake had been inside Brainforth for just over four hours and already it seemed a lifetime. As a gust of cold wind brushed through the wire onto his face Jake looked up and noticed Conrad standing at the open window of the chapel taking a sly smoke. He was in conversation with someone hidden behind the stained glass windows. Blowing the blue cigarette smoke out of the window he glared down on the exercise yard; his domain, his patch.

"Fancy a game of chess afterwards?"

Feeling a presence over his left shoulder Jake turned around to find the face of his cell-mate smiling up at him. "No."

"It's a prison institution, chess."

"You should be in an institution." Jake's yawn blew a burst of grey fog.

"You can have white. White goes first."

Strolling off Jake's fingertips brushed along the wire fence. It wasn't long before he heard footsteps behind him. "I don't know what your trouble is Jake?"

"Work it out."

"Oh I see. Feeling sorry for yourself are we?"

Jake's patience was ready to snap. Catching the look on Jake's face the prisoner jumped in front of him. Clenching his fists he took up the stance of a boxer ready to sweat a good ten rounds. "Be very careful Jake never judge a book by its cover. Not so long ago I was a good boxer; a south paw. I was a very good boxer. I used to prize fight at the fair. Thirty or forty fights. Never put down on the canvas once, I only had knock outs."

Both men eyes pierced each others.

"That's the second time you've put your fists up to me. Let it be your last."

If he hadn't looked such a pathetic figure with his patched-up specs Jake would have burst out laughing. He looked like he couldn't fight his way out of a paper-bag never mind prize fight for money. "Do yourself a favour and leave me alone." Throwing a couple of dummy punches into the face of the prisoner Jake huffed and continued his walk along the wire. Another burst of sunshine swept across his face and for a few seconds he was back with Carol in the back garden.

Conrad's eyes were glued on the new inmate.

Once again Jake shielded his eyes from the sun and looked around at his new surroundings. Bricks. Millions and millions of bricks. Conrad was still at the window. For a few seconds the two men locked eyes with each other before Conrad flicked the burning butt of the cigarette out of the window and disappeared into the darkness of the chapel.

Then the hour was up. Sixty precious lost minutes.

That noise. Unforgettable sounds. For as long as he lived Jake would hear that iron door slamming shut behind him. The key turning in the lock.

Sitting on the bottom bunk the prisoner sat waiting with anticipation. Laid out in front of him was a chess board, the pieces ready for action.

"I told you outside I didn't want to play chess. You don't bloody listen and it's starting to piss me off."

"Outside you were in a funny mood. I thought the fresh air would have taken you out of the doldrums."

"Well you're mistaken."

"You can go first." Catching the prisoner's grin he gestured for Jake to take a seat opposite him. "Come on, it passes the time. What else have you got to do?"

Resigning himself to a game Jake sat down. "Anything to shut you up." Picking up a black and white pawn he put them behind his back; shuffled them around in his hands, then brought them out, both pieces concealed in his clenched fists. Looking across the chess board Jake waited for some sort of decision.

Breaking the silence Jake snapped. "Well! Black or white?"

Contemplating, the prisoner went into a daydream. "White, like the White Knight; like the White Star; like White Wine; Snow White."

Bringing the ramble to an abrupt end Jake leaned forward into the prisoner's face. "Cut all the chat or you can play chess by yourself. Got it?"

"Loud and clear – Dib, dib, dib." Jake gave him a look.

"Only joking. You want to learn how to take a joke, Jake." With that he pointed to the right hand. Opening his clenched fist Jake's palm held a black pawn.

"I don't mind. I'll have white, if you want to?"

Turning the chess board around 180 degrees Jake felt like a cigarette for the first time since he had quit smoking six months previously. "I'll have white. I don't trust you."

"Alright Jake, take it easy, it's not as if we're playing tennis in the Vatican with the Pope as the line judge, now is it?" Licking the tip of his index finger he held it up to the wind. "I smell rain."

"I smell bullshit."

Leaning back in the chair Jake glanced through the cell window. A second look; rain drops. Startled, he gave the prisoner a puzzled expression.

Giving him a wry smile the prisoner sat relaxed. "I believe it's your move Jake."

"I know it's my move."

Contemplating his first move Jake could feel the prisoner's eyes upon him. Pretending not to notice, he picked up a white pawn directly in front of his queen and moved it two squares forward. Quick as a flash the prisoner moved his pawn, copying the same move. Jumping his knight across the front row of his pawns, Jake moved it towards the centre of the board. For a few seconds the prisoner's light fingers wrestling with each other before he mirrored Jakes move. Looking across at his opponent Jake could sense he was playing mind games.

Ok, if that's how you want to play it.

Moving his thumb and index finger across the tops of the pieces Jake moved his pawn one square in front of his king.

Without blinking an eyelid, the prisoner copied the move.

"Hold on; you're making the same moves as me."

With a yo-yo smile the prisoner clasped his hands across his chest but said nothing.

"Cut it out, alright." Moving his knight forward Jake watched as once again his move was copied. "What are you doing?"

"I've never played chess before, Jake."

Sweeping the palm of his hand upwards Jake tipped the chess board over sending the pieces flying across the stone floor. "Bloody hell!"

"Take it easy Jake I never said I could play chess. You just took it for granted I could. I guessed white went first being a primary colour, but that's all."

Jake paced the cell. His chest pounding.

"I'm sorry! Jake, I can see you didn't appreciate my ambiguity."

Rearing his head backwards Jake opened his mouth and howled like a werewolf. "Somebody get me out of here and bring a straight-jacket!"

Shaking his head the prisoner looked bewildered and somewhat annoyed by the outburst.

"Bloody hell, you'll be having me running up and down the landing playing knock knock next."

"Very funny Jake, have you ever thought about taking up a career in Vaudeville?" Dropping to his knees the prisoner started searching the floor for the chess pieces. "And if that was an impersonation of Lon Chaney as the werewolf it wasn't very good." Picking up a castle he scrutinised the chess piece for damage; every speck of dirt was cleaned from the piece before he placed it back into its small wooden box. After meticulously picking up all the pieces the prisoner folded the chess board, closed the box and slid them under the bed, then, breathing deeply he became calm. Sitting back down on the bottom bunk he rearranged his glasses and started reading a small, green, leather-bound book. Embossed on the book cover in flaking gold leaf was a small sailing ship and an old man with scraggy white hair and white beard and the title; 'The Old Man and the Sea'.

Claustrophobia was something Jake wasn't used to, but lying on his bed with his roman nose at arms length from the ceiling, he could feel it slowly settling over his body like morning dew. Turning to the wall he looked at a small photograph of Carol and himself. It was taken about six months ago in Hyde Park in London. They were sitting on the grass; Carol's head nestled on his lap; in the background the Royal Albert Hall. Both were laughing about something. He tried to remember. It was a sunny photograph in more ways than one, a photograph that at the last minute he had wrestled with himself to take it inside. It was a sad reminder of what could have been.

Wondering what she would be doing and where she was, he let his mind wonder. Who would she be with? What would she be wearing? Running his fingers through his hair Jake agonised. This was the first night inside Brainforth. God-only-knows what it's going to be like after ten years. Paranoia as well as claustrophobia?

Jake had made it crystal clear to Carol that he didn't want her to visit him or write to him inside prison. "Let me be." He said. Leaving her sobbing uncontrollably in the room at the back of the court he could still feel the touch of their fingers brushing each other. At that time it was the only way he thought of how he could survive. She had pleaded with him, but her cries for help had fallen on deaf ears. He was determined to lock himself away from the outside world. For everyone's sake, particularly hers. "Get on with your life. We'll both be different people when I come out. You won't know me. I won't know you."

The rest of the day callously dragged.

No goodnights or pleasant dreams in this place. Listening to the officers voices as they made their way along the landing he counted the keys rattling in the locks. It would become a nightly ritual; an annoying habit. Then, apart from a shimmer of the cell's red light, the bright lights of the prison were diminished. All Jake's fears suddenly became a reality. Clasping his hands behind the back of his head he closed his eyes and tried to deflect his mind-set. Somewhere a prisoner coughed. From the cells he heard shouting, laughing. Outside a dog barking. Rain.

"Nighty – night Mr Conrad you fat bastard!"

"I hope you ears turn to arseholes and you shit all over your shoulders!"

"Give Mrs Conrad one for us!"

The prisoner's laughing was drowned out by a plane flying overhead. Wondering where the plane was going, Spain, America, South Africa, Jake could taste the passengers first in-flight drink on his lips. A gin and tonic; a cold beer, a few hours to glorious sunshine.

For a few precious minutes Jake had been alone. Then his voice returned. "That's an A20 Airbus flying overhead. It weighs the same as twenty African male elephants."

"You're joking, male elephants, not female elephants; you must have been an albatross in a previous life flying alongside aeroplanes taking notes."

Opening his eyes Jake looked to the left and spotted the prisoner's silhouette at the window. Staring up at the blackness of the sky he seamed once again lost his in own little world. He cast a sad figure. "It's flying due-west; it's a couple of minutes late tonight."

"Do you know the times of the trains as well?"

"Once again your dry wit precedes you Jake."

If nothing else Jake hoped that the prisoner's paraphrasing; his inscrutable tone and his outpourings of oratory would help him sleep. Closing his eyes again he was mistaken. Sleep would have to wait.

On hearing a match strike Jake's eyes shot open. Looking down over the side of the bunk he saw the prisoner light a candle; then another candle and another; his face slowly illuminating to the flickering of yellowy, white light. Shadows moved around the walls. Some solid, some vanishing through the bricks. A candelabra holding three candles was placed on the table next to the plant and cassette recorder, giving of a waxy scent.

Turning around the prisoner gave Jake a wink of satisfaction. "Who needs electricity when you have candles? One of the good things about being inside Brainforth I suppose is no electricity or gas bills." Hypnotised by the glow of the candlelight he continued talking in a silky voice. "It's amazing what you can get in here Jake. Newspapers, televisions – some prisoners even get wacky-backy smuggled in."

Rolling over onto his side Jake spoke with an air of acceptance. "I'll need something stronger than wacky-backy if I'm in here with you much longer."

Seeing the funny side for once the prisoner seemed to snap out of his trance. "You can be very witty; has anyone told you that Jake. I bet you make your kids laugh?"

Facing the candlelight Jake propped himself up on his elbow. "I don't have any kids."

"You should have them before it is too late; they bring so much into your life. Time goes so quickly. Before you know it you'll be changing the water in the glass which holds your teeth."

"You're a real bundle of laughs aren't you?"

A scraping noise at the door made Jake sit up. An eye peered into the cell through the eyehole in the door. It was the eye of a Cyclops, a green flickering eye. Then it disappeared.

"You're on suicide watch Jake. That little green eye will appear all night long. On the hour; every hour. First night inside they like to look after you. If there is a suicide with a new inmate it normally happens on the first night when the reality of where you are and how long you're in for, sinks in."

Leaning down the prisoner reached behind the bunk and produced a bottle of dark lemonade like a magician fashioning a rabbit out of a hat. Inside the prison the noise intensified with the darkness of the night. Shouting, coughing, metal on metal. Somewhere a police siren. The noises seemed exaggerated beyond reproach.

"You'll get used to the noise." The prisoner tried a reassuring voice but Jake wasn't convinced. Swinging his legs over the side of the bunk Jake felt dead to the world. Rubbing his eyes he focused on a tin mug being handed up to him. "It's not beer; we'll just have to pretend its beer." Jake watched the prisoner take a large gulp and realised it was as if he was talking with two different people.

"Delicious." Running his tongue across his thin lips the prisoner wiped his mouth with the back of his hand. "Delicious, delicious, delicious."

Looking down at the brown, black liquid swirling and bubbling Jake slowly brought the mug up to his mouth and took a sip. It brought back a sharp reminder of his childhood. The acid flavour of the drink bringing tears to his eyes. Waiting for a reaction the prisoner stood wide eyed, a smile strewn across his face like a comedian waiting for the audience to stop laughing before he belted out another gag. "It tastes good, and by golly it does you good." Shaking his head Jake coughed and looked down into the prisoner with watery eyes. "I haven't had Dandelion and Burdock since I was kid."

"Everyone knows what dandelions are but do you know what burdock is?"

"No, but let me take a guess who's going to tell me."

"Burdock is a weed like a dandelion. So in reality, we're drinking two weeds." Wearing a know-it-all-grin the prisoner took another sip, contemplating how dandelion and burdock was a gift from the Gods. "Delicious – So what is happening with your appeal?"

"I don't know if I want to appeal."

"You should. The British legal system moves in mysterious ways. When we first come inside we all feel sorry for ourselves so for the first year it doesn't cross our minds. What if I said I know a way to appeal that had never been done before in this county?"

A false dawn drifted across Jake. "I'm not interested."

"Oh you will be."

"Are you hard of hearing?"

"No, but this place has a reputation for swallowing you up like a Venus Flytrap. It wouldn't do you any harm just to listen would it, after all your going nowhere."

Shuffling across the cell the prisoner stood with his back to the door, took a sip from the tin mug and composed himself. Head down he paced the cell, spinning on the balls of his feet one way then the other, transfixed in his own thoughts like a barrister about to deliberate on a major murder trial at the Old Bailey.

"Your appeal will be based on your genes, genetics. You know what genetics are, don't you Jake?"

Biting his lip Jake was blurred in thought. Gulping the last of the pop he dropped the mug down onto the bottom bunk. "I know what genetics are." His voice was stern, annoyed, instant, tired. "I'm not stupid you know."

"I didn't say you were stupid. We established the fact that

you're reasonably intelligent ages ago. So let's move on other wise we'll be here all night; excuse the pun – we'll be here all night, get it?"

"And you say I'm the comedian."

"Just trying to bring some light relief to the proceedings"

"Get on with it." Jake shot a cutting look.

"Alright. Where was I, I've lost my train of thought now, ah, right, so your appeal would be based on genetics and that through your blood line you were destined to be violent and develop antisocial behaviour."

"I'm not antisocial or violent."

"With all due respect Jake the courts think you are. That's why you're in here, please don't interrupt me anymore; you'll ruin my train of thought. Let me tell you about two instances involving such a court case that went before the Federal Supreme Court in America. The two names of the men who appealed have escaped me but it doesn't matter; you can always get your lawyer to research them when they are compiling your case notes." Jake's sigh could be heard in the next cell block. "I'm tired."

Becoming agitated the prisoner continued. "I asked you not to interrupt me. This is for your benefit not mine."

Suddenly a large wave of tiredness swept over Jake's body. He was too weary to listen. Too shattered to argue. Resigning himself to the prisoner's dulcet tones sending him to sleep he lay down on the bed and closed his eyes. But there was no stopping the prisoner. He was on a roll, a mission. Along came another speech.

"The first case was of a man in Atlanta. For no apparent reason this man walked into a fast food restaurant and ordered a bucket of chicken. The girl serving him asked him if he would like a drink with his meal. He replied in a southern drawl, "Coke.""

As the pretty girl, who was working her way through University turned to collect his order the guy pulled from the inside of his bomber jacket a revolver and shot the girl in the back of the head. In his defence his lawyer said he suffered from a mental disorder which affected the chromosomes in his brain. He was sentenced to the electric chair. But Jake, this is where the case gets really interesting and that's where your appeal comes into the equation. Appealing against his sentence the man who pulled the trigger realised that he knew at the time it was a genetic act of violence but he had no logic as to why he committed the unprovoked killing. Delving into the history of his family, the jury learnt about his father who had been imprisoned on a number of occasions for unprovoked violence. On one occasion biting the ear off a traffic cop. His grandfather and his mother both had a history of drug-related crimes and he had been sexual abused as a child and was in and out of foster homes all his life. Developing tics, he was diagnosed with a brain disorder called caritozan which causes self inflicted injury. Then for no apparent reason, one day as a child he just strangled his dog in the back yard of a foster parent."

Looking out of the corner of his eye the prisoner checked on Jake. He was listening to every word. "However his appeal wasn't successful and he is still on Death Row as far as I know or already has been given the electric chair. Did you know Brown and Kenneally invented the electric chair?"

Jake sighed, "I'm tired. Where is this going?"

"Listen to case two. A Native American Indian, who worked as an insurance salesman, swindled his insurance company out of millions of dollars. Working as a bingo caller at night to drip feed his cocaine addiction he was caught with his fingers in the till and was sent to trial. In his defence he said that he was the fourth in line of a family with a history of alcoholism. His father, his grandfather and his great grandfather were all alcoholics and it was inevitable that he would become one himself. But Jake, amazingly enough his trial was a success; he got off with just a warning from the judge and was given a suspended sentence. It was the first time in American legal history that a case like this had ever happened and was a success. You see Jake, you're history. You. It's not your fault."

Turning onto his side Jake's gaze disappeared into the flames of the candles. "How do you know all this stuff?"

"In here you get to read enough stuff to last you a lifetime. Gulliver's Travels, the Bible, War and Peace, magazines, newspapers, old and new. You see Jake, your behaviour, it's genetic. It's not your fault. Get yourself a good QC and you'll be quid's-in one way or another. Although money won't buy you happiness. What did Sitting Bull say about Custer?" Remembering he continued. "They say I murdered Custer. It was a lie. He was fool who rode to his death. Don't become a Custer Jake. The way I look at it, even if your appeal isn't successful, you'll be able to sell your story to one of the national newspapers or even write a book. Many prisoners have written books inside; it passes the time and I think in your case, it could be a God-send. What do you think?"

"I'll sleep on it."

"And another thing, when you appeal keep shtumm, walls have ears and there are plenty of them in here."

Slipping off his trousers Jake crept under the covers of his bed. The sheet felt rough on his skin like cardboard and smelt of industrial detergent. Reaching under his pillow he slid out the photograph of Carol. Removing the chewing gum from his mouth he stuck it to the back of the snap and pressed the photograph onto the wall. A tear crept into his eye as he looked at the smiling face looking at him. The prisoner noticed.

"A few words of advice Jake. If you do the jigsaw puzzle in here of the Leaning Tower of Pisa there are three pieces missing and please don't have the eggs; they are full of hydrogen sulphide. The cells are small, if you know what I mean, and don't feel sorry for yourself too long; life has presented us both with a bill, that's why we are in here."

"Very profound now please let me get off to sleep."

"So your first day inside hasn't been that bad after all has it?"

"If you say so." There was a tremor in Jake's voice. He could hear it, it wasn't hard to conceal. At the same time Jake felt sorry for his new cell mate; eccentric, absentminded, his eyes held sadness and he seemed dispirited at the same time, his voice holding loneliness. As cell mates go they were custom-made for each other. The bickering had stopped and had been replaced by an unspoken truce.

Three blows came from below the bunk. The candles died and the cell fell into darkness. Jake could smell the vapours from the candles and he caught sight of the smoke drifting across the red night-light above the cell door. Closing his eyes he listened to a couple of prisoners shouting insults from one window to the next against the backdrop of a barking Alsatian dog. He thought about Carol. For Jake, his first night inside Brainforth would be the same every night for the next ten years of his life. Ashamed, embarrassed, Jake buried his head into his pillow trying to muffle his sobbing.

"Not to worry lad, in years from now, nobody will remember you and nobody will remember me. An act of God can take us anytime and all that will happen is that daisy's will be growing up from both our graves."

Who ever the prisoner was, he never asked any questions; he never cast aspersions; all he showed was humanity.

Drifting off to sleep Jake escaped as Brainforth bled itself into the night.

CHAPTER SIX
The dream inside Brainforth was so vivid, so real.

A kitchen; a dark kitchen, soot smeared walls, the room lit only in patches from the dying embers in the hearth of the open fire; the smell of chicken boiling in a pot. Sitting at the back of the room a man scratched at his scraggly beard which drooped down to the first button of his black woollen suit. Facing the fire, his pupils reflected the glint of the fire, circled in black his eyes held troughs of fears. A cape hung from his thin shoulders, the occasional glint of colour swishing from its red silk lining. Across the room a young woman sat sleeping. Slumped forward in a solitary wooden chair, strands of hair dropped across her forehead and ashen face. Wearing a grubby, cotton dress which hung down just above her ankles, a baby boy was draped across her lap, his head tilted backwards over the arm of the chair. Both were asleep, seemingly. No breathing, no sound.

His kiss on the baby's head was tender sweet.

Closing the wooden door behind him, the man disappeared into the darkness of the night.

Outside a pea-soup fog clung to the wooden buildings and cobbled streets. Hunched forward, the man's fingertips skipped across the wall of an alley as he followed it towards the sounds and twinkling lights of the river. His face was hidden under the rim of his top hat as ghost-like figures loomed out of the mist. Drifting past him most looked through him, their faces as white as emulsion, their black eyes sunk deep inside their skulls. Two policemen holding batons appeared in the gloom.

Then a woman's haunting screams.

"That's him, that's him! Get him, get him!" Police whistles cut through the smog and the man turned and ran for his life. As he ran his cloak floated behind him. His panting became exhaustingly heavy. Turning a corner he skidded, his boots splashing through the black puddles. Voices in front of him, violent voices from behind. Yelling hit him from out of an ally; a corner; a turn. Finding refuge in the dark doorway of a butcher's he wrapped himself inside his cape then crouched down. Turning himself into a bundle of rags he listened to the crescendo of shouting. They were close. Very close. He could hear them breathing. Heavy boots on cobbles, a mob, eager, hungry for blood, and then more police whistles.

"Don't let him get away!"

"A shilling for anyone who gets him!"

"I'll double that!"

Then they were gone. Stillness.

Creeping out the doorway the cloaked figure turned left and avoided the gas lamp at the end of the street. Figures were gathering. Shooting down a back ally the man walked panting, his cape held close, his sight fighting the pitch dark of the night. Rats around his feet. From all sides they were near, closing in. He could feel their breath on the back of his neck. Then he saw a number of small yellow lights from the windows of a pub. A pub he recognised. Somewhere he knew he could blend in.

Inside held smoke and a yellowy glow. A group of men with faces like their pit bulls terriers stood drunk at the bar. On hearing the door swing open they turned and ogled the dark, mysterious figure as he stepped inside. The rims of their pewter mugs sticking to their bottom lips. A serving wench, with milky white breasts smiled revealing her little black teeth. Smacking a mug full of foaming beer onto the wooden table the man handed her a penny which the woman disposed of down her cleavage.

Through one of the small bottled windows the figure could see the policemen outside scurrying around in the dark shadows. Lit only by the flickering gas lamp, he watched as their cheeks blew in and out; their whistles gripped between their lips; purple lips. Holding torches which lit up the night, a gang of men, women and children ran past.

"The coppers will get him this time, if not, the mob will. There's too many of them."

"They'll never catch him. Your mother or your wife will be the next one. Mark my words." Egged on by the drunks they suddenly became confused by the wench's squawk. "It's him. I swear it!" Finding himself the focus of the bars attention, eyes widened. Across the room a slot machine stood in one corner it's flashing lights reflecting off the inside of the black windows. To the right of it a blackboard advertised a race night on Mothers' day. One of the drunks smiled across at the figure before looking at his wristwatch. Then the figure noticed a woman with short grey hair walking towards him across the bar. Aged around sixty; she was small, square, a smoking cigarette nestled between her red lipstick. Her eyes drove into him. Then the figure noticed the t-shirt that she was wearing. Printed on the front was a picture of a haunted face, his face. His eyes were red; his gaunt face skulking under the rim of his top hat; his shoulders hunched forward; the collar of his cloak turned up showing part of the red lining. Running across the top of the woman's t-shirt were the words 'Jack the Ripper'.

For someone inside Brainforth it was to become a recurring, confused nightmare. One day, for someone, it would be like waking up in a coffin.

TRACY JANKOWSKI
AGED 17
AMERICAN
JANUARY 1965

CHAPTER SEVEN

1965
They say lightning doesn't strike twice.
Nineteen years later it did.

The young artist who had murdered the waitress was now in his late thirties. He had put on a little weight around his waist as most men do at that age and his hair was starting to recede at the temples. He was about to strike again.

Throughout the airways of pirate radio stations The Beatles and The Rolling Stones were giving a flavour of the swinging sixties. On their TV sets Americans were watching Ed White's first space walk and in certain parts of Europe; disillusioned youths frustrated with their countries lack of modernization, looked at places like Carnaby Street in London as the promised land. Poland was changing; but at a snails pace. Restoration of museums, schools, hospitals and churches were the government's main priority. Buildings or people's lives? Poverty was still evident across the country and in the hard fought winters there were still reports of starvation.

Krakow was enveloped in a thick covering of snow. Stark trees stood like black monsters against the white city. In the district of Stare Miasto the killer booked into the modest hotel under the pseudonym of Rafel Majewski. At reception he was contemplating making at tentative enquiry about the guided trips to Auschwitz when the glass doors swung open and a group of American students burst into the main lobby. Flooding the marble floor with their rucksacks, Majewski found their excited chatter and vigour energising. In a blasé manner Majewski picked up a few tourist pamphlets and pretended to flick through the pages. Turning his good ear towards the adolescent teenagers, he picked up on their American accents and sneaked the odd glance at them in the refection of mirror at the back of the reception desk. A minute earlier Rafel Majewski had no intention of murdering again. This was a sentimental visit to the city; a pilgrimage. But now, sixty seconds later, he had become engrossed in one particular face, one particular accent which he'd only heard in the movies. Instantly that happy, happy face would be his next victim. Those American kids had no idea that their lives were about to change forever. For the rest of their lives they would have nightmares. They would never forget their trip to Krakow. And he wouldn't let them forget. Catching his own reflection he appeared nondescript. It was just how he liked it. One of the tutors, a long haired woman in her early forties with a waxy complexion paired the students off into rooms, her high pitched voice overtly irritating. Another tutor, an overweight man in his fifties with receding gums and shoulder length hair, walked to the desk and confirmed the group's reservation to Auschwitz the following morning.

Majewski had already started planning.

That night he slept well.

As the students hovered around the breakfast tables deliberating on the fish or sausages Majewski sat alone at a table pretending to be submerged in the pages of a Polish guide book. Occasionally flicking his eyes to the girl he had chosen, he took a side glance out of the hotel window at the whiteness of the snow capped buildings. Apart from the students and their two tutors, there were about a dozen other tourists who had booked for the trip to the camp. Mainly middle-aged couples, they sat eating their breakfast in sombre silence, lost in thought about what lay ahead.

In that hour's drive to Auschwitz in his hire car Majewski could only hear one voice in his head and could see only one face. Absorbing everything before they left the hotel Majewski had sat in the breakfast room and eavesdropped on the girl relating her story about her grandfather who had died inside the camp. Tears filled her eyes as the other students around the table encouraged her to drink the coffee as if it was some sort of magic potion which could help her with the grief. A comforting arm around her shoulder from her teacher. He watched as she drank a glass of water instead and became intoxicated.

As the bleak countryside flashed by, Majewski drove through lines of naked linden trees which held the thumb prints of bird's nests in their branches. At times the glare of the deep snow made him pull down the sun visor, his grey breath evident as it rolled up the inside of the front window of the car. Occasionally stopping to study the road map. He had considered following the coach but he couldn't take the chance of being seen and set off an hour earlier. Spinning along the roads he looked at the farmhouses dotted across the countryside. Single lines of smoke spiralled upwards from their chimneys and he thought of the farmers and their families huddled around open fires. Continuing, he passed a number of green dome churches. Some of the churches seemed familiar, but he questioned whether it was just his imagination playing tricks with his memory. He was enjoying the drive and it gave him time to scheme.

Sitting in his car Majewski smoked a Polish cigarette. Picking the tobacco out of his teeth he saw the coach pull into the car park of the camp. As the icy snow crunched under the heavy wheels of the coach it jerked to a stop. First off were both the tutors. Then one-by-one the students stepped off the coach. Stubbing out the cigarette into the cars ashtray Majewski buttoned-up his overcoat then slipped on some glasses. Pulling on a woollen hat he tucked the loose strands of his hair behind his ears. Climbing out of the car he followed the group of students and the guests of the hotel as they moved towards the barbed wire fences of Auschwitz. Unintentionally he could feel the hate and the revulsion which had murdered the waitress all those years ago had returned. Consuming his body and his soul Majewski could feel himself slowly becoming excited. Passing through the main gates it was hard not to stop and look up at the letters that were set in a wave of iron up above them.

'Arbeit macht frei – work makes you free'

Taking a step backwards always heedful, Majewski avoided being asked by one of the tutors to take a group photograph of the students. In the spot where a Jewish orchestra was forced to play a recital welcoming the thousands of doomed prisoners who passed through the gate into the camp, he watched as the students huddled together ready for the snap. It was a quiet, respectful, sombre gathering but one of the girls stood out. She was loud, giggly and posed for the photograph as if it was a day out at a funfair or a day trip to the zoo. It was the same girl that Majewski had first clapped eyes on in the reflection of the mirror back at the hotel. The same girl whose voice he had listened to back at the hotel. His obsession was making him drunk.

Majewski was becoming an expert at eavesdropping.

During the tour of the camp Majewski kept his distance straggling behind at the back as the group. Walking through the camp they approached a line of red bricked buildings. All were numbered. The first building held a handful of British Soldiers who escaped. Rubbing a mixture of petrol and Russian tobacco over themselves they evaded the Nazi dogs who were put off their scent. Re-captured, and to their amazement they had found themselves reprieved from a firing squad. Inside the second building an exhibit of human hair stretched the length of the building behind a glass wall. Another building held thousands of spectacles, another hut, thousands of shoes. As the guide recalled the story of the holocaust through the camp Majewski caught some of the students sobbing but he felt nothing. He had other things on his mind.

On the drive back to Krakow Majewski thought about the hundreds of photographs which had been taken during the day. Many would finish up on college notice boards or framed inside the houses of certain loved ones back home over the Atlantic. But for one family their daughter would never have the joy of presenting them with a photograph or relating the story of her adventure. Listening again he overheard when the students were leaving Krakow and also their itinerary. The day after tomorrow they would be travelling through Poland by train to Italy. Stopping at Rome, before flying on to London. They were excited about seeing The Coliseum, Big Ben, shopping up the King's Road. But that youthful joy would be snatched away from them. Having got away scot-free with one murder why not another. For Majewski there was no time like the present.

That night Majewski bought a pack of polish cigarettes from a kiosk, lit one and lingered. The temperature had dropped and it was icy cold. Every now and again to keep warm he would walk round a small garden keeping an eye on the entrance to the hotel. Back in the camp he had strained to hear the tiptoed whispers of the students. Out of earshot from the tutors they were planning to have a secret party that night in one of the hotel rooms and vodka was mentioned. This was his chance. At some point they would have to come out of the hotel and Majewski would be waiting.

After an hour the first to appear were a couple of boys. Scuttling across the snow they went over to the kiosk then concealing the bottles of spirit under their overcoats they sheepishly shot back into the hotel. A couple of girls came out of the hotel; one of them slipping over on the ice with excitement. Tomorrow there would be a few heavy heads.

Then he spotted her.

She was alone; she was confident; a rebel; a kindred spirit; Majewski had picked her out and he was right. An electric current shot through his body. As she bought a bottle of vodka through the small hatch of the kiosk he sidled alongside and engaged her in conversation about the trip to Auschwitz. Tempting her with the taste of cherry vodka, she decided to buy a bottle. He could almost taste the cherries on her lips. Slightly drunk she took the bait to impress her friends even further and agreed to go to another kiosk 'just around the corner' to buy the vodka. She was small, like a china doll, her brown eyes dominating her face and pale skin which held two rosy cheeks under the hood of her duffle coat. Majewski looked around conscious of making the girl nervous and being discovered. Breaking the silence by cracking a pathetic joke, it surprisingly made the young girl at his side giggle, making her more alluring.

Turning the corner by the side of the hotel he wiped the smile off her face.

Pouncing like a wolf he threw his arm around the girl's neck and clamped his leather glove over her mouth. Lifting her body off the ground. The bottle dropped from her hands exploding onto the ground. As her legs kicked furiously Majewski dragged the young girl into the murky fire escape doorway. For a little girl she was strong and he winced as her teeth cut through the leather of his glove. Pulling her hood downwards he ripped her woollen hat off her head with his teeth. Another jerk another twist of her neck and she was finished. After the violence her body became limp. The life sucked from her tiny body. Lowering her to the ground Majewski could feel his heart thumping the sweat running around the inside of his shirt collar and down his back.

Picking up the woollen hat he stuffed it into his pocket. Lifting the girl with a heavy grunt he slung her body over his shoulder like a sack. Walking to the corner of the building he stopped and looked around the car park. Strips of blue and yellow light streaked across the ground from the hotel rooms high above. For a few seconds the place where he had parked the car had slipped his memory. Adding to the panic of the kill he then heard voices. Spotting his Volvo he took off. Slipping on some black ice his heart raced as he heard a police siren in the distance, then laughter from an open window high above. Flicking open the boot of the car he leaned forward sliding the body off his shoulder all in one movement. Closing the boot quietly he blew a sigh of relief. Hearing a door open and voices he quickly crouched down. Taking a peak around the side of the car he watched as two kitchen hands shared a joke and a cigarette. As he waited in the shadows he looked up at the hotel windows and thought of the girl's friends. By now some would be drunk. Some of the girls would be kissing their boyfriends. Kids on holiday. Smiling a crooked smile he wondered what the tutors would be up to.

It was well after four in the morning when Majewski arrived

back at the hotel. Avoiding suspicion was of the utmost importance. Parking the car in a side street he walked the small distance to the hotel. Apart from some workmen salting the pavements the streets were deserted. After the long night the assassin couldn't afford to get caught now. Through a small window at the side of the hotel he watched the night porter yawning on the front desk. Tubby, lethargic, the porter resembled a panda gorging on bamboo shoots as he smoked, chewing on a stick of liquorice at the same time. It would be hard to move him. The city was waking up and Majewski had to make a quick decision. Rapping the window with his knuckles he crouched down and ran round the side of the hotel. Seeing the porter move from behind the desk Majewski shot around the corner of the hotel, along the front and through the front doors. Then, quick as a flash, he ran past the front desk making the flight of stairs and skipped up two at a time. At the end of the third floor landing he opened his hotel room and found sanctuary.

Placing his head on the pillow his eyes closed and his mind wandered back to him driving the body of the young girl across the River Wista. Rafel Majewski had found himself sobbing uncontrollably. In the tomb of the derelict warehouse he had stripped the girl then hoisted her up. Wincing as before when the collar bones dislocated he felt paralysed. His body hadn't moved for over an hour and he felt at any second that his heart would explode out of his chest. Staring into her brown eyes that had once been full of life they now looked like they were about to pop out of their sockets. After stripping the girl he then shaved her head. After tying a piece of symbolic cloth around her forearm he then meticulously tattooed the girl's arm with the letters that meant so much to him.

HWEIILNLRIIACMH HMIILMLLEERR

Calculated; meticulous; evil; cunning; a schemer; callous; a henchman; the devil. Majewski slept for three hours, showered, and then went down for breakfast in the hotel restaurant.

Drinking black coffee he tucked into slices of bread and honey, hard boiled eggs, then fish cakes. As always he watched and listened. As the American students filed in bleary-eyed from last nights secret vodka party he heard Tracy Jankowski's name being mentioned by the tutors. Flustering around the tables asking the students when they had last seen her, their voices harboured concern. Finishing his breakfast with a small sponge cake and three finger-size pastries Majewski lent back in his chair, sipped his coffee, unloosened his trouser belt and watched the drama of the missing student unfold before his eyes. Satisfied, he smiled to himself with a calm heartbeat. Murder had given him a hearty appetite. Now he decided to walk it off with a leisurely walk around Krakow.

CHAPTER EIGHT

Jake's eyes flickered open. For a spit second he thought he was back in the comfort of his own bed with Carol and then reality dawned. Facing the wall his first sight of the day was of Carol's face in the photograph. Rolling over onto his back he looked up at the ceiling, yawned, stretched out his legs and took in the sounds of the prison waking up. Although the previous day had left him wanting and considering it was his first night on an unfamiliar mattress he was surprised how well he had slept. Turning to the left he saw a thin shaft of daylight tiptoeing its way through the cell window. Filtering through the thick walls he heard the rumble of traffic outside the prison. Then the flutter of a bird the same Alsatian's bark, prisoner's voices, a shout, cell doors.

Swinging his legs over the bunk he looked around the cramped cell. Confused, he frowned. The amaryllises and the cassette recorder had disappeared from the table along with the pile of books which had been stacked in the corner. Leaning forward he took a peek into the bottom bunk. The bed was empty, just the plain mattress, there was no sight nor evidence of the prisoner. He had gone.

Lowering himself down onto the stone floor the cold shook the soles of his feet. Sitting on the lower bunk Jake pulled on his socks and surmised that the prisoner had been moved during the night. Or perhaps the prisoner had been taken ill? But why strip the cell of his belongings? Perhaps he'd died in his sleep, or had he been sedated. The logic was he had been sedated; sectioned; after all, the prisoner was off-the-wall in more ways than one. He had slept like a baby and heard nothing.

Exercising his limbs Jake used what little room there was inside the cell to limber-up. It was daily ritual for him to get the blood circulating around his leg since his accident. Slowly the blood returned but the disappearance of the prisoner started to play on his mind. Crouching down he looked under and around the bed as if he had lost something. No sign of the delicious drink or of the candelabra that had turned the cell into a grotto of light the previous evening. Puzzled, he felt a surge of goose pimples consuming his body. Something didn't sit right in the pit of his stomach. Suddenly his eyes flashed to the cell door as the key rattled inside the lock. A flash of daylight made him squint as Conrad's large frame appeared silhouetted in the doorway.

"Good morning Jake."

"Good morning."

"I bet you're hungry aren't you?"

"You could say that."

"After breakfast you'll meet Mr Simpson, he's our vocational advisor. We need to get you working pronto. You better get some trousers on."

Lifting his jeans off the end of the bunk, Jake stepped into them, then in a matter-of-fact way spoke. "Where has the guy gone who was in with me last night?"

Frowning, Conrad's voice dropped. "I'm sorry lad; I don't know what you're talking about?"

"The guy who had the bottom bunk?"

Conrad's frown grew, his eyebrows rising. "I think you're mistaken; there was nobody in here with you last night."

Hitching up his jeans Jake swung round and locked eyes with Conrad. "There was a guy in here with me all day yesterday. He was off his head. I don't mean on drugs or anything. Or possibly he was on something, I don't know, he was just…more eccentric."

Conrad shook his head with a condescending grin.

"All his possessions were in here." Gesturing to the table Jake continued his voice becoming more and more frustrated. "On the table was a plant and a cassette recorder. In the corner was a pile of books. You must have seen him when you brought me in here?

"Doesn't ring any bells."

"Chinese music was playing on the cassette recorder."

"Sorry Jake you must have dreamt it and dreams can turn to nightmares in this place."

"I didn't dream it!"

Conrad gave him a dubious look. "Come on now we'll talk about it later."

With a clouded expression running across his face Jake lapsed into silence, slipped on his shoes and stepped towards the door. Before following Conrad onto the landing Jake turned and gave the empty cell one last look. A moment passed and he felt a slight breeze brush his face sending a shiver through his body.

Following Conrad's impatient walk Jake was oblivious to the other prisoners and voices which carried along the landing. His mind was everywhere. *I bet he's watching me now, a few yards away, playing games? Him and Conrad playing games more like it?*

Then it twigged and a smile followed. "Oh I see it's a Brainforth initiation test?"

"What?" Conrad spoke over his shoulder.

"An initiation test for the new guys?"

"If you say so."

"You got me there."

Conrad stopped, turned and gripped the handrail with his left hand, his arm blocking the way. "What are you muttering on about lad?"

"I get the joke, its ok."

"It's too early in the morning for all this. What joke?"

"Slipping the guy in with me and then sneaking him out in the middle of the night. Trying to make me think he disappeared into thin air, very funny."

Again that frown shot across Conrad's face. "Sorry Jake, as I've said, nobody, and I repeat nobody, was in there with you last night, you must have been dreaming it." Removing his grip from the handrail. Conrad continued walking as Jake sheepishly followed. Thinking twice before continuing Jake watched as Conrad caught a few nods and a couple of smiles from passing officers and prisoners alike.

"I tell you Mr Conrad, there was someone in with me last night." Conrad ignored the voice from behind but could feel Jake's eyes digging into the back of his head.

"Did you hear me. I said I didn't imagine it?" Conrad turned once again into Jake, stopping him with the back of his hand across his chest. Making sure he was out of earshot he was calm and relaxed. An officer in complete control. "A word of advice. You've been in here less than twenty four hours. If you're going to survive the next ten years keep yourself to yourself. If you didn't know already there are a lot of bad bastards in here. I for one want an easy life and so will you."

"I know that, but why don't you believe me?" Conrad put his hands on his hips, irritation drifting into his eyes. "Ok, what did he look like?"

"He was aged about forty, slim, short, wore glasses, with a plaster holding them together."

"Is that it?"

"No, he wore slippers, tartan slippers, he was well read, over intelligent if you know what I mean?"

"What do you mean?"

"I said to you before he wasn't mad; more eccentric."

"Did he have a name?"

Searching for an answer Jake's voice was trapped as the awkwardness turned into embarrassment. "He didn't say."

"He didn't say." Sarcasm was Conrad's second name. "So you were in with him all night and it didn't occur to you to ask him his name?"

Embarrassed Jake shook his head; his throat felt like sandpaper.

"Well I don't think both of you will be going anywhere so you've got ten years to bump into him again." Conrad smirked, his eyes having perfected the art of looking through a prisoner like glass. Turning on the soles of his boots Conrad continued walking along the landing.

Regretting it instantly, Jake pulled him back by his arm.

Snatching his arm away Conrad spun into Jake his hand poised on his baton. "You touch me again; or any officer for that matter and you'll be put on report! Look, I'll check out your story with Mr Rose and the other officers who were on watch last night."

Walking into the canteen, the rattle of cutlery on breakfast plates and a crescendo of chit-chat echoed around the bare, grey walls. Sunlight streamed through two large barred windows onto a hundred or more prisoners sitting in lines of regimented tables. The warm smell of eggs mixed with prisoners BO; great.

Watching Conrad swaggering off through the tables Jake joined a line of prisoners shuffling along towards a counter of hotplates. He felt alienated. All the time he looked for that familiar face. Picking up a breakfast tray he once again searched for the prisoner, but he was nowhere to be seen. All that he saw were faces; just faces, some vulgar, some lost, some impassive and bored, it was just another day for them, another long day that lay ahead inside. For Jake it was a threatening day.

Taking in a waft of fried food Jake moved along the line and felt as lonely as he'd ever felt in his entire life. Suddenly he felt nauseous. The putrid smell which lingered everywhere had now become a stench and already he could feel it impregnating itself into his prison clothes. Placing a plate onto his tray he waited to be served and glanced again for the second time over his shoulder. On the opposite side of the room Conrad was talking to the prison priest. As they talked their heads bowed into each other like a couple of old woman chatting over a garden fence. A serious look troubled their faces and Conrad was in full flow when suddenly both men shot their gaze across at Jake. For a few moments the priest ogled Jake and he could see he looked ill at ease, his eyes eventually turning to the floor. Well over sixty the priest was all skin and bones, his gait carrying a large weight around the shoulders. Wearing a shabby, black suit, threads of snowy white hair drifted over his bald head and without the support of his walking stick he looked like a slight wind could have blown him over at any second.

"Hey good looking, guess what we've gotta cooking?"

Resting his hand on his hip and with a serving spoon held up like magic wand in the other the prisoner who had blown him a kiss across the landing the previous day stood serving behind the hotplate. His name was Fruit Shot and his partner in crime was called Kit Kat. They were to make an impression on Jake's life in more ways than one.

"Eggs?"

"Sorry?"

"Do you want eggs darling?"

"Er, no just toast."

"Go on have some eggs?"

"I don't want any." His voice returned for a second. *Don't have the eggs.*

"Go on."

"No."

"You'll love them when you taste them."

"I know what eggs taste like."

Fruit Shot threw his arm around Kit Kat's broad shoulder and fluttered his eyelashes. "Go on have just one egg for me, pretty please?"

"Have a bloody egg mate and shut them up otherwise we'll be here all day."

Looking to his left Jake was met by hungry, pissed-off prisoners. Talk about trying to keep a low profile.

Fruit Shot suddenly became over excited and turned to Kit Kat who Jake recognised as the guy wearing the pink dressing gown. "One egg for our gorgeous new inmate coming right up. Scrambled? Fried? Boiled? Poached? I'm sorry we don't do scrambled or eggs-benedictine." Kit Kat spoke with a high pitched Welsh twang. Both men wore a hint of mascara and blusher, their lips painted bright red. White aprons hung over their blue checked trousers and their hair was concealed under chef's hats which stood up on their heads like pillar-boxes. The question about the eggs had come at him with the speed of a gattling gun.

"Poached."

"What did I tell you, I said he was a poached man." Fruit Shot blew him a kiss then threw his hands on his hips and tilted his head to the right. "My name is Fruit Shot. What's yours?"

Jake looked at the two faces staring at him across the steam of the hotplates. "Jake."

"And this is Kit Kat."

"I can introduce myself thank you." Kit Kat thrust out his hand. The two men shook hands across the hotplates of food. Finding his grip strong, clammy and greasy, Jake discreetly wiped the palm of his hand down the side of his jeans. A few prisoners waiting to be served give him a prickly look as Kit-Kat slipped two poached eggs onto Jake's plate.

"I knew you were a poached egg man all the time." Kit-Kat gave him a wink his granite jaw tightening.

Gripping his breakfast tray Jake walked away with poached eggs on toast and a plastic mug of coffee. Pausing for a moment he looked around for an empty table; that familiar face.

"Any chance of getting a breakfast here?"

Stopping for some cutlery Jake caught Kit-Kat and Fruit Shot ogling his backside both men were leaning into each other wide-eyed. They smiled. A prisoner, a big burly bastard banged his plate on his tray and stared at the two cooks, his voice deep and gravely.

"Any chance one of you two puffs serving breakfast sometime today!"

His nickname was Dutch and he was legend for all the wrong reasons.

Kit-Kat fired back. "Watch who you call a puff, you tosser?"

Dutch responded. "Mr Tosser to you Kit Kat."

Fruit Shot raised his voice for everyone's benefit. "I love the smell of testosterone in the morning."

Finding an empty table, the top bearing the scratch marks of past prisoners initials, Jake sat down picked up his knife and fork and questioned how hungry he was. Staring down at the two eggs which looked like two dead man's eyes looking back up at him his appetite quickly disintegrated. Already his plate had grown cold. On hearing the chair move opposite him he found the warming smile of the priest. Folding up his walking stick he smiled. His voice was loose; solemnly deep; with a whisper of a private education. "Good morning, I'm Father Tom Nolan."

On closer inspection his face was heavily lined and large bags hung beneath his sunken eyes which held the secrets of a hidden past. "Please don't let me to stop you from eating your breakfast, that's if you can call it breakfast in this place, although I have to say the food has improved in here over recent years."

Followed with a smile he clasped his hands and rested them on the table as if he was about to start praying.

"Is this where you tell me father that if I want to go to confession you'll only be too happy to listen?"

"That's one of the roles I play in here but not the only one."

"Save your breath father, I think I've used up all my Hail Mary's." Jake took one bite of the egg, grimaced and pushed the plate away from him.

"You'll get used to it." The priest wore a grin of resignation. "Mr Conrad told me your name, Jake isn't it?"

There was a cunning glint in his eyes, Jake wasn't soft, of course the priest knew his name. Jakes' eyes roamed around the canteen. "I'm sure he told you more than just my name."

"I'm not here to judge."

"Thanks father but I think I'm past absolution."

"Mr Conrad said your surname was Jacob?" His watery eyes drove into Jake's as his bony fingers picked at a hangnail on his thumb.

"Now you're going to tell me Jacob is a biblical name."

"Who decided on your name, your mother or your father?"

Jake's response was muted. "My mother."

"Does she go to church?"

"Every Sunday but it hasn't done her any favours."

"Why do you say that?" The priest's face held an odd expression.

Jake looked directly into the priest's eyes. "Because she's dying."

"I'm sorry."

Jake shrugged his shoulders. "I know the Lord moves in mysterious ways."

Standing, the priest cast a long, thin shadow across the table. Crossing himself he looked down and smiled. "I know when I go to see my maker there will be things I want answers to, things I don't understand, but don't give up on us just yet Jake. You never know, we could come in handy one day. God bless you." Jake resigned himself to the sermon.

Hobbling on his stick the priest made his way through the line of tables muttering over his dog collar. Looking for disciples, some of the prisoners who saw him approaching buried their heads into their breakfasts. Once again Jake scanned the room but all he saw were bored, blank expressions. Mouths chewing without taste or enjoyment, faces lost in the vapours of their breakfasts. Slouching back in his chair Jake brought the cup up to his mouth and sipped the coffee; surprisingly it tasted half-decent. Surreptitiously looking over the rim of the cup his eyes watched the canteen in motion. Kat Kat and Fruit Shot slopping food onto plates, mouths chewing, slurping, the priest only to happy to find a listening ear. *Look calm, stay calm, don't attract attention.*

Then out the corner of his eye Jake saw him. It was if he was walking in slow motion. There was no mistaking him. Slamming the coffee mug down on the table Jake sprung to his feet and followed him out of the canteen.

Daylight flooded the well of the prison from the large skylight that ran the length of the roof. Adjusting his eyes to the brightness Jake searched the landing. Hunting for the prisoner with the tang of coffee and egg lingering in his mouth a heavy set officer orchestrating a work detail trudged out of the canteen behind him, the daily bind evident in his body language and voice. "Get a move on now lads, you'll have it dark."

There he was. At the far end of the landing, the prisoner was leaning on the hand rail and looking directly at him with a smile across his face. Opening his stride Jake side-stepped prisoners and for seconds momentarily lost sight of the prisoner. Flustered, he found himself alone at the end of the landing were the prisoner had been standing. Then he saw him nip inside a cell. It was if he were playing a game of cat and mouse. Jake smiled to himself. At last he felt a sense of relief. Now he had him cornered.

Peering into the cell Jake found a young prisoner sitting on the toilet with his trousers around his ankles. Engrossed inside the sports pages of a daily tabloid he looked up with a scowling expression. If looks could kill. "What the bloody hell do you want?"

"I'm looking for someone."

"Well go and look somewhere else."

"He came in here, I just saw him."

Searching, Jake's eyes widened. The prisoner had vanished into thin air.

"Piss off and let me have a crap in peace!"

Taking a step backwards Jake caught the smell of strong bleach as it drifted along the landings. A couple of yards away a seasoned prisoner was mopping the floor. "Did you see a guy come out of this cell?"

"Yes, he said if you want him he'll be sunning himself in the South of France." His laugh was loud, raucous, his teeth rotten. Then he spotted him again disappearing into cell 43. Keeping his eyes glued to the cell Jake barged past the prisoner knocking over his mop bucket.

"Watch where you're going you prick!" Jake was making friends fast.

Cell 43 was empty.

Feeling like an abandoned baby who had been left on a doorstep Jake stood alone in the centre of the cell. Pulse racing, his brain felt like it was on fire. Minutes before he had found himself scurrying around on his hands and knees double checking under the bunk exploring every nook and cranny for something, a clue, but he found nothing. Hearing the sound of heavy heeled footsteps behind him he turned around. A giant of an officer with an unfamiliar face ducked under the fame of the door.

"My name is Mr Rose; I've come to escort you to your new abode." His voice was soft, Irish. Originally from the West Coast, Rose shadowed the cell with his large frame. Early forties, a black moustache with flecks of grey ran under his bulbous, ruddy nose. Bushy eyebrows merged like two caterpillars over his brown eyes, his chubby face holding a burnt, razor-blade complexion. Both his thumbs were tucked under his leather belt like an American line dancer. "You don't have to move far, just across the landing."

"Why do I have to move?" Rose tugged at the right lobe of his cauliflower ear, a legacy from playing prop-forward for the past twenty years. "This is a holding cell; new prisoners are put in here on their first night inside until we can allocate a suitable prisoner for them to shack-up with."

"I got along fine with the guy who I was in here with last night, where has he gone?"

"Mr Conrad has apparently spoken to you about that."

"I've just seen him."

"Can you gather up your stuff please." Looking uncomfortable the top of Rose's hair was inches away from brushing the top of the ceiling. "Come on now sonny Jim, quick as you can." As Jake started to gather up his bedding he caught the smell of last night's aftershave mixed with earth. Looking down he noticed blades of wet grass stuck to the side of Rose's highly polished boots, fresh grass from cutting the lawn maybe, or from playing a round of golf? Observations. Where had this come from?

"You must know who was in here with me?" Rose ignored the question as Jake continued to gather his stuff. The uncomfortable silence between the two men appeared relentless; it was an unnerving silence that Rose eventually broke by coughing then saying. "Got your entire kit lad? Ok follow me please." Rearranging his tie Rose ducked through the door. Jake felt like he was sleepwalking. Picking up his bedding and toilet bag he looked around the cell for one last time.

On the landing Rose gave him a stern glare his eyebrows joining his hair line. "What's that number Jake?" Rose tapped the knuckle of his right index finger on the iron door. The faded number 43 in peeling, cracked white paint was barely visible.

"43."

Rose's jaw tightened his voice frustratingly hoarse. "Cell number 43. If you look down the landing at the numbers on the doors you'll see that they have three numbers but not this cell. It has been here for donkey's years. In Brainforth it's legendary. It held prisoners the night before they went to the gallows. Before capital punishment was abolished they used to hang murderers outside in the yard. Hence rule 43 in the prison handbook. Every prisoner on their first night inside can request being put in solitary confinement or an officer can suggest it. You were watched throughout the night. One, for your own protection and two, suicide watch, you are no different from the hundreds of prisoners, past and present, who have spent their first night inside Brainforth. You were all alone last night and you slept like a baby. How do I know? Because I was the one who checked on you. On the hour, every hour."

Jake's heart missed a beat. Bafflement. A sense of self loathing swept through his body as everything sank in.

In his life Jake had made mistakes this was one of those times. A moment he regretted instantly. He had been warned. You never touch an officer. Like the flicker of an eyelash it was a moment that zipped so fast it became a blur. Someone hit him from behind. It was hard, so hard Jake could still hear the back of his skull crack.

CHAPTER NINE
Someone inside Brainforth had that dream again.

Heavy inside, so, so, heavy. The aroma of metallic paint mixed with sanitation. Bright white; a stinging glare; an instant headache. Slowly coming into focus, a cobweb in the corner of the ceiling, bars on the window. Jake felt like his temples were about to explode. Louder and louder the throbbing noise of a pulse booming inside his head. Through the veins in his body a relentless agonising ache slowly crawled under his skin. Such an effort turning to the right. Straining his neck, he stared at the fork-lightning flickering across the black horizon to the monitor of a cardiovascular machine. A tube ran out of his arm and up to a drip. Trying to move, his arms felt numb, sore, no feeling in his legs. Looking down he saw that both his arms were secured to the bed by heavy leather straps. So were his legs. At least he was alive. Or was he? He wept before passing out.

Doctor Leman suffered from overpowering bad breath which blended in with the rank stench that drifted around the hospital.

His thick blond hair swept back over his austere looks while his white coat hung like a drape over his tall, skinny frame. 'A high state of agitation, becoming delusional', was why four orderlies had held Jake down and strapped him to the bed. Concussed, he was confused and angry. Given a sedative Jake had been slipping in and out of consciousness for the past two days. When he woke up he found the doctor standing over him. Writing notes onto a clipboard, his smile was unconvincing. "My name is Doctor Leman you're in a secure hospital ward. You've taken a pretty bad blow to the back of our head."

A thin ray of light was shone into Jake's pupils. "Do you feel nauseous?"

Only from the doctor's breath he thought. "Yes."

"You need to drink plenty of water."

"I have a headache."

"I'm not surprised."

"Do you remember what happened?"

"Vaguely."

"You had a run-in with an officer."

Jake pondered a response. "I thought I was going mad."

"Only time will tell if you're a madman. First day stress inside Brainforth has a history of doing that to prisoners. You won't be the first I've seen and you won't be the last." There was a hint of ambiguity in what he said. Scribbling more notes onto his clipboard he stood over the bed and only glanced up once when the branch of a tree brushed against the window.

Unbuttoning his shirt collar the doctor loosened his tie and looked down at Jake his voice provincial, eloquent. "If I unbuckle you, do you promise to behave yourself?" Jake nodded.

Leman started unbuckling the thick leather straps that had pinned Jake down for the last forty eight hours. The relief was instant.

"There you go, free at last."

"I hardly think so Doc."

"A Freudian slip."

Rubbing his wrists Jake lifted himself as the doctor propped a pillow behind his shoulders. Light headed Jake felt the back of his head.

"You'll have a lump there for a while. You have suffered concussion, nothing to worry about." The words that filtered out of Leman's mouth hardly gave Jake confidence.

"How long will I be in here?

Checking his blood pressure, pupils, chest and the inside of Jake's mouth, the doctor sighed. "You won't be going anywhere for a week or two so get some rest. I'll pop in and see you later." Leman left closing the door behind him.

Over the next couple of weeks the days and nights merged into one. Finding himself sleeping for long bouts and fighting waves of depression the time of day became irrelevant and on more than one occasion he found himself sitting naked on the cold floor with his back up against the tiled wall. With his knees tucked under his chin he would rock back and forth like a newborn muttering to himself. Delusional and covered in sweat he would scream out and would have to be restrained and sedated. Inside a prison hospital the orderlies have little sympathy, to them every prisoner is just a biological statistic which went wrong. Give them a number. Stitch them up. Write a report; then move them out until the next nutter comes in screaming and bleeding.

Slowly Jake recovered, but what had happened to him in cell 43 gnawed away at his insides. Eating well, his blood pressure and general health were checked daily and he found watching television a reprieve. During the day he sat looking out of the window across the Oxfordshire countryside with a copy of the book 'Compendium of Movies' on his lap. Flicking through the book certain films brought back memories; his first date, a moment, a film he went to see with his mother or with Carol. But during this time of soul searching he had time to think, to ponder but still that face wouldn't go away. Was it just a bad dream? Could it have been his imagination, the stress of his first day inside Brainforth making him delusional? Was the prisoner an illusion or an illusionist? After all Houdini escaped from a prison cell with the worlds press watching.

In between the self analysis Jake had sessions with the psychiatrist who finally diagnosed that he might have suffered a small mental breakdown. After a month's rehabilitation, Jake was eventually passed fit and once again let loose into society, that's if you could call Brainforth a society.

On the day Jake was discharged from hospital he found himself on report. It had never crossed his mind that he had to prepare himself for a battleground of abuse. According to the official report Jake had pulled Rose back by the arm and pushed him against the wall resulting in the officer fracturing his left wrist in two places. After the alarm was raised the two officers who came to assist Rose found the prisoner leering over the officer. Fearing for the officer's safety Jake had to be restrained by force, the force being a baton.

Hauled before the Governor, Jake stood pensively as he was read the riot act in no uncertain terms. A talcum-powder light shrouded the office which overlooked the exercise yard. Down below the chatter of prisoners filtered into the room through a small open window. On the walls were old black and white photographs of how the prison used to look. Brainforth was a Victorian prison and had been due for demolition for years. The establishment could be smelt in the cement that had bound the prison bricks together and as always inside Brainforth you survived or you rolled over and died.

Terence Hall was just about to turn sixty and had been sitting in the hot seat of Brainforth for the past twelve years. A lover of books and literature his lasting legacy inside was writing a paper on an educational reform within prisons that encouraged prisoners to gain degrees in modern English and Mathematics. Hall was finishing a telephone conversation when Jake noticed one of the photographs on the wall. Lifting a pile of ledgers from a chair Conrad clicked his fingers ordering Jake to sit as if he was training his dog. In the black and white photograph there were three men. A priest; a man with a bushy moustache wearing a three piece suit looking at his fob watch. But Jake's eyes were drawn to the third man, the one on the left of the photograph. Wearing a shirt and tie with his sleeves rolled he was holding a thick rope with a noose at the end. Then in the corner of the photograph there was a date scribbled in faded pencil; 1946 and the words, 'The Last Day of Hanging.'

Correctly dressed Hall's sigh came from deep inside his gut as he replaced the receiver. Looking across the leather-topped desk Jake caught the smell of cigars and coffee that lingered in the air.

Hall was tired and pressed, his voice hoarse. "Calmed down a bit have we Mr. Jacob?" Looking over the rim of his glasses Hall strummed the desktop with his long fingers as he waited for response, it wasn't forthcoming. "Would you describe yourself as having always been a violent person Mr. Jacob?"

"No."

"Well unfortunately your record says otherwise, you are, after all serving ten years for armed robbery and we can't ignore the fact that you have assaulted a prison officer, resulting in serious injury. Not a very good start inside my prison is it?"

Standing with bad posture Hall removed his jacket and slung it over the back of his chair his black pointed shoes looking at odds with the rest of him. Walking behind his desk he stole a look down and consulted his notes, his sighs manifesting. On the windowsill was a small cherry tomato on a side plate. "This tomato was grown inside this prison. It was nurtured from a seed, then from a shoot; then it was re-potted until it grew into a rich plant bearing fruit." Turning to Jake Hall gave him a look which would turn anyone to stone. "You have a choice inside my prison Jacob, you can be like this tomato and grow and learn or…" Picking up the tomato Hall popped it into his mouth. "Or you can be eaten up by the regime or establishment where you will never learn or win." Running his tongue around the front of his upper teeth Hall continued. "Less than twenty four hours you were inside my prison before you once again turned violent. You will learn that this sort of behaviour will not be tolerated."

Jake was just about to defend himself when, Hall raised his hand to silence him. "You will serve an extra year which will be imposed on your current sentence. This is not open to debate; negotiation or appeal. Also you will spend the next ten days in solitary."

Trying to explain was pointless.
Before Jake had time to defend himself judgement had already been passed. Like a thespian flicking away a fly in an amateur dramatic production Hall settled his eyes back into a report before waving Conrad to remove Jake from his space.

Conrad had stood behind Hall throughout the five minute hearing listening and yawning with a pensive, sometimes pedantic expression. He'd heard and seen it all before. Behind Jake another officer stood with his back to the door arms folded across his chest. He was there, just in case.

Punishment was passed and for the next ten days Jake sat alone in solitary confinement like a condemned man and it felt like ten years. All privileges, if you could call them privileges, were denied. Seeing a counsellor was compulsory only to tick the right boxes as to judge whether he was criminally insane or that this latest bout of violence behaviour was just a one off. His counsellor was a funny man, young and intelligent and Jake found the sessions a welcomed break from the tedious monotony of his own company. Their talks varied from Stanley Matthews mazy runs to Nelson Mandela's incarceration on Robbin Island; from putting the first man on the moon to the Kennedy assassination and flashing between his childhood memories, was Carol and his upbringing.

As for that first night inside Brainforth it was always at the back of his mind. Sometimes he could smell him; sometimes he could hear his voice. Time and time again the conversation between the prisoner and himself turned over and over in his mind. For the rest of his stretch inside solitary confinement one thing kept coming back. Like a tape recorder rewinding then playing back the same thing. It was how the prisoner was insistent on him appealing. It was like being forced to watch the thin line of sand dribble down in an hour glass day after day as Jake wrestled with the demons which had camped inside his head.

On the day of his release from solitary confinement, Jake surprisingly found himself as a minor celebrity back on B-Wing. An act of violence was nothing new inside Brainforth, lockdown was a daily event but seeing ghosts or having abberitions was a different story. In the seconds that he waited at the security gate to open Jake took in a deep breath puffed out his chest clenched his fists and was determined to avoid eye contact with anyone. On seeing Jake back on the Wing many of the hardened criminals just scoffed and turned their backs, but most of the inmates were intrigued to hear more tales about the Ghost Boy. They say time is a healer. Not in Brainforth it isn't.

At ten past nine on the morning of the same day Jake sat opposite Conrad. The room was bare and dark. Overlooking a small courtyard which held a clinging mist the bars of the two pokey windows had been replaced with wire netting. Studying a report for almost five minutes Conrad eventually lifted his eyes and spoke. "You're a smart cookie Jacob, a university degree in politics. What went wrong?"

"It's a long story."

Conrad continued with small talk. His tone dismissive and evasive. Jake said nothing.

For a few silent seconds Conrad inspected Jake across the table without blinking then in a derisory voice that held a cold tone he tried to sever his subconscious by reiterating what Hall had said to him ten days earlier. Writing notes he interjected occasionally with his own statements always conscious of his professional gravitas.

"It's a new start for you Jake and we'll let bygones be bygones." *Easy for him to say, tell that to the rest of the prison, we'll see about bygones.* Within the hour Jake found himself back on familiar ground.

The Ghost Boy had returned, now we'll see.

It was like a magnet. Across the landing, Jake stared at the locked door of cell number 43. He wondered who was inside. Standing on the threshold of a cell Conrad tilted his head slightly to the right and gave Jake a comforting look. "We've put you in with somebody whom we think is compatible." Two doors down Fruit Shot and Kit Kat appeared and pierced the air with a couple of wolf whistles for Jake's benefit. If Jake had any thoughts about trying to keep a low profile he could quickly forget about it. Welcome back.

Kit-Kat who was broad and athletic from hours of lifting weights gripped the handrail with both hands. "Can the Ghost Boy read our horoscopes Mr. Conrad?"

"I don't know you'll have to ask him."

"He can read my palm and my tea leaves any day." Fruit Shot's smile was infectious.

"Take it easy girls." Conrad's smile broadened into a wide grin and Jake caught sight of a gold filling in one of his side teeth. Taking a step inside his new cell Jake was met by another prisoner doing press-ups. Conrad's voice followed. "This is Vince, like yourself he's a non smoker, I'll leave you to get acquainted." As Conrad strolled away Jake once again glanced back over his shoulder and looked across the landing. The door to cell number 43 seemed to hold an energy which drew him towards it.

"You must be the nut job everyone is talking about. Just my luck. Yours is the bottom bunk."

Vince grunted as he struggled with the last couple of his push-ups. Tipping his kit onto the unmade bed Jake looked around at the girlie posters on the wall and caught a waft of stagnant water from the toilet and wash basin. Observations. There were five bars on this window instead of four in his last cell; the only thing different from the previous nights cell where that the bare bricks had been replaced with mauve painted walls. From what Jake had been used to it was like being at the Ritz Hotel. "Eighty!" Rolling onto his back Vince grabbed a towel and started wiping the sweat from his neck and face, his hairy chest pounding up and down. "What did, Conrad say your name was?"

"He didn't, but its Jake."

"I'm Vince." Sitting up his hand shot out like a gunslinger

drawing a six shooter. His handshake was strong and clammy.

"You don't look nuts."

"I'm not."

"I don't give a shit anyway, who isn't in here?"

Muscular framed Vince was short and lean. A tattoo of a dagger piercing a heart was evident on each of his muscular biceps and Jake noticed a track of needle holes running up the inside of both arms. His short, cropped mousy hair had recently been cut and his blue eyes shone out against his white complexion like a husky. He had a confident cock-sure manner in the way he held himself, his voice which was surprisingly high-pitched, held a Yorkshire twang. "What you in for?" Mockingly crossing his eyes, Vince stuck out his tongue from the side of his mouth and gargled inaudibly like Quasimodo. "Apart from being bonkers?"

Making his bed Jake replied with a muted tone. "Let's say, I deserved what I got."

"I robbed one house too many. The last job, two bloody big Dobermans came from nowhere and set about me, the bastards nearly ripped me apart. Don't like dogs never have done, bloody shit-machines. One of them dug his teeth into my arse. Look eight stitches." Dropping his trousers Vince presented his war-wound with a sense of pride.

"Did the court take that into consideration, did they bollocks!"

Gathering that Jake wasn't listening, Vince could see that he was transfixed on that cell across the landing.

"I was put inside there on my first night."

"Were you alone?"

"Yes."

"Did you see anything in there?"

"What do you mean did I see anything? Hey don't be freaking me out."

"They put me in with someone, but according to Rose, Conrad and everyone else, I was in that cell by myself."

Vince gave him an inquisitive look. "There must be an explanation for it."

"They were adamant I was alone."

A delayed laugh sprung from Vince's mouth. "You know what they are doing don't you? They're winding you up; they're playing a game with you. Some of the screws in here can be real wind-up merchants."

"I thought that at first."

"Did you see the initials engraved in the brickwork?"

Jake shook his head and once again stared back through the cell door across the landing. Hypnotised, the cell enticed Jake's gaze, drawing him inside once again. Wrestling with the demons inside his mind he felt himself becoming more and more agitated, helpless.

The lure of the cell door was broken when two figures stepped inside unannounced.

"A welcome present for you handsome." Handing Jake an orange, Kit Kat stood in the doorway as Fruit Shot parked himself on the bottom bunk. Kit Kat's teeth were whiter than white, his red lipstick complimenting his olive skin and jet-black hair. Ringed with shadows his black eyes looked as if he had last tasted sleep a lifetime ago. Born just outside Manchester he was one of a small number of Muslims inside Brainforth. Fruit Shot on the other hand was a Roman Catholic and had been raised in South Wales. They say opposites attract. Both men smelt of loose tobacco mixed with Brut aftershave. Their smell which clung to their clothes reminded Jake of the spices in Istanbul where he had once gone back packing as a teenager. How he longed for those years of freedom to return, if only he knew then what he knew now.

Uncomfortable with the two transvestites Vince's shoulders had dropped and a shadowy frown had replaced his cheeky grin. Clasping his hands over his right knee Fruit Shot rocked nervously causing the springs in the bed to creak. His lips held a permanent pout and two lines of old sweat had cut its way like tram lines through the thick foundation on his right cheek. As his foot bounced up and down, his blue painted toenails deflected the drabness of the stone floor. Kit Kat's scarred knuckles rested on his hips, legs apart, with the stance of a swashbuckling Errol Flynn he coughed before he spoke. "The orange is our little way of welcoming you as our new neighbour."

"Thanks."

Fruit Shot sighed and move his eyes above waist level. "Ask him something interesting then." Scowling down Kit Kat's voice rose up an octave. "You ask him something interesting!"

Sighing sarcastically Fruit Shot's head slumped to one side. "So handsome, how would you describe yourself? A maverick? A scholar? An auctioneer? And do you know what a maris piper is?"

"Don't take any notice of these two, they'll drive you mad Jake. No pun intended." Vince had finally relaxed. Crinkling-up his face Fruit Shot huffed back at Vince then looked up at Kit Kat. "Is that an interesting enough question for you darling?"

Taking a few seconds before continuing, Kit Kat looked back at Jake. "I think he knows what maris piper is."

All three men looked at Jake waiting for a response. "It's a potato."

Leaping to his feet Fruit Shot slapped a high-five with Kit Kat. "So tell us about the ghost?"

With as sombre look Jake spoke with little uncertainty; it was if the moment never existed. "He wasn't a ghost. He was just out of the ordinary. Sometimes I have questioned what happened and sometimes I don't believe myself." As soon as

Jake opened his great big mouth; a great hole appeared. One he was digging for himself and one that was getting deeper by the second. "I'm telling the truth." Kicking himself he thought it would only be a matter of time before this latest episode of self-destruction made its way around the prison. He was mistaken, it already had.

ANNA VAN READ
AGED 30
POLISH
JANUARY 1969

CHAPTER TEN
Red sky at night, Shepherd's delight.

The corpse laid out on the marble slab which had been milky blue was now slowly turning pink. Three hours earlier Detective Lech Adamski had stood watching as a specialised police unit had cut around the woman's body and lifted her out of the River Wista in a block of ice. Around the body there might be a lead, any lead, hope.

The dungeness room was depressing and cold but not as freezing as the snow blanketed roads that covered Krakow outside. The winter had hit Poland hard and with a cutting wind of minus-ten outside Adamski was only to happy to be indoors, even if it was inside a mortuary. Claustrophobic, void of any ventilation, the damp clung to the walls as the ice melted around the body. Already the tops of the woman's toes, her nose and the nipples of the breasts were becoming evident as the water dripped like a leaky tap from the table onto the stone floor. It would only be a matter of minutes before the nauseous smell of decay would seep up from the body. Adamski was shivering; he felt a cold coming on and sneezed into his handkerchief. The hours on the river bank as he watched the body being cut from the ice then hoisted onto the back of a wagon had gnawed into his bones. Fifty, short, bald, with sharp features and dark rimmed glasses Adamski stood over the frozen corpse and examined the ice. If she had been moved after her assault there might be debris. But there was nothing. Reaching inside his heavy overcoat he slipped out a postcard size photograph and laid it on the ice next to the head. Pushing his glasses back up his nose he refocused and studied the girl's face. At first he was sure it was her. High cheekbones; each earlobe pierced. He looked on curiously but there was only a vague resemblance. Being in a freezing river her face and body were bloated beyond recognition, her eyes were wide open, bulging out like table tennis balls. Resting his hands on the table he looked away for a few seconds as his stomach churned. Bringing his handkerchief up to his mouth he coughed as he caught the putrid smell of death.

Struggling to take in air he started walking around the body, contemplating. He had lost count of the amount of times over the past three weeks the dog eared photograph had been shown to potential witnesses, taxi drivers, hotel receptionists. All vacant faces who just frowned shrugged their shoulders and shook their heads back at him. Every minor clue which had given a glimmer of hope had been wrenched back turning the murder hunt into another dead end.

Auburn haired, smiling, with piercing blue eyes, the woman in the photograph was beautiful; the world at her feet. In total contrast to the woman on the slab whose head had been unceremoniously shaved, her body now ravaged by the river and that of the killer.

Lech heard the rhythm of footsteps over his shoulder. Suddenly the ungodly silence was broken as the double doors swung open sending a bright yellow light into the room and a cutting wind into the back of Lech's neck. That's all he needed.

"Sorry I'm late. How are you today Lech?"

"Cold as usual."

"It wouldn't be Krakow in January without the cold."

Wearing a leather surgical apron which hung down below his knees Wojtek Jaruzelski was in his mid forties. Tall, thin, he wore the beard of a prophet. Resembling an albino his complexion matched his pallid arms and waxy neck. Almost translucent the fringe of his shoulder length hair continually dropped over his face which Adamski found irritating as he couldn't see his eyes. Along with his many peculiarities Adamski also knew that the pathologist was a secret brooder who drank too much. Flicking his hair from off his forehead Jaruzelski's long legs took him across the stone floor to a large glass cabinet that held an array of ancient surgical instruments and jars of embalming fluid on its shelves. Crouching down he sheepishly opened the bottom draw and removed a bottle of cherry vodka and two shot glasses. With a twinkle in his eye Jaruzelski poured the vodka then stepped back into the room. Handing a glass to the shivering detective he once again lifted the hair from his eyes.

"Here's to a wounded Poland and to the German soldiers who never got time to dynamite and blow up our magnificent city before its liberation!"

"Always the optimist Jaruzelski, you make Poland sound like it floats along on a white cloud."

"We have to believe that the poverty in our country will one day be eradicated. You should join our Socialist Party; resentment to the rest of Europe is on the agenda for the next meeting. If you don't like the debate just come along for the vodka and you never know you might even meet a woman to keep you warm at night."

Jaruzelski slapped Adamski on the back before the two men clinked glasses and gulped the vodka down in one. Instantly the spirit warmed their insides.

"You look worn out Lech."

"It has been a long night."

"And you look cold."

More vodka was poured.

Jaruzelski looked down on the corpse, his voice monotone as if he was reading from a shopping list. Descriptive analysis of a corpse was nothing new to him. "Right onto the business of this unfortunate soul; I would say she is aged around eighteen to twenty years of age. I can't make out any injury to her skull, temporal or parietal and as far as I can make out there are no signs of epidural haemorrhage and I would hazard a guess she hasn't been sexually assaulted. You know all to well that I can't make a final analysis on anything until the body is completely thawed out. With the body being bloated and her lungs full of ice I would say she has been in the water for well over twenty four hours even before the river froze over. The ice has preserved the body but once it melts the decomposition will be rapid. Count yourself lucky she wasn't buried in the earth the decomposition would be eight times faster. She would be a skeleton by now but because she was found in the ice, the bacterial and enzymatic action in the body has preserved it almost like a mummy." Taking another drink Jaruzelski then continued. "If you want to read some more on mummification and decomposition there's a book around here about Casper's Law, I don't know why I'm telling you all this because you know it already being a seasoned detective; basically I've told you all you need to know at the present time." Taking a deep intake of breath he continued. "Both her collarbones have been dislocated. I can't see any cuts or abrasions apart from around the wrists which indicate she wasn't knifed or bludgeoned to death, but the bruising around the wrists indicate to me that she had been bound with rope or a flex of some sort. The way the head is laying flat against the back it's my guess she's had her neck broken, just like our American girl. I can confirm everything that when the x-rays come back."

"Do you think it could be her?" Adamski handed the photograph to Jaruzelski who studied it before looking into the ice. "Could be, who is she?"

"Her name is Anna Van Read. She's been missing for three weeks. We're trying to contact her parents now to come in. Will you be here?"

"All night my friend." Filling the detective's glass with more vodka Jaruzelski raised his eyebrows, smiled and brought some relief into the room. "How is your son, is he still at University?"

Adamski was elsewhere, then after a few seconds he answered. "Yes, he's doing well, thank you."

Leaning forward Adamski held the handkerchief hard against his mouth and peered through the ice scrutinizing the body. Around the girl's bicep he made out a piece of cloth that had been tied tight and knotted. Digging into her skin the cloth was washed out with a thin blue stripes and scantily sewn onto the fabric was a green triangle. Moving his eyes downwards he followed the overlapping veins which ran down the girl's thin arm. Tilting his head sideways he leaned forward rearranged his glasses and studied the outside of the girl's arm. A tattoo of undecipherable letters ran from her wrist up the outside of her right arm.

Jaruzelski looked over Adamski's shoulder. "Normally the numbers were tattooed on the left arm. When some of the numbers were added up they represented words like 'Hebrew'.

There were thousands and thousands of tattoos done in the camps like this one." Frowning, Jaruzelski sighed. "I have no idea why numbers have been replaced with letters and what they mean."

"It's a code of some sort."

"The tattoo, or should I say the cuts to her arm, are scratched in with a tool a blunt instrument like before. Possibly a rough blade or the end of a nail. They're repetitious to the branding and the material which was tied to the Yankee girl's arm. I'll have a better idea when I can get something under the microscope."

Jaruzelski took the glass out of Adamski's hand and poured him another restorative shot of vodka. "Once again he has left is trade-marks. Congratulations Lech, you have a serial killer on your hands."

It was two o'clock in the morning before Adamski sat down at his desk and switched on the desk lamp. Cold, hungry and tired, his cold was taking a hold and a sick fear was pulling at his heart. He wasn't happy. He would wait for the phone to ring from Jaruzelski with his report then he would get some well deserved sleep. Removing his scarf from around his neck he unbuttoned his overcoat and looked down at the file in front of him.

Unsolved.

Tracy Jankowski.

January 1965

At the end of his desk courtesy of the records department was another file which hadn't been opened for the past twenty years. Adamski had woken them at one in the morning – they hadn't been happy. Slumping into his chair he lifted his glasses and pinched the bridge of his nose, closed his eyes for a few seconds and yawned; it had been a long twenty four hours.

Opening the file in front of him Adamski's eyes focused on the report and he began to read.

Name: Tracy Jankowski:
Age: Seventeen
Eyes: Blue.
Hair: Auburn.
Height: 5'- 2"
Nationality: American.
Religion: Jewish.
Next of Kin: Mother, Anna Jankowski.
Father, John Jankowski.
Address: 124, South Warbosh Drive, Massachusetts, USA.
Discovery of body: January 18th 1965.
Identification of the body: Professor Graham Carter, Head of History, Massachusetts University.

Pathology report: Dr Jaruzelski

The body of the woman is aged between eighteen and twenty years of age.

The body had been frozen for approximately four to seven days before discovery.

The cause of death was a broken neck.

The body on first inspection was bloated indicating she had been in the water for approximately a week before freezing.

An examination of the woman's vagina and anus indicates she had not been sexually assaulted.

Both her shoulder blades have been dislocated.

Around both wrists there are deep abrasions indicating that at some time the woman had been bound, possibly by rope or flex.

It is suggested that the victim could have been strung

up by her wrists with her arms tied around her back, resulting in the dislocation of the shoulders.

Lacerated into the victims left arm were cuts of letters replicating the Nazi's tattooing of Jews in the death camps, such as Auschwitz and Birkenau. In this case the cuts were letters not numbers. The abrasions were done by a sharp implement such as the end of a knife.

<u>Witness Interview 1:</u> Bruno Cieply. Aged 70. 45, Krzemionki, Krakow. Retired shopkeeper.

The retired shopkeeper discovered the naked body under the ice in the south bank of the River Wista whilst walking his dog along the footpath by Kotlarski Bridge. As far as he was aware there was nobody else in the area. The footpath was deserted and he immediately informed the police.

<u>Witnesses Interview 2:</u> Michelle Levitz, aged 20. Address supplied by Massachusetts University. The American student was a close friend and room mate of the deceased.

Tracy had said she was going to the kiosk to try and buy some chocolate and some vodka. She didn't like the Polish food. She knew that food was in short supply but we were used to hot food and we didn't like the cold ham or cheese which they served for breakfast. We laughed at first but then we had a craving for chocolate, I don't know why. We tossed a coin as to who would go to the kiosk. It was freezing out there. She was wearing jeans, black boots and a beige duffle coat with dark brown fur round the cuffs and neck. She also wore a woollen hat that she pulled down over her ears that her grandmother had knitted for her as a going away present. It didn't match her coat, it seems insignificant now. It was the last time I saw her. It was about six in the evening when she went out, but it could have been around seven. It was dark. I wish it had been me who had lost the toss of the coin.

Witness Interview 3: Eva Shultz. Aged 58. 23, Kollatja, Krakow.

The owner of the kiosk never recalled any American girl coming to the kiosk or purchasing any chocolate of which she had none anyway. She remembered two boys who came and bought vodka and cigarettes and said she would have remembered anyone asking for chocolate as it was in short supply. She closed early at eight and during that time she sold only cigarettes and only to the Poles.

Witness Interview 4: Boris Haman. Aged 60. Taxi driver. 113A, Skateczna, Krakow. The taxi driver was parked outside the hotel between the hours of five and seven. He stated that apart from a few people walking past he didn't remember seeing a young girl by the kiosk or go in or out of the hotel as he was busy reading a newspaper. His first fare was taking two elderly English ladies to another hotel across the city.

Summary: On interviewing the students and professor of the deceased it was found that Tracy Jankowski was a very popular student. In a long distance telephone interview with the girl's mother, she said that she had no idea who would wish their daughter any harm. This was also confirmed by interviews with the girl's friends and her two University Professor's who escorted the group of students to Krakow.

Case on going.
Detective Garrett Haman. Head of Krakow Police.

Adamski reflected on the report.
Detective Garrett Haman had been killed in a car accident two years earlier.

Closing the file on Tracy Jankowski, Adamski paused for a cigarette; exasperated, the report had made hazy reading. Through the black windows he caught the first sight of dawn. The sun casting a pink glow across the snowy rooftops. Brushing the palm of his hand across the particles of dust clinging to the file's cover he read the faded words:
Unsolved
Klaudia Matyjas
February 1946
Inside the file held just a single piece of paper. It was faded with time and at the bottom it was signed by a Detective Bogdanovich. Now deceased.
Adamski felt wounded.

Name: Klaudia Matyjas.
Age: 30
Nationality: Polish.
Religion: Jewish.
Address: 10, Chopina, Nowa Wies, Krakow.
Body discovered in the Wista River on the 6th February 1946.

Crime Report: The naked body of Klaudia Matyjas was discovered frozen in the ice floe of the River Wista by a number of labourers who were working on repairing the river bank. After an examination by the pathologist he found the neck of the body had been broken. Her head had been shaven and both shoulder blades had been dislocated. Letters were cut into her left arm.

She had worked as a waitress at the Grodzka Café and after leaving work on the night of 19th January 1946, she never returned. It was the last time the owner had seen the woman and he knew nothing about her, other than that she lived by herself. On interviewing her landlady, as to whether she had a boyfriend, friends or family, she said the woman had kept herself to herself and apart from 'rent day' she never saw her during the week or with anybody.

Signed: Detective Bogdanovich.

Adamski closed the file, yawned and looked out at Krakow waking up to another day.

Both files were empty of anything that could get him going. All he wanted was a single clue. He understood why the file of Klaudia Matyjas was thin. It was 1946 just after the war and crime was still rife. People were starving, lost souls trying to build their lives after the war. Souls searching for something. A corpse pulled out of the River Wista was nothing unusual. Bodies were turning up everywhere. Some were lukewarm, some unrecognisable. A common grave waited for them along with the other hundreds of other unidentified bodies. That month Detective Bogdanovich was investigating over fifty murders involving firearms alone.

Stretching his legs Adamski looked through his office window. Behind the rolling clouds the sky was a vibrant red. Over the months he had wrestled about giving the killer a name.

It would make communicating easier. Then it came to him. As a choir boy he recalled only a handful of psalms, one of which had stuck in his mind. Psalm no 23. 'The Lord is my Shepherd.' The red blood sky hanging over Krakow had triggered a name for the killer. 'The Shepherd'.

The file on the American student, however, held some hope with this new murder. Adamski realised one thing. It was either a copycat murder, or the killer was the same man. But why wait for years to strike again for the third time? Adamski lit another cigarette and went over the both files again. Had he missed something? One clue that's all he wanted. One solitary clue. All the women's heads had been shaved. Their neck's broken. All had the same series of letters cut into their arms, in the same order and their shoulders had been dislocated. This latest body had all the hallmarks of the same killer.

Checking the missing persons file with Jaruzelski the detective was grateful for the pathologist's time. Identification of the body was down to a number of possibilities and Adamski clung to the hope that one of them was a young woman who had disappeared in the last three weeks. The relatives of the missing woman had been informed and they had been asked to come in and identify the body.

The phone rang.

Jaruzelski had woken Adamski at his desk at four in the morning. He sounded drunk and coughed loudly down the phone before speaking. Adamski had to move the receiver away from his ear.

"Lech there's been a positive identification. It's the same woman in your photograph. Anna Van Reed. The one who has been missing for three weeks. Apparently she worked as a guide at Auschwitz and Bergen."

Anna Van Reed lived with her parents on the outskirts of Krakow; she travelled in her modest car to work every day and was always on time, returning home at the same time. Every day of every week. Every week of every month for the past four years. Her life was a routine. As far as her parents knew she lived a single life and apart from meeting an old school friend for coffee in Krakow at the end of every calendar month she didn't socialise very often. It was simple; one day she left for work as usual but never returned home. Her parents rang the camp and discovered she hadn't gone into work that day. The woman in her office surmised she must have been suffering from the flu or some other ailment. Before the day drew to a close her parents rang the police and notified them that she was missing. A report had been taken and filed.

Adamski had once heard that the sky over Auschwitz and Bergen had died from the gas that drifted upwards from the gas chambers and that the birds which once flew overhead had disappeared forever. Now he would have the chance to find out for himself.

Adamski washed and shaved in the toilet of the police station. It wasn't the first time. Throwing on the same clothes he had been wearing for the past two days he made himself a quick cup of strong black coffee. Five minutes later he climbed behind the wheel of his car. The urgency inside had set him on fire.

Leaving Krakow behind in the rear view mirror Adamski tried to recall when he had last journeyed out into the countryside. It was when he was about twelve with his uncle who took him with him to buy a truck from a farmer. They travelled by bus and returned in a flat back truck with the windows open. Both of them had urinated behind a scarecrow. With the wind on their faces Adamski laughed at his uncle singing dirty songs. They were good memories.

As the wipers pushed away the snow, Adamski drove down the narrow lanes, through small villages, passing frozen ponds and painted churches. Outside Krakow the people were poor. Deep in thought he blew into his hands, for months he had been meaning to have the heater in his car fixed. Now he was suffering. Shivering, a wave of despondency swept across him like a snow drift. He would ask the same questions and see the same shocked expressions as before. "Was there anything unfamiliar with Anne Van Reed prior to her disappearance? Was there anything unusual about her or did she say anything out of the ordinary? Did she mention anybody she was meeting?"

Stopping twice to read a map he noticed a Polish flag fluttering from a house. Then turning a corner Auschwitz came into view for the first time. Surrounded by woodland the camp was circumspectly hidden. Pulling into the car park Adamski's mind fixed on the children's faces in a photograph which he had seen a hundred times or more. It was of a group of children wearing ragged striped overalls. Standing behind the wire; it was a haunting image.

Auschwitz was an abyss, a silent horror, void of soul. Climbing out of his car Adamski lit a cigarette and watched as a group of elderly people filed past. Holding flowers and candles, every step, they quietly cried. An old man with a strong kind face brushed his arm and handed him a single flower. A line of Polish medals on his lapel and unforgiving eyes telling their own story.

Without taking a smoke he stubbed out his cigarette and followed the group towards the wire fence. Underfoot the snow crunched as if he was walking on the bones of a million corpses. To his left a line of wooden watch-towers shadowed the once electrified fence. A sign with skull and crossbones was imbedded into the earth. His stomach churned as his ulcer rumbled inside his gut. Reaching inside his overcoat he discreetly removed a pill bottle and popped a tablet. Gulping hard, he coughed into his hand.

As the group walked towards the main gate Adamski looked up from the apocalyptical landscape and looked for life.

There were no birds overhead. Just a motionless sky.

CHAPTER ELEVEN

Five fifteen, November 24th 1947.
The day after the warehouse fire.

Immersed in the moment one of the policemen who had dragged the suspect from his bed stood with his back to a barred window which held the blackness of the morning outside. His jaw ached from a punch from the man he helped arrest three hours earlier. Every word spoken echoed around the brick walled room as Detective Stone stared at the man across the table. Stone had a face resembling his surname, his expressions soaked in whisky from over thirty years of service to the boys in blue.

STONE: Right, let us start again.

MAN: Why? I've told you everything.

Lighting a cigarette Stone leaned back in his chair which creaked of old age and took in a deep intake of smoke into his lungs.

Seconds later smoke hung across the room like a blue cloud.

STONE: Why did you kill her?

MAN: I didn't.

STONE: There is a reliable witness.

MAN: He's lying.

STONE: He said he saw you.

MAN: He's lying.

STONE: I think he's telling the truth.

MAN: He's lying.

STONE: But you're not denying you were there?

MAN: I've told you a hundred times that I was there.

STONE: Right, let's go back to the beginning.

Stone took another smoke then looked down on the observations he'd scribbled into his notepad over the past two hours of the interview, although the man across the bare table would have disagreed, seeing the interview as an interrogation. A few seconds passed as a frowning Stone struggled to comprehend his own handwriting. Spreading his nicotine stained fingers out like a fan across the table he eventually spoke, his voice a whisper.

STONE: You said that you had broken into the warehouse through the back door.

MAN: The skylight.

STONE: The skylight. Because you knew there was a large amount of money in the safe?

MAN: Yes.

STONE: Then what happened?

MAN: I told you.

Stone unbuttoned his shirt collar, loosened his tie and stubbed out his cigarette.

STONE: Tell me again.

MAN: I jumped down onto the top gantry and then made my way down the stairs onto the shop floor.

STONE: Then?

MAN: Then I saw a light under the door of the office where the safe was held.

STONE: How did you know there was a safe in the office?

MAN: Because I used to deliver wood there before the war.

I knew the layout inside the factory. You know all this. I've told you a dozen times.

STONE: Then what did you do?

MAN: I thought there was someone in there, someone working late, like a manager or someone, so I decide to leave. Then I heard crying from inside the room.

STONE: You said whimpering?

MAN: Whimpering, crying, what's the difference?

STONE: Because it's different from your original statement – continue.

Taking a deep breath, the man shuffled uneasily around in his seat.

MAN: I opened the door and saw the back of the man I've described crouching down over the girl.

Stone removed another cigarette from its box. Lighting the cigarette he inhaled and coughed; blue smoke streamed from his nostrils. Thinking before he spoke he leaned across the table.

STONE: My problem here is that it's your word against his, as the girl is dead.

MAN: I'm telling you the truth.

STONE: So you've said.

MAN: Why don't you ask him what happened?

STONE: I have done.

MAN: Well he's lying.

STONE: What's confusing me; is how the girl got into the factory?

MAN: I don't know. Ask him.

STONE: The way I see it you broke in to the factory, then went back out onto the street to bring the van round the back.

MAN: No.

STONE: Then by chance you saw an opportunity.

MAN: No.

STONE: An opportunity to grab the girl.

MAN: No.

STONE: And you took it.

MAN: No.

STONE: Or perhaps it was a bit of both. She caught you in the act, breaking in so to speak. She was a pretty young girl, it was dark and you pounced like an animal.

MAN: No.

Stone smiled flicking cigarette ash onto the stone floor. Silence for a few seconds. Stone looked at the policeman who stood listening and who had been present throughout the interview. Returning his gaze across the table Stone's voice hardened.

STONE: Do you like young girls?

No answer.

STONE: Can you answer my question.

MAN: If I say I like young girls what would that make me?

STONE: You tell me?

MAN: You asked the question.

Stone mulled over his next line of questioning.

STONE: We've known about your dealings for a long time. We just haven't been able to catch you.

MAN: You said it 'dealings'. That's what I do a bit of wheeling and dealing and that's all.

STONE: I think the girl caught you breaking in and she got in the way.

MAN: Think what you like.

STONE: What else do you want me to think?

MAN: Do me for breaking and entering but not for murder.

STONE: You're pretty sure of yourself aren't you?

MAN: I'm sure of one thing, as God is my witness.

STONE: The pavements are paved with good intent as the Devil said.

MAN: Are you religious?

STONE: Not really.

MAN: As God is my witness, was a metaphor.

STONE: And you think a metaphor about God will save you from the rope?

MAN: To tell the truth and nothing but the truth, so help me God.

STONE: You seem bright enough, so you can see my dilemma – a common thief, the main witness a pillar of the community who has identified you in a line-up and saw you running away from the factory.

Stone stood up and walked around the room.

STONE: The scales of justice are weighed down in who's favour would you say?

Outside the police station Stone pulled up the collar of his heavy overcoat and shivered as he finished off the last of his cigarette. A cold dawn was breaking over the East End of London. Across the terraced rooftops he listened momentarily to the sound of the docks waking up to another day. A milk man passed and tipped his hat, the hooves of the horse pulling the cart echoing on the cobbles. He thought about the charred remains of the young girl's body lying on the mortuary table and the gravel that shook in her father's voice as he identified his daughter with only by the hem of her flowery dress and one of her lace-up shoes as identification. Stone had taken him to the same interview room where he had just charged the man with his daughter's murder. As the father held a mug of tea in his shaking hands he looked across the table and caught Stone's eye and pleaded with him.

"Have you charged the bastard?"

"Yes"

"Will he hang?"

"Yes."

"Please, make sure when you hang him the noose is as tight as possible."

The father's wishes would be granted but as for Stone he was unconvinced that the man was guilty. He would go to his grave an alcoholic and a broken man in more ways than one.

CHAPTER TWELVE

Ten thirty on the morning of the 6th of November 1976.

An icy wind severed the exercise yard, cutting the hardest of prisoners. Lost in thought a spot of rain hit Jake's cheek as his name was called out and ordered to report to the gate. Met by a crescendo of whistles and smart remarks directed towards the Ghost Boy, the new celebrity of Brainforth, Jake was met at the gate by an officer called Thorpe. Escorted across the yard to a hail of spiteful sarcasm from behind the wire Jake tried to keep calm evading eye contact and the temptation to return fire.

"Where are they taking you, for ride on the ghost train?"

"Give Mrs Minniver one for us."

Thorpe found it amusing.

Short, bald, heavy set with an anvil jaw line, Thorp's blazing eyes didn't suffer prisoners lightly. Looking up with a pinched expression Jake watched as a glint of sun sneaked from behind a number of heavy rain clouds. Catching the priest's gaze looking down on him from the chapel window, it slowly closed.

"We must tell him."

Rubbing the frown lines across his forehead with the tips

of his fingers Conrad's voice was full of frustration. "We've gone through this a thousand times; there is no need to tell him anything." A wave of blue light flooded the chapel as an eerie silence took hold of both men. Three cells had been knocked into one to make the place of worship and even in the hottest days of summer a strange coldness hung perpetually in the air. With a high, mock wood beamed ceiling, ten plastic chairs sat each side of a thin aisle which faced a small altar with a single, heavy brass candlestick. At the back of the alter Christ hung from the cross and on the far wall was a tapestry made by former inmates of Brainforth depicting the Raising of Lazarus.

From the window the priest turned to Conrad. "He has the right to know."

Conrad sat down and raised his right foot over his left knee. His shoulders tightened, agitated, his right foot shaking nervously. "He's in here for ten years for armed robbery and he's assaulted an officer. He has no rights."

"I took an oath over forty years ago – the priest found himself being interrupted.

"Which, you have suddenly decided to question after all these years?"

"Well, I'm questioning my faith now."

"When it's time to meet your maker you can ask him then. Now is not the right time."

"I have questions I want answers to. Serious questions."

"Well I'm sure you'll see the light then."

"But this is wrong, very wrong."

Seeing the priest's eyes enlarging Conrad leapt to his feet kicking out with his boot sending a number of chairs hurtling across the room. Lurching forward he grabbed the lapels of the priest's suit jacket. His voice was hysterical, rising to a falsetto. "You listen to me; you say nothing or I'll nail your feet to the floor, understand?" Blazing breath and specks of saliva scuffed the priest's face. "I'll take the blame when I meet God almighty."

Pressed against the window the priest's arms fell to his side the palms of his hands clinging to the wall for support. He could feel his brittle body shaking but from somewhere he found the strength to stand his ground. His voice quivered. "You have a choice. You tell him or I will."

Little did Jake know.

Five minutes later and with the prisoner's abuse still ringing in his ears Jake sat nervously in a wooden portable cabin. Situated at the far end of B-block the large cabin consisted of a number of small, dark rooms that led to a tight, creaky corridor. The wooden floorboards smelt earthy and when the drawers were slid open in the metal filing cabinets the plywood walls shuddered like an earthquake. Kept waiting for over an hour Jake observed the clerical workings of the prison service before Thorpe dragged his feet inside and started warmed his hands up against a paraffin heater which bellowed out unhealthy heat. It was like sitting in a funeral parlour.

"Bloody hell it's cold out there." Recognising the voice instantly Jake swung around in his chair as Rose walked into the room. It was the fist time the two men had seen each other since the incident. Thorpe powered his cumbersome frame across the creaking room and slumped behind his desk with a heavy thud. His life was regimented and uneventful. Clasping his chubby hands together on top of the desk his stern purple complexion matched the shot veins at the end of his nose.

Wheezing, grey mist came out of Thorp's thin, letterbox mouth. "Mr Rose would like a word with you Jacob."

Choosing his words carefully Rose was unruffled as he closed the door behind him. Nerves swept over Jake as the room fell silent. Pulling up the sleeve of his jacket Rose revealed a surgical support on his wrist. "This still hurts, a little like this." Putting the support at the back of Jake's head he pressed down hard. Wincing, Jake's forehead was forced down onto the top of the desk, his hands gripping the side of his chair.

Rose released his arm with a final violent shove. As Jake recovered twenty seconds of silence followed. Tapping the end of his pencil against the front of his teeth Thorpe spoke. "It seems one of our baton's has left its mark." A grin spread across his face. "Next time you won't get up again."

Rubbing the back of his head Jake looked across at Thorpe, a shift of light crossing his face from a tiny skylight above.

"Your wife wants to pay you a visit Jacob."

"I don't want her to visit." Leaning back in his chair Thorpe's fatty paunch sprung forward and flopped over his thick leather belt. "Why?"

"That's my business."

If telephones were being answered through the thin walls it didn't register. With some effort Thorpe lifted his heavy frame from out of his seat and was already on his feet when he said. "Don't you think you're being slightly selfish?"

"As I said, it's my business."

Rose was feeling the heater warming his backside. Opening his mouth nothing came out; he then thought for a second and said. "I think you'll change your mind."

"I won't." But there was no conviction in his voice. Taking his eyes from Rose then back to Thorpe Jake watched as Thorpe ran his index finger around the inside of his tight shirt colour. Both officers stuck to their ritual. Shrugging his shoulders Rose turned his back, crouched slightly, and held the palms of both hands up to the heater.

"This might change your mind." Thorpe dropped an envelope into Jake's lap. Opening the envelope Jake read the letter. Carol had applied to visit him in two weeks time, he had no choice; his mouth void of words.

Rose smiled, bringing an end to the proceedings with a sarcastic footnote. "You look like you've seen a ghost Jake."

CHAPTER THIRTEEN

January 1972.

Lech Adamski had been retired from the Krakow police department for almost three years when he received a phone call from Kuba Lewandowski his old chief of police.

"The Shepherd's struck again."

Replacing the receiver Adamski propped up his fishing rod back in the corner of the room; a day on the lake would have to wait until tomorrow. He needed to get some air, quick.

Walking outside his chest tightened, that old feeling he thought had vanished forever had returned. For an hour he started pacing the perimeter of his wooden house with disturbing regularity. Underneath his boots he could smell the dampness of the earth beneath the snow; a shine of silver still evident across the blanket of white. Hearing of the latest discovery his mind instantly returned to those dark days and the faces of the young women. Some people remembered them; some people recognised their photographs but nobody could give the police anything significant, every minor clue was in vain. Hour after hour he had spent examining and re-examining the paperwork which had filled a store room stacked high with cardboard boxes and which were filed in numerical order. The room may as well have been nonexistent, a white elephant.

Shielding his eyes with his hand from the early morning glare of the sun he looked across the frozen lake which shone like a plate of glass, the blackness of the water moving hypnotically under the thick ice.

Meandering down a winding path towards the wooden jetty where he moored his small rowing boat during the summer he admired a heron flying over the lake. Across the expanse of water he watched as a father and son trudged along the snowy bank. For a few seconds it reminded him of when he took his son fishing. Smashing a hole in the ice they would cast their lines into the hole and pull up fish after fish. A father and son. Good times.

Instantly the memory and the tranquillity were broken. Haunted by the case, the women's faces trapped inside the ice flickered inside his mind. Closing his eyes he felt dizzy and took in a deep breath. Holding onto the wooden handrail of the jetty for support, he embraced the warm sun on his face. Over the years he had learned how to handle the panic attacks. This was the first in a long time. Taking early retirement which had been forced upon him, his mind had been wandering. "You're becoming too close to the case and it was clouding his judgment Lech. We need a fresh approach." Their words, not his. Now they needed his help, to pick his brains, rekindle everything that he had tried to wipe from his conscience. Hypocritical.

Late afternoon two police officers arrived at Adamski's house which had been about an hours drive outside Krakow. As the snow started to fall a black Volvo pulled up outside the house. Pulling back the curtains Adamski took in a deep breath. All day he had been on tenterhooks, drinking coffee, watching television, checking outside and walking the house.

Climbing out of the car Adamski recognised Dariuz Kuszcak as the up and coming rookie policeman who was hell bent on climbing the promotional ladder of the Polish police force as quickly as physically possible. From a long line of law enforcers Kuszcak was on a mission from the first day he set foot inside a police station. Tall, weathered, his salt and pepper hair was unkempt and he looked like he had been sleeping in his dishevelled suit for a week. Slouched, he trudged up the snowy path towards the house with the world on his shoulders. He was the so called 'fresh approach' but the three years he had been trying to solve the women's murders had taken its toll. At his side was another detective whom he didn't recognise.

An open fire illuminated the modest furniture in the large living room. A number of books lined one wall and a few family photographs sat in silver, ornate frames on a wooden dresser. There was a neatness to the room, although at the same time there was disorder.

Both detectives sat slouched on a couch opposite their host. Adamski recognised himself in the men's faces; it was a mixture of anxiety and defeat, all three men carried another ten years and it showed in their eyes. Pouring the coffee Adamski offered the men some homemade cake, both declined. Kuszczak's sidekick, Sikorski looked subdued, worn-out and scratched his scraggly, ginger beard throughout the conversation.

"So how is retirement treating you?" Kuszczak's voice wheezed asthmatically.

"The fishing is good, even in the winter. Do you fish?"

"No time, you know how it is. Perhaps one day."

"Perhaps, is a word that can catch up with you."

Kuszczak smiled and sipped his coffee then cut to the chase. "The body was found yesterday in the Wista."

"Where?"

"On the south bank, between Kotlarski Bridge and the railway bridge."

"Let me guess a young woman – twenty to thirty?"

"Guess again, not this time. The body is male, white, aged around twenty."

Adamski found the surprise on his expression hard to conceal. Confused, intrigued, he poured himself some more coffee.

"The body was found under the ice around seven yesterday morning. Once again the head was shaven, a series of letters cut into the arm."

"The same as the others?"

"Yes."

"Are the letters in the same order?"

"Yes."

"Are you sure?"

"Yes."

Turning the coffee cup around in his fingers Adamski leant back in his chair. "Who found her? Sorry, him?"

"The body was spotted from Kotlarski Bridge by a couple walking to work. They thought it was some sort of animal at first."

Adamski contemplated his next trail of thought. "I'm not trying to be evasive in any way but I need you to tell me every detail. It doesn't matter how trivial or insignificant it might feel."

The two detectives glance at each other. Kuszczak stretched his legs and spoke. "I assure you everything has been done by the book. The body cut out of the ice. The riverbanks searched. As usual a piece of cloth was tied around his right bicep, although this time there was a pink triangle sewn onto the fabric."

"Pink?"

"Pink. Not the green one like the rest."

"So he was a homosexual."

"Homosexual?" Both detectives took another glance at each other.

"The Nazis colour coded every prisoner who came into Auschwitz with a triangle. Green for Jews, another colour for Romany Gypsies, another for Polish soldier's etcetera. Anyone who they presumed to be a homosexual was marked with a pink triangle."

Kuszczak nodded his head. "I know." But Adamski wasn't convinced that *he did know.*

"Have you been to Auschwitz?"

"Yes." It was an abrupt answer and once again Adamski wasn't convinced.

"Where his collarbones dislocated?"

"Yes, like the rest. Everything is identical except the body is male."

Adamski asked himself two questions. "Why would he have changed to a man? What if it was a random killing?" Turning his attention back to the detectives he continued. "Do you know what nationality he is?"

"Not yet."

"I suppose you'll know when he's reported missing." There was reluctance in Adamski's voice.

"The pathologist should have a report for us by the end of the day."

Adamski brought the coffee up to his lips. Before sipping he said. "So why have you come to see me?"

"The boss thought it would be good to share a few notes."

"Ah, how very considerate of him." A crooked grin came across his face. "I was never on his Christmas card list."

"It was his idea, not mine."

A minute of silence followed before Kuszcak spoke again.

"You said in one of your reports."

"I wrote hundreds of reports, took hundreds of statements."

"I know, I have read them all."

"You flatter me."

"Well in one of the files you wrote that you thought 'The Shepherd' would eventually slip up, as if he wanted to get caught. What did you mean by that?"

"It was a long time ago. All I can say is that I thought the killings might be ritual."

The other detective spoke for the first time. "Ritual, what sort of ritual?"

"I didn't mean it in the sense that it was a killing to some sort of ancient sun God, but I had to hang onto the hope that at some time the killer would slip up. Whether he would do that on purpose or by mistake now makes the latter more conceivable. The shaving of the heads, the symbolic lettering up the arms resembling the tattooing of serial numbers the Nazis carried out in Auschwitz, the victims not being subjected to any sexual abuse but at some time they had been suspended by their wrists which indicted to me some sort of a ceremonial killing."

To Adamski it was, at least, half true.

"Why go to all that trouble of killing someone the way he did then disposing of the body into the water just before it iced over?" The more questions that were asked the more the case became confused.

As the conversation meandered, Adamski caught the reflection of the fire in Kuszczak's glasses. "Is the artist working on a mug shot?"

"It will be in the papers tomorrow." Kuszcak slipped his hand inside his overcoat removed an asthmatic inhaler and squirted it into his mouth. Sucking in hard, he then breathed out heavily and coughed.

"Would you like a glass of water?"

"No thank you, coffee is fine." Taking a sip he composed himself before continuing with slight irony in his voice. "I'm sure the public will be delighted to know that the killer is still at large."

For the first time Adamski became sympathetic to the detective. "When are you doing the press conference?"

"Tomorrow at noon."

"High Noon." The two detectives were too young to remember the film 'High Noon' and Adamski was too drained to enlighten them on the western classic. The mention of the press conference took him back to the time that he had sat in front of a number of reporters and said that an arrest was imminent. Imminent, a word that would come back to haunt him time and time again. At times the two detectives blank expressions had made Adamski nervous throughout the afternoon. If they thought he had the answers they were mistaken.

A tense silence wrapped itself around the men as another pot of coffee was brewed. For two hours the three men searched for something. Discussing the numerous profiles of the murders from the pathologist to psychiatric reports they delved into the misogynistic and pathological fantasies of the serial killer and on more than one occasion their eyes clouded over with the endless superficial evidence that didn't exist.

Adamski measured his words carefully. Since retiring he was getting used to being heard but not necessarily being listened to. His appraisal was grim. "Since the discovery of the first body there have been three other murders; the waitress in 1946; the American girl in 1965; the tourist guide in Auschwitz in 1970 and now the fourth the first male; a homosexual in 1976. Four murders over a forty four year period and nothing." The silence and melancholy looks between them said it all.

Adamski eventually reflected. "Over the years I have tried to build a profile of 'The Shepherd' in my head. Is he like us, a man who visits the dentist for regular check-ups? Does he have a family doctor? Does he have a family? You know sometimes when I sat in a coffee shop I thought I could feel his eyes on me. I would quickly spin around to try and catch him out but there would be nobody there. If I heard somebody laugh in the street I would think it was him laughing at me. One day a man stopped me in the street and asked me directions. I looked at him without speaking. He walked off. Take my advice, don't leave it too long before you pick up that fishing rod."

Drained with the lack of evidence the case had become an enigma inside the corridors of the Krakow police department. On many occasion the detectives minds went blank with the frustration and speculation regarding the case. Constantly hounded by the press for any 'new developments', the killer had remained a phantom; a ghost, for the detectives. Whoever committed the murders had just evaporated; he didn't exist.

At the door Kuszcak turned to Adamski. "Who nicknamed him the name 'The Shepherd'?

Adamski shook his head. "I have no idea."

As he watched the two men walk back to their car Adamski was overwhelmed by a sense of sadness. Their spirits had been dampened and he couldn't stop thinking that both the men were lost souls. Just like himself.

JAMIE FISHER
AGED 40
1972
ENGLISH

CHAPTER FOURTEEN

Jake's fate waited.

Unable to sleep, unable to dream, Jake turned onto his side and looked through the window into the darkness outside. Time had been irrelevant all that evening when he stood and stared through the same window at a glorious sunset that could have been ripped from the canvas of a Turner painting. For an hour or so a couple of bats had kept him entertained. Swooping and dive bombing in circles he had become engrossed. They had reminded him of a dog fight from 'The Battle of Britain', a film his uncle Billy had taken him to see when he was a young boy. When the bats eventually disappeared along with the sun behind the walls of the prison walls Jake unknowingly sank into a fit of despair. Rolling over onto his back he rubbed his eyes and looked up at the ceiling. Thoughts of his mother played on his mind and a game she played with him when he was young. On both index fingers she stuck a small piece of paper and then recited a rhyme:-

> *Two little dickie birds sitting on a wall.*
> *One named Peter one named Paul.*

Fly away Peter.
Fly away Paul.
Come back Peter.
Come back Paul.

By switching fingers the paper would disappear then reappear again as if by magic. Then his mother's laugh; he could see her smile and he wanted to wrap those memories around himself forever.

Oblivious to Vince snoring underneath and the rock music thumping through the walls his thoughts flashed to when Thorpe handed him the envelope. For a spit second Jake had looked up from reading the letter and caught Thorpe grinning across at Rose as if he anticipating a hysterical or violent reaction. For those few seconds his grin became unnerving, Thorpe seemed to be one of those officers who like to play games with prisoners, winding them up was a good way of passing the time but Rose had taken him by surprise. Up until the incident he had come across as an O.K. officer, an ordinary, run of the mill officer, but he was mistaken. Thorpe's voice had become a weird mix of triumph and sarcastic despair. It could have been insignificant and just his way of grinning but either way it was playing on Jake's mind. Inside things can become larger than life; paranoia was part of the game. Jake knew it was the prisoners against the officers; reds verses the blues. His mail was read before it was given to him. They knew his business. It was just a matter of fact. Prison life. Protocol. But after much deliberation he agreed to Carol's visit.

Sleep was a priceless commodity inside prison, with a lack of it, prisoners became edgy and that could become dangerous. For Jake during the short time he had been inside he hadn't had one full night's sleep and cruelly time had dragged. That night it felt close, heavy, and it wasn't long before thunder rumbled in the distance. Counting to seven, Jake waited for the light show.

Right on cue, thunder crashed and a crack of lightning blasted through the window of the cell. A ghost. At first he thought he was seeing things, standing in the corner, he was there then he disappeared into the darkness. A baby. Another crack of white light and the child was back. Then blackness. He had the face of an angel. Gasping for air, Jake sat up. As the rain drummed on the prison roof he tried to focus into the darkness of the corner. Clawing at the bed sheets he held his breath. Another roll of thunder. No light. Blackness. Jake's mind flickered back to when he was a young boy and how he cowered under the bed covers frightened of the thunderstorm. Comforted by his mother he could feel her hand stroking his brow. "It's alright son, it's just God moving his furniture." Closing his eyes all he could see was the child's face. Drifting off to sleep, he once again questioned his own sanity.

Just after dawn Brainforth once again sprang into life to the sound of the guard dogs barking. Flickering open, Jake's eyes were lead heavy as the child's face once again flooded in to mind. Rolling over onto his side he was surprised to see the cell door was open. He hadn't heard a thing. A line of prisoners were drifting past along the landing to breakfast. Stripped to the waist Vince had shaved and was washing as best he could in the small wah basin. He spun around when he heard the movement on the top bunk.

"Bloody hell, Sleeping Beauty has finally woken up." Dabbing his face with a hand towel Vince's voice suddenly deepened. "Captain's log says it is breakfast time."

"I'm not hungry."

Throwing on a t-shirt, Vince then moved towards the door. "Ok, see you later, I'm starving. Popping his head back round the door Vince said drolly. "Oh, by the way, our friend the priest dropped a welcome present in for you."

On the table next to yesterdays newspaper was a bible.

"God loves a trier." Vince left with a spring in his step.

Swinging his legs over the side of the bunk Jake dropped to the ground. Yawning, he picked up the bible. On the cracked leather cover a faded cross in gold leaf was barley visible. Flicking through the gospels Jake smelt the must clinging to its pages. Slipping out of the pages a single sheet of card floated to the floor. Crouching down Jake picked it up. It was a prayer card. Embossed with small dried flowers, Jake turned it over and read the back.

Beware of men who speak well of you.

Shrugging his shoulders Jake went to place the bible on Vince's book shelf and noticed the same bible sandwiched in-between Pele's autobiography and a book on Self Enlightenment. The priest got around.

Over the next month life was dreary and full of routine. Counting the minutes; the hours and days; the nights closed in around him like a black mist. Allocated a job in a small store room cramped with filing cabinets Jake was told to file and keep filing. Void of any natural daylight there were no windows. The days lost their names.

Then after two weeks Carol arrived.

After being body-searched at a number of security gates Jake slipped on a yellow bib and was told to wait in line down a corridor. Scrubbed-up, hair combed, the prisoners smelt sweet. As the door opened up in front of them Jake found himself silently shuffling into a large room with a high ceiling. An officer allocated each prisoner to a table which were numbered in lines running the length of the room. The room was warm and humid reminding Jake of university; just before he turned over the exam papers. Swamped in anxiety Jake looked around. He wasn't the only one perspiring. Light crept in through three barred windows which were streaked in condensation. At the end of the room a sign listed prison regulations.

No explosives.
No guns.
No knives.
No drugs.
No electrical appliances.
If caught, culprits will face at least a two year prison sentence.

Then the sign that every inmate dreaded.

If you are planning to separate from your husband/boyfriend please notify the prison office before your visit.

Reading the warning sign Jake never considered that Carol was paying him a visit to tell him it was all over. He felt sick. Chatter was spasmodic, sparse amongst the tables. Then the room fell silent. It was almost time. Lining the walls the officers clasped their hands behind their backs like soldiers, at ease on a parade ground. Waiting, watching, Jake found himself staring up at the wall clock as it ticked timelessly.

Filtering into the room the prisoners heard the voices of excited children. Sitting up Jake ran his fingers through the fringe of his damp hair. At the far end of the room an officer unlocked the double doors. Slowly the room came to life as a sea of loved ones filed in. Wide eyed, children with confused faces searched for their fathers. Teenagers dragging their feet clung to the sides of their mothers; girlfriends with tears in their eyes; nervous friends trailing behind. Embraces; the shifting of chairs; laughter; more tears. A deafening noise took over the room as the officers chatted amongst themselves always vigilant.

Then they found each other.

The warmth of their touch, the relief to be loved, held no bounds. Hugging each other, their bodies shook with pent-up emotion. Carol's lips brushed Jake's cheek. Holding her face in his hands he watched the tears flow. Her face had changed from that of a young girl to that of a woman.

Carol's voice broke first. "God, I miss you."

"I miss you too."

"You've lost weight."

"You said I needed to." She smelt sweet, like fresh flowers, her kisses were a blessing, sweeter than sweet. Dabbing her running mascara with a tissue Carol composed herself. Her voice shaky as Jake reminded himself how to smile. An officer walked across the room. "Could you sit down please." Feeling like two scolded children they laughed at each other. They had always shared the same sense of humour and in that split second they were reunited.

Trying to put Carol at ease Jake spoke. "His nickname is Doris, he's like an old woman, but for a screw he's alright. You look great."

"Thanks."

"You've done something with your hair."

"I feel like I've come on the back of a motorbike."

Her smile lit up the room. They stared at each other. A minute passed.

"Don't shut me out again." That's what Jake liked about Carol; she was always straight to the point.

"I'm sorry."

"So am I."

"Why, you've done nothing."

"I could have kicked up more of a fight to get your sentenced reduced."

"Don't beat yourself up about it."

"I've got another meeting with the solicitor next week. We are going to get you out Jake."

"I'll still have to do time. You know that."

"I know."

Mesmerised by her surroundings, Carol's eyes were everywhere. A couple of nervous kids sat opposite their father fidgeting in their seats. He was asking them questions about school, their mother prompting the answers. It was an alien world to them, to Carol. Jake was concerned how Carol would react. He could see it in her eyes. Inside his emotion slowly turned to embarrassment. They sat for a moment not speaking, glancing around the drab room, the silence uneasy. Understanding why Carol looked at odds with herself Jake watched as her troubled expression turned into a false smile. Returning her gaze back to Jake she spoke quietly. "I'm pregnant."

A lump lodged in Jake's throat.

"Well say something."

Jake eventually found his voice. "I'm just shocked."

"Good shocked or bad shocked?"

"It's fantastic."

Reaching inside her handbag Carol slid a black and white photograph across the table. "It's too early to tell whether it's a boy or a girl."

Studying the ultrasound scan Jake made out the foetus. Reaching across the table he took hold of Carol's hand. "My God I'm going to be a father."

"And I'm going to be a large person."

"I want you to sell my bike."

"You love that bike more than you love me Jake."

"Please, I want you to sell it. You should get about three grand for it. It will help, you'll need the money."

"I'm ok at the moment." The emotional gulf in her voice was evident.

She smiled with that gorgeous smile Jake had fallen in love with all those years ago.

For a second time the couple shared a smile but it was short lived. "Do you think you can come here for another ten years?"

"We'll get through this together." Glancing over Carol's shoulder Jake watched as a young boy was being given a lesson by his father on how to fight back in the school playground. Tears were streaming down the young boy's cheeks as his dad handed out instructions how to throw a right hook, then a left, followed up by another right. He recognised the prisoner from the previous day in the exercise yard. He had sat alone reading. He had looked frail, a loner, frightened to get eye contact with anyone. Now he was trying to impress his son by playing the big man, the king of the castle.

Jake's eyes drifted from the soft skin on Carol's neck to her eyes. He thought of all the missed opportunities, missed opportunities that had followed Jake around all his life.

Then as soon as she had arrived she was gone.

Just over an hour later Jake found himself back inside his cell. Listening to the chit chat regarding the next door neighbour, a school report or a family ailment was the easy part, but for the prisoners and visitors alike the hour dragged. Jake was the exception. His hour had flashed by and he knew that one day he wanted to die in Carol's arms as an old man.

"Until the next time my love." That's what Jake had found himself saying as he kissed her sweet lips goodbye, the love of longing. But would there be a next time? Inside, hardened men became broken men after visiting time had ended. Back in their cells some prisoners cried themselves to sleep. Some wanted to take on the world. Some wanted to take their own life.

That night Jake reflected on the visit. He couldn't stop looking at Carol and thinking what his child would look like. Would he be tall; his face reflected in his own looks. What if the child was a girl? Would she have her mother's eyes? Jake had noticed that on more than one occasion during Carol's visit that she took her gaze from his in an effort to hold her patience. Over and over again in his mind he went through their moments. Then from nowhere he heard that voice again. "Appeal Jake and if it doesn't work at least it it's a good way of passing the time."

Jake went to work.

It occurred to him that trying to find a loop hole in the legal system wasn't new inside Brainforth or any other prison. The librarian who passed the books over had seen that look of hopefulness many times. Then by page five all likelihood of optimism and expectation turned into despair. But Jake was determined. By page thirty he found the legal jargon intriguing. Over the next couple of months he immersed himself in law books and kept fit by using the gym every day. His mind became sharp. Assigned to certain workshops he did everything from filing, packing breakfast bags in the kitchen, to working in the laundry. Anything to keep his mind occupied, anything to pass the time, and every spare minute was spent buried in the volumes of law. It was a Herculean task.

Attempting to turn a metal bar in the machine shop his mind wandered from case study to case study when the file slipped from his grip whilst using the lathe. The palm of his hand came down on a jagged piece of metal as his blood spilt onto the floor. Eight stitches were sewn across the life line of his right hand by the prison nurse. And all for one pound fifty an hour.

On the days he was relieved of work duty Jake grabbed the opportunity to immerse himself in law. Inside the library he found the tranquillity he needed to read; to concentrate, to try and find that loop-hole in the legal system which might grant him his freedom or at least reduce his sentence. Embracing the challenge it took him back to his days at university where he'd burnt the midnight oil studying the history of Middle Eastern politics. It was an ambitious subject but learning had been his life and so it was to become again. But trying to read and sharing a cell with Vince wasn't that easy. Accepting the daily routine of prison life Jake equally accepted the conversations he had with Vince whose repertoire varied from the mundane to the world in one. Both of which he knew little about. As Jake tried to bury himself in the British legal system Vince would continually challenge articles in the daily newspapers. Become exasperated, his opinions on a world leader or a footballer would develop into him gesticulating from an imaginary soap box. When Vince rambled with enthusiastic vigour about a topic that had caught his interest Jake would pretend to listen. With his head submerged inside a book he hoped that Vince would realise that he was otherwise engaged and stop talking but he never did. Like chalk and cheese, an unusual friendship grew between the two men and sometimes they would pass the time by playing board games; scrabble, chess, draughts or backgammon. Vince had one main ambition in life and that was to reach the stars.

"When I get out of this shit-hole I'm going to re-invent myself."

A nine-to-five-job was out of the question; Vince knew he was unemployable and he wanted to do something exciting, so he made the conscious decision that he was going to enter every game show on television and earn himself a small fortune.

When Vince was released, Jake missed him. Underneath the persona of being a hard act Vince was a troubled character. He had dreams and nightmares like the rest of the prisoners inside Brainforth and on more than one occasion Jake had been woken in the middle of the night to Vince shouting out in the cries of a little boy. "Get off me, please, please, don't." Some nights he sobbed in his sleep. One day over a game of chess Vince opened up about the recurring nightmare which had been torturing him for years….

….Vince's veneer of toughness slowly peeled away, as he unfolded his story.

"When I was a young lad I was in and out of boy's homes. They call them care centres now. My mum and dad had split up in more ways than one. All I can remember is them battering each other when they came home at night drunk. Sometimes I got in the way. In one of the homes we had a man who slept over. He was like a warden come youth worker. His name was Jamie Fisher. He was older than he looked; had mop top hair and always seemed to dress in red for some strange reason. I can still smell him, a mixture of stale aftershave and burnt chip fat. One night I got up to go to for a piss and I heard a noise coming from one of the boys rooms down the corridor. The door was slightly open and I took a sly look inside his room. A skinny kid, around the same age as me, was stripped and being forced upon by Jamie. He had his hand across the kid's mouth and had his trousers round his ankles. The previous night he had done the same to me and it hadn't been the first time. I remember saying to myself, enough is enough. I picked up a fire-extinguisher which was in the corridor and barged into the room. It was heavy but somehow I found the strength to lift it over my head. Take that you bastard! I brought it down on the back of his skull. I can still hear the crack now, not only in my dreams. It was like a delayed reaction before he slumped onto the bed. Slowly blood started flooding out the back of his head onto the cover of the duvet. The other kid and I where shaking uncontrollably. We tried to lift him off the bed but he was too heavy so we woke up the rest of the lads in the home. There were about ten or twelve of us all together; we were like those kids on that island in that film. I can't remember what it was called. All of us stood around the bed just looking at him. I've never seen so much blood.

Then one kid said, "Come on lads, we need to get him out of here!"

It was weird in some ways, I can't really explain it but all of us never thought twice. We started wrapping him up in the blankets. Then all of us carried his body out of the back door of the home and across the corn fields. Apart from the lights of the housing estate which swept up one side of the hill that ran to our left it was pitch black. You should have seen us carrying this bundle on our shoulders; we must have looked like a giant caterpillar. One of the kids started laughing hysterically when we got him stuck on some barbed wire. Another kid whacked him across the face and he started crying like a baby. At the end of the corn field was a small wood. We debated as to where we should dump the body. Some of the lads said we should bury him but we had no shovels so we decided to drop him into a shallow stream. It was about one in the morning and I remember the moon had sneaked out behind some clouds and that I had no shoes on. It never crossed my mind to put any shoes on, it was that mad. The moon was so bright it lit up the bank of the stream like a searchlight. Fuck me we were scared out of our wits, it was freezing. Then, just as we unrolled him out of the blankets, his eyes shot open and he groaned. One of the older lads, Garry I think his name was, who smacked the kid, picked up a large rock to smash over his head. Then this other lad stopped him. He said if he was found by the police they would know he'd been murdered because his head had been smashed-in at the front and at the back. Talk about the mind of a murderer. Thinking back we were older than our ages; that's because we had no choice but to grow up fast. A couple of the younger lads pissed themselves. Then this other lad, who was just standing there with his hands in his pockets, said we should drown him. So we dragged his body to the river's edge. His eyes were wide open and he was shaking and groaning. We rolled him over onto his back and it took all of us to hold him under the water. We could feel his body wriggling. The river was icy cold, freezing. Blood was coming out of the back of his head and floating down the river. I slipped and fell over to one side; my hand went into some dog shit. Its funny how certain things stick in your mind. I'll never forget Jamie's face under the surface of the water, it was grotesque; his head was shaking to the right and left, merging with the blood. Three or four of us pushed him further under the water. Two of the lads were sitting on his chest; some were holding down his legs and arms. Then the bubbles which were coming out of his nose and mouth eventually stopped and he stopped wriggling so we let him go. Grass and mud were entangled in his fingers where he had been clawing at the earth. We stood in silence and watched his body drift off in the slow current, a trail of blood following him from his head. The only sound came from the branches of the trees as they groaned in the wind. We picked up the blankets and all of us legged it back to the home. When we got back we made a cup of tea and had a pow-wow round the canteen table. We all had jobs to do; change our clothes; wipe the mud off our shoes. In my case my feet; clean the fire-extinguisher; change the bed; burn the sheet and blanket we carried the body in, somewhere, well away from the home where it would never be found. Two of the lads went back with a torch to the barbed wire fence to see that nothing had been snagged on it; we even went to the point of brushing away the odd footprint on the bank of the river. Then we all ate toast and made a pact. We swore more than once on our lives, cut our thumbs and joined our blood. It was a little like that film; that film; what's it called? That's it; 'The Lord of the Flies' when they killed Piggy. Then we covered our backs by deciding on what time we went to bed, that we slept two to a room all night, and that none of us had left our rooms; we didn't know or hear anything. For all we knew Jamie was in his room all night and when we woke in the morning we were surprised he wasn't there. In the morning when the other youth worker came in, I forget his name; he asked us where he was? We just shrugged our shoulders and tucked into breakfast as if nothing had happened, we were good, very good, convincing. A few days later the body was found about a mile away, floating against a sluice gate next to an old mill. A few coppers came round to the home to question us. A social worker came with them a big woman who resembled Margaret Rutherford, you know the big actress in those old black and white movies. Anyway, we stuck to our story. They never suspected a thing from us baby-faced angels. From that day forward we never mentioned what happened that night. The only downside was a week or two afterwards when one of the boys became ill. At first the doctor thought he just had flu but then he contracted jaundice. He was taken to hospital where he was diagnosed with Weil's disease. It's funny how you remember certain words as well as certain things. His eyes became itchy and he eventually lost his sight. He died. I remember where and when we were told. It was late evening and we were playing darts and pool in the utilities room of the home. Our world seemed to stand still for few seconds; he was one of us. We never spoke about it, but we all knew. We heard he got the disease from the river. The waterway ran through a dump up stream and was contaminated with rats piss apparently. We all wept at his funeral but it just wasn't for him it was for ourselves, a sort of absolution. Every boy in that home had been raped by that bastard Jamie, including me. The way I look at it he had it coming…

Vince was fractured, old before his time. Tortured, the words had poured out of him; his voice weary and toneless; he seemed to be one of those people who would never find happiness anywhere, even if he tried.

But there was another reason why Vince had confessed his story to Jake. And it was quite simple. For the past twenty three of his thirty three years Vince had put what happened subconsciously to the back of his subconscious. Vince described his recurring nightmare. All I see is Jamie's face under the water. His eyes are red, bulging and look like there about to explode. Bubbles of air are streaming out of his nose and mouth, his head shaking from side to side. Then suddenly his hands shot out of the water and grabbed me around the neck.

Over the years the nightmares stopped. They only reoccurred on his first night inside Brainforth when he spent it alone. Inside cell number 43.

CHAPTER FIFTEEN

The Ghost Boy.

Throughout the prison Jake was commonly known as the Ghost Boy. Supposedly in cloud-cuckoo-land, the name followed him around like a bad smell, not just from the prisoners but from the officers alike. After his supposed apparition it was understandable that the majority of prisoners were reluctant to be around him. Reluctant to engage in conversation with anyone Jake kept to himself as best he could and carried on reading law. But as much as he tried to keep a low profile thing's only became worse. Around the exercise yard, on the landing or at work; Jake was subjected to the snide remarks, the loony tune, the basket case, the nut job. There were the guys who were waiting for him to snap, the ones looking for a dust-up. Fast becoming a prize catch for a prisoner who was out to make a name for himself Jake felt as if the air was being sucked out of his lungs. Vince had been released and keeping himself to himself was becoming more difficult by the day.

Then there was Kit Kat and Fruit Shot.

At first, Jake thought it would be best to stay clear of the two of them. Being known as a crack-pot was bad enough, knocking around with two transvestites was suicidal. But as much as he tried to ignore them they kept on coming back for more. They seemed to take a shine to him and smuggled all sorts of contraband into his cell. Chocolate, fruit, a magazine, a clean razorblade, you name it, if they could get it, they got it. Uninvited they would park themselves in Jake's cell for hours. Fancying himself as a bit of a card shark Kit Kat would regularly challenge Jake to a game of poker. As he shuffled the pack Fruit Shot would religiously stand behind Kit Kat and brush his hair. The two of them seemed to have full reign of the block and Jake never worked out how they acquired the goods, so he never asked. They were like a couple of modern day spivs, what ever Jake requested it would arrive within the hour, no questions asked.

But there was one underlying reason as to why Jake put up with the two of them. Apart from watching his back Kit Kat was as hard as nails. Shoulders like a wrestler, his thuggish features presented an aura of invincibility which glowed around him like an electric pulse. Confront him at your peril. Three men had tried and three men had failed. Taking a shower three prisoners thought they would try their luck and jumped him. Their luck ran out and they were given a good-hiding. Two of them spent a month in hospital, one with a broken jaw, the other with a fractured cheekbone, as for the other prisoner he found himself on a life support machine. Kit Kat was tried internally and pleaded self defence. He was found not guilty. Nobody messed with him again. As for Fruit Shot he lived every day in a fairy tale. He was the princess and Kit Kat was his prince charming. Holding a pose like a manikin his general knowledge and strong opinions of everyone and everything were priceless; from politics, to movie stars, sport trivia, the Russian Revolution to

Lindbergh's first flight across the Atlantic in the 'Spirit of St Louis'. When released his dream in life was to travel to New Orleans. Not for the Mardi-Gras like normal people, but to study 'the wonders of voodoo' as he called it. He thought it would be fun to stick pins into dolls. Cupid had fired his first arrow bringing Kit Kat and Fruit Shot together.

One day over a game of stud poker Kit Kat accused Fruit Shot of undressing Jake with his eyes. It caused an argument and both men spilt out onto the landing accusing each other of being their own personal anti-christ who had been sent inside Brainforth to persecute the other. After their tongues went into overdrive they never spoke to each other for a week. When they kissed and made-up, they came back to Jake like two love-lorn teenagers who had promised their eternal love to each other. Apologising to Jake for being caught up in their love tiff they insisted by celebrating their reunion with chocolate cake which they had pilfered from the kitchen. Within an hour after stuffing their faces with cake it was as if nothing had happened. Then, overnight, like magic, the dark hours and the resentment that had surrounded Jake lifted. The word had gone out. Anyone who wanted to give Jake a bad time would answer to Kit Kat. If looks could kill.

He was always there, never far away. That prisoner who he shared the cell with on his first night inside. His face was vivid; those eyes. Sometimes he could see him swaying to the music from the Orient. Appeal Jake, appeal. Jake continued to study; to read in hope.

One day after the next, one month after the next, passed along with each dawn and every setting sun. Eventually, every brick, every crack in the white paint on the ceiling over Jake's bunk became as familiar to him as the lines on his face. But all the time he had to watch his back. Kit Kat had left his 'mark' and the tension was ripe. Like a country village or a small community hooked on small talk and gossip, inside Brainforth was no different. Everyone likes an incident and when Jake was sedated on his second day inside the story spread along the walls of the landings like wild fire. He wasn't a paedophile, a rapist, a nonce but he was the basket-case who saw things in cell number 43.

Then the Ghost Boy remarks returned.

For something to do, to idle away the hours, he once again became a good notch on someone's belt. Like a category A prisoner serving life; killing him in defiance of Kit Kat would be 'high-fives' all round, until the next one. Kit Kat knew it, Jake knew it and the prison knew it.

And taking up the mantle was Harry Kuyt.
'The Dutchman', as he was nicknamed had a bland face like his personality and was a well-known mental case. A notorious 'head-the-ball' with a reputation for everything including gang rape and grievous bodily harm. Violence was his second name, his forte, you name it; everything was in his locker. The rumour inside Brainforth was that on one occasion he had walked into a city centre bar in Oxford with a Stanley Knife and sliced the tendons from behind the knees of two guys who didn't take a shine to his pet dog. The men were unable to walk and were reduced to being pushed around in wheelchairs.

"You better smile at The Dutchman's dog or that's what happens to you", they were the words rumoured on the street. Tales of The Dutchman were legendary.

Blonde hair sat above his collar and his cold, hazel eyes could give you a thousand yard stare which would liquefy the hardest of men. Everything and everyone was a challenge to him and Jake was to become another face-off, his next cold case. With a line of freckles that ran over each cheek, blonde stubble littered the chin of his baby face sitting on his thick neck which swept down to his broad shoulders. Running up both arms were tattoos of scenic Holland. Windmills; tulip fields, clogs. Weird. The funny part was that The Dutchman had never set foot in the Netherlands. His three bodyguards or 'Tulips' as they were christened accompanied him everywhere and preyed on the weak, which included one or two officers who were only to happy to turn a blind eye to his menace.

Jake had heard about his reputation, tried to avoid him and saw him coming. Pulling up a chair opposite Jake in the canteen his inquisitive eyes shot daggers across the table as he brought his coffee up to his lips. Avoiding eye contact with the Tulip's sly eyes, which peered down at him, Jake froze as he watched Dutch slurp his coffee. For a second Jake caught eye contact with Fruit Shot and Kit Kat across the hot-plates and for another split second he nearly stood up and left the table, if not for the blood in his body turning to lead.

The Dutchman leaned forward and produced a smile which wrinkled his long face. His voice held meaning and aggression.

"So you're the famous Ghost Boy?"

Jake cleared his throat. "I don't know about being famous."

"What did the ghost look like?"

"He was just an ordinary prisoner."

"Like me?"

"Not really."

"So, I'm not ordinary?"

"No." A dry burning sensation crept up from Jake's stomach as he searched for something else to say. His fear sharpened. Tilting his head sarcastically to the right The Dutchman slouched back in his chair and waited for more of a response, his eyes as wide as his grin.

"So, did you see a ghost or not?"

Trying not to stammer Jake found a strong answer. "If I saw

a ghost they would lock me up wouldn't they?"

Glancing over each shoulder Dutch smiled at his 'Tulips' as he continued. "I like this guy, he's funny. I also like ghost stories. Why don't you tell me what happened?"

"Nothing happened."

The tone of Dutch's voice changed, intimidation in his eyes. "Don't bullshit me."

Suddenly Kit Kat appeared from nowhere and started wiping the table top with a cloth that smelt of strong bleach. Chewing the inside of his mouth Dutch gave him a look; a look of anger mixed with mutual respect. One hard nut to another. But that look; that split second stare between the two of them, was about to start World War Three.

Dutch had become fixated with Jake as his temper seemed to fade. "You're lucky. Today I'm in a good mood, but something tells me that tomorrow I might not be."

Sensing Jake was under the protection of Kit Kat he left the table shoving a young skinny prisoner out of the way in the process. That, as they say, was that. The moment had past but Jake was under no illusion there would be another.

Over the next few days Dutch could think of only one thing. An obsession took over him. He became fanatical about the guy who saw the ghost. A bullet now had Jake's name on it, The Dutchman was determined to have his moment and Kit Kat and Fruit Shot were instrumental in his decision. Homophobic, he couldn't come to terms with the fact that a gay guy could be stronger than him; both physically and mentally. Paranoid about his status wavering inside Brainforth amongst the prisoners who might be thinking he was all right bullying the little guys but taking on Kit Kat was a different matter he became violently agitated. All that mattered to him was being number one. Unaware, Jake had become the catalyst. And so the war started.

At first Jake had told Fruit Shot and Kit Kat to stay out of it. It was his fight but in Kit Kat's words, "You have no idea what he's capable of. He will cut off your balls as soon as look at you. Anyway, Dutch has got it coming." It would only be a matter of time and Kit Kat was convinced that the previous attack on him by the three guys in the showers had been instigated by Dutch.

Jake wondered why God had sent The Dutchman into his world.

The following day in the canteen you could cut the atmosphere with a knife. It was like the pianist who stopped playing when the two gunslingers squared up against each other in a saloon. It was Kit Kat who took the bait and stepped into Dutch's shadow.

"You and me Dutch?"

"When?"

"Tomorrow."

"I'll look forward to it."

Guns were drawn; my dad's bigger than your dad. For the next twenty four hours the tension became unbearable. Kit Kat became morose, cracking his knuckles and staring into space, psyching himself for the sound of the first bell. Fruit Shot was beside himself with worry and stood behind Kit Kat massaging the shoulders of the prize fighter. Like the constant humidity along the landings the prison waited for the thunder. The fight was to be in the laundry at twelve thirty when the officers changed shifts. A knife was to be hidden behind the first tumble dryer on the right, on top of the first pipe that ran across the ceiling. It had to be ready, easily snatched at any given second. Fruit Shot had made sure it was there. He knew Dutch would play dirty, he couldn't take any chances.

"Can't fight your own battles can you Ghost Boy?"- "Hey Ghosty, getting the puff to fight your battles for you?"

Once again Jake found himself the centre of attention. Along the landings, in the canteen and at every angle of the exercise yard. If this was how it was today and Kit Kat was beaten, think of how life would be tomorrow. Throwing-up. That night Jake didn't sleep. The choice was made for him. He hoped tomorrow would never come. But it did.

After vomiting again one step led to two and he was on his way. No turning back, come what may. Breathing heavily, his legs turned to jelly and his heart raced so fast that he thought it would explode out of his chest at any second. Pushing open the kitchen door Jake stepped inside.

Silence.

A number of kitchen hands stepped to one side. Pumped up, ready for a scrap, Dutch stood at the end of the kitchen. Stripped to the waist his fists were bound in bandages, clenched tight; at the ready. Overhead, to the right of Jake, the knife waited. Dutch, flanked by his three 'Tulips' stood like the Four Horsemen of the Apocalypse. Throwing a few punches into an invisible opponent, sweat stuck to Dutch's body. Seeing Jake a line of spittle sprayed out of his mouth. "What do you want?" The two of them locked eyes for a few seconds before Dutch burst out laughing. "Don't tell me the faggot's shit himself?" Dutch looked at Jake there was something in Jake's expression that just wasn't right. "Fancy your chances do you Ghost Boy?"

There and then, Jake signed his own death warrant.

Punching the Tiger with eyes. Be first, be quick.

Head butting Dutch; a surging pain shot through Jake's forehead as it landed onto the bridge of Dutch's nose with a tortuous crack. Stunned, Dutch wobbled backwards. Sliding along the aluminium work top, pots and pans were sent clattering to the floor. The noise was deafening. Snatching up a mop one of the 'Tulips' turned back towards the door and slid the wooden shaft through both door handles. Another 'Tulip' helped Dutch to his feet. Shoving him aside Dutch laughed wiping the blood from his nose with the back of his hand. His manic laugh was surreal. Then the laughing stopped; his eyes narrowing, the veins in his forehead throbbed; a smudge of blood across his cheek. Dutch wasn't going to let Jake leave the kitchen alive. *Be quick.* Stepping forward Dutch fists came at Jake, the swish of air from his fists flying inches from Jake's head. One strike would be deadly. Ducking, swinging wildly, Jake's fist thudded into Dutch's bare stomach. Groaning, lunging forward, Dutch went berserk. Hatred filled his eyes; his nostrils flaring like a bull as his fists rained in. *Be quick, move.* Seizing an opportunity Jake swung his knee up between Dutch's legs. It was sweet. As Dutch buckled over onto his knees it was now or never. Quick as a flash Jake grabbed a pan and thumped it across the side of Dutch's head. Adrenalin shot through Jake's body as Dutch grabbed his leg and buried his teeth into his thigh. Bringing the pan back over his head Jake brought it down with a thump onto the back of Dutch's head. A gasp shot around the kitchen as Dutch keeled over. "Get him."

Side-stepping the burly one of the three 'Tulips', Jake watched as he stumbled over and fell forward cracking his temple on the corner of the work unit. As the floundering figure joined Dutch on the ground Jake followed it up with a volley of kicks to his ribs. *Keep them down.* Groaning Dutch had rolled over onto all fours. Gripping hold of the oven door Jake brought it back once, then twice, then three times, smashing the door onto the crown of Dutch's head. As Dutch rolled over to one side, Jake stood above the two groaning men. Sweat streamed down his face as his heart thumped.

Then from nowhere, blackness followed by pain; stars and near death.

As the knife gathered dust Jake was taken straight to intensive care. After the guards broke down the door to the laundry they found the 'Tulips' trying to drag Dutch off Jake while the kitchen hands looked on. Unconscious, Jake's body lay broken as Dutch rained in kick after kick. He was like an animal.

At first the guards found it hard to identify the prisoner. The blood and swelling around his face making him unrecognisable.

For three months afterwards Jake found himself outside the prison walls in an intensive care unit in the local hospital. Sipping liquids through a straw, his jaw was wired, his nose broken. Along with three broken ribs, twelve stitches started on his left cheek and ran under his left ear like rail tracks. A ruptured eyes socket caused the most concern. After two operations the physicians fought to save his sight and retained it, just, but it would remain bloodshot and his sight blurred for the foreseeable future. During his rehabilitation his torso turned back from being black and blue back to its normal colour. His doctor's words struck a cord.

"You're a lucky young man. One more blow could have been fatal."

Finding himself in the local hospital Jake sat for hours in his room overlooking a public park and a number of football pitches. The park was flanked by woods and a housing estate sprawled along the surrounding hills. Some days he'd watch people walk their dogs and he looked forward to Saturday afternoons and Sunday mornings where he had his own grandstand seat for Match of the Day. It took him back to kicking a ball around the streets as a rough and tumble kid and he looked back on those days with a fondness. What a mess he'd got himself into. Not just the face that stared back at him in the mirror but in his life. Memories came into his mind like the pages turning in a book. Carol swimming in the sea; Carol painting her toenails; Carol dancing; Carol smiling. Her smile was always there. She was never far away from his thoughts along with him becoming a father for the first time. And he read.

After two seasons had vanished unnoticed Jake was transferred back to Brainforth. As the prison van pulled out of the hospital gate Jake looked through the window of the van and noticed the building next to the hospital which also backed onto playing fields and woods. A sign read 'Grantham's Child Care Centre.' It was the boys home, now re-named, where Vince had spent part of his ill-fated childhood. The football pitches had once been fields of swaying corn, the woods still holding their dark secret.

Bad or good timing, take your pick.

Charged with grievous bodily harm along with his side kicks, on the same day Jake found himself back inside Brainforth, Dutch was being transferred to another high security prison. Still bearing the facial scars of the beating Jake was escorted through the prison by Conrad. Feeling as if he was daydreaming Jake was stopped at the exercise gate and came eye to eye with Dutch on the other side. Handcuffed, two officers stood either side.

"Well, well, well, look who it is, the Ghost Boy."

Conrad raised an eyebrow. "Ignore him Jake you won't be seeing him again."

Stepping to one side Jake and Conrad watched as Dutch was led through the gate. Jake could almost feel his breath on his cheek and taste his venom. Looking over his shoulder Dutch wrestled between the two officers "Hey Jacob as the song goes *we'll meet again some sunny day.*"

As the gate was locked behind them Jake's shoulders dropped. Resisting the temptation to turn and give The Dutchman one last look he spotted Kit Kat and Fruit Shot through the wire of the exercise yard. Both greeted him by raising their right fists in a triumphant victory salute A few prisoners clapped; some offered him cigarettes, some chocolate, some kitchen hands who had witnessed his beating turned away in embarrassment, embarrassed at being weak. Every prisoner's face told their own story. As from that day The Ghost Boy was dead and buried.

Three minutes after the adulation in the exercise yard Jake found himself being led into an interview room. The phone rang. Thorp picked up the receiver looked at his wristwatch and wrote something down. Standing by the window the priest turned and looked at Jake grim faced. Jake looked puzzled.

Thorp hung up and looked at Jake his expression remaining. "Sit down."

Stepping away from the window the priest played nervously with the wooden crucifix which dangled around his neck. His mouth dropped at the corners. 'I don't know how to break this to you'. He crossed himself before taking a deep breath. "I'm sorry Jake but your mother has died."

A hero's welcome return. Jake's mind darkened.

JIM ABBOTT
AGED 35
ENGLISH
1946

CHAPTER SIXTEEN
Unexpectedly the girl's screams would sneak up on him.
Then he would smell the stench of burning flesh.

Nine days before Christmas Day in the bitter corridors of justice, Len Hutton sat waiting for his name to be called. In five minutes time Len Hutton would be standing in the witness box and would be asked to describe in detail to the sea of faces in the courtroom his recollection of that night, that night in late November; that night which had haunted him for the past three weeks.

Although the High Court was busy with clerks and barristers, upstairs in the public gallery it was packed to the rafters. Hanging over the front row of the gallery where two ladies who had travelled miles by public transport. It was their fifteen murder trial and they had brought their knitting. To the right of them a newly married couple who had queued through the night in the pouring rain held hands. This trial had touched everyone. It was front page news.

In the oak panelled courtroom thousands of questions and answers had brushed the faces of criminals who had pleaded their innocence for over fifty years. Inside the courtroom the atmosphere was electric. This was no ordinary trial. It had held the public's attention for weeks and a large crowd had gathered outside. Jim Abbott had arrived inside a police van and been smuggled inside the court through the back entrance. A blanket covered his head.

Judge Boot sat pensively and adjusted his horse-hair wig and red gown before loudly coughing; it was his way of bringing the court to order. The room quickly fell silent.

Len Hutton swore on the bible to tell the truth and nothing but the truth, and the courtroom hung onto his every word. Although Len was very descriptive, his rhetoric surprising the majority of educated men, he was extremely nervous and apart from making a best-man's speech at his brother's wedding he had never spoken in front of so many people before. Across the room, the eyes of a condemned man who was about to be sentenced for the murder of the young girl watched under hooded eyes.

Listening intently to Len Hutton's account of that night in November the courtroom's imagination became embroiled in the pictures that he painted. At times they found themselves helpless; their feelings wrenched one way then the next. Len Hutton had recalled the night, saying that he had sat in the window of 'The Blazing Stump', watching, waiting.

"Watching what?" Asked the prosecuting barrister.

"The warehouse."

"Why?"

"I was waiting for someone."

"Who?"

"Jim Abbott."

"Why?"

"Because we had conspired to steal from the warehouse. I was a look out."

"Was Jim Abbott in the warehouse?"
"Yes."

Drinking heavily to combat his nerves Hutton described how he was on look-out and in collaboration with Jim Abbott to steal. He was the night watchman for the warehouse. But admitting his involvement in planning to rob the warehouse didn't prove Jim Abbott was guilty of murder. Pleading guilty the following week Len Hutton was sentenced to five years imprisonment.

Up until the second day of the trial the jury were at odds with themselves. The prime witness, a young policeman, was called to the stand. Questioned by a barrister named Andrew Cummings-Jackson who was a stalwart of the establishment. He had come to prominence ten years earlier with a case that was now legendary in legal law. Defending a man for stealing books from the local library, Cummings-Jackson listened as the defendant who was asked to read from the card and swear on the bible. "I can't swear on the bible your honour because I can't read the card." Cummings-Jackson had his wings clipped. In legal circles he was admired by his peers as being the prima-donna of defence lawyers but also a barrister who defended a man for stealing books, books he couldn't read.

The young policeman, spotless in his uniform, stood straight-backed on the witness stand and swore his oath on the bible.

ACJ: How long have you been a policeman?"

PC: About eight months, sir."

ACJ: Why did you want to become a policeman?"

PC: I wanted to help people."

Cummings-Jackson turned and faced the jury with the glint in his eyes of a mischievous boy.

ACJ: Very commendable. You wanted to help people."

Cummings-Jackson readjusted his wig and turned back to the young policeman; his serious tone meaning business.

ACJ: "Now let me take you back to the night of the 23rd of November last year. Could you tell the court in your own words exactly what your recollections are of the evening?"

PC: "It was a cold evening and I was walking down Grove Street just off the Dock Road. I was checking the doors of the factories."

ACJ: You had done this before?

PC: Yes sir. It was part of my job.

ACJ: "Were you alone?"

PC: "Yes sir."

ACJ: "Have you walked the beat alone before?"

PC: "This was my fourth time sir. Twice previously I was accompanied by my sergeant."

ACJ: "So you had some experience of being on the beat. Please continue."

PC: "Half way down Grove Street I noticed a light, a dim light coming from under the back gate of the factory. It was unusual for this time of night so I tried the door and found it open."

ACJ: "Did you see anybody hanging around outside?"

PC: "No sir. The only life was the noise from the Blazing Stump across the road."

ACJ: "So the street was deserted.

PC: Yes sir.

ACJ: Was the door forced or was it just unlocked?"

PC: "At the time I didn't know, but later on our investigations found the door to have been forced."

ACJ: "Please carry on."

PC: "I went into the factory and saw that the light was coming from an open door at the end of the factory."

ACJ: "Was it dark inside?"

PC: "Yes sir, but not dark enough not to see, if that makes sense?"

ACJ: "So it was dark, but light enough to make things out, obstacles, if you like. You're making perfect sense constable. Continue please if you would."

PC: "I went to investigate the source of the light. At first I thought it was most probably the night watchman, but then I heard crying."

ACJ: "Could you be more definite in your description. Was it the crying of an injured dog, for example, or that of a person crying?"

The policeman took a long breath and looked across at Judge Boot who was as engrossed as the rest of the courtroom.

PC: "It was a young girl crying sir."

ACJ: "Then what?"

PC: "I pushed open the door and saw a man….on top of the girl."

ACJ: "Could you see his face?"

PC: "Not at first sir."

ACJ: "Why?"

PC: "Because he was on top of the girl and he was covered."

ACJ: "Covered? I know this is difficult for you, but could you explain how he was covered?"

PC: "He had on an overcoat which was pulled up back over his head."

ACJ: "What else was he wearing?"

PC: "Nothing."

A gasp from the public gallery.

ACJ: "This is very important constable. Was he naked apart from the overcoat. Were his trousers round his ankles?"

PC: "Yes sir."

ACJ: "Thank you constable, I think we get the picture. Then what did you do?"

PC: "I went to the young girl's aid sir. She was in some distress."

ACJ: "Commendable, very commendable. I realise this must be very difficult for you constable but please could you describe to me and the court exactly what happened next?"

PC: "I grabbed the man by his collar and dragged him off the girl. It was then that I recognised the girl."

ACJ: "Her name? How did you recognise her?"

PC: "I recognised her as Heather Brown. She worked in a shop that is on part of my beat."

ACJ: "Distressing, very distressing. You then saw the man's face?"

PC: "Yes sir, that's if you can call him a man."

ACJ: "Did you know him as well?"

PC: "No sir."

ACJ: Did you recognise him from somewhere?"

PC: No sir.

ACJ: "Could you recognise him again if you saw him?"

PC: "Yes sir."

ACJ: "A positive identification?"

PC: "Yes sir."

ACJ: "Can you recognise that man in this courtroom today?"

PC: "Yes sir."

ACJ: "For the benefit of the jury can you point him out to us."

From behind his back the constable swung round his arm and pointed his index finger across the court room to Jim Abbott standing in the dock.

"Murderer!"

"Silence in court!" Judge Boot looked up at the faces of the hungry mob baying for blood in the public gallery. "Any more disturbance from the gallery and I will have it cleared."

Judge Boot had a reputation for sending twenty prisoners to

the hangman's noose and was looking like he was up for twenty one.

After the 'summing up' by the barristers the jury retired and took less than an hour to reach a verdict of guilty. Away from the courtroom's glare, Judge Boot's rheumatic fingers had fiddled nervously with a triangular piece of black cloth which was draped over his chubby right knee. Throughout the trial in the privacy of his chambers he had struggled to hold a brandy glass. A tipple he privately toasted after he had sent a prisoner to their death. Passing sentence Boot along with the courtroom watched Jim Abbott sway and he gripped the sides of the witness stand for support. The case was made for Boot and his ego. The headline on tomorrow's front page was already written.

Bringing the rim of the brandy glass up to his thick purple lips Boot toasted the sad, beaten figure being escorted across the cobbled courtyard towards the prison van.

"May God have mercy on your soul." It was a ritual he repeated religiously. One he had said minutes before in the courtroom and now to himself when he had sent a man or woman to the gallows. As the shot slid down Boot's throat he looked down from the window of his chambers at Jim Abbott who was standing at the back of a prison van. Momentarily Boot became mesmerised by the grey smoke puffing from the van's exhaust pipe. After Boot had passed judgment he never gave the prisoner a second glance. Like all the summings-up of a callous murderer he addressed the courtroom like a Shakespearian actor delivering Henry the Fifth's rallying speech at Agincourt.

But certain things about this case played on his mind. There was something different about this case, Jim Abbott. Quietly proclaiming his innocence Jim Abbott had spoken articulately and said only 'his maker' could pass judgment on the man who had really committed the crime.

"Murderer! Murderer!" once again bellowed down from the public gallery. All the prisoner could do was to shake his head. Not in shame, but at the savagery of the moment.

"We find the prisoner guilty!" For the first and last time Judge Boot questioned the legality of the sentence which was a unanimous verdict by the jury. It rested on his conscience and the brandy was of little solace. It had been snowing for a while, flecks of white clinging to the window and the tops of the sandstone wall which squared the courtyard. Peering down Boot unexpectedly caught the condemned man's gaze as he looked up. For some strange reason Boot felt empowered, raised the brandy glass and toasted the prisoner. There was a look of haunted resignation across his face then within seconds Jim Abbott disappeared from view into the back of the prison van.

As the van drove through the gates of the courtyard Boot was drawn to the lines of footprints in the snow, they were the last footprints of a preordained man who would never see daylight or feel the sun on his face again.

The following day at his gentleman's club whilst reading 'The Times' newspaper, Judge Boot was drawn to the grandfather clock as it chimed midday. Just about to have a lunch of fresh salmon he reflected on the prisoner. Walking his final steps, he wondered what went through a man's mind when he was about to die. He had heard stories of course. Accepting the 'last-rites' the prisoner was led out of a holding cell where the prison governor and his executioner stood waiting. Given a shot of brandy to tighten his neck he was positioned over the trap door. Gulping hard; a hood; then a noose were slipped over his head.

"Your usual Napoleon Brandy Judge?" Looking up at the waiter, a shudder went through the Judge's body as Jim Abbott plummeted through the trap door.

CHAPTER SEVENTEEN

For a little while afterwards Jake took on some sort of bizarre hero status inside Brainforth. Some new prisoners stepped aside as if they might catch a bit of something that he had. The turn of events had become surreal; from the ridiculous to the sublime, the melodrama of him being nicknamed Ghost Boy had been replaced with the status of him being a different type of nut case; a hard hitter who wasn't afraid of anything or anyone. Most of the time he got the looks he knew all to well, the looks that said, "I don't want to know. Keep your distance". Occasionally he was met by stares and whispers. Still, the threat was obvious.

But it was the death of his mother and grief that really took a hold of him. It seized his insides with a firm grip and wouldn't let go. For the next week he kept himself to himself and avoided any conversation which came his way. Kit Kat and Fruit Shot kept on raising their right fists in a triumphant victory salute. It was their way of saying, "If you need us, we're here", they knew he wanted time alone, time to grieve.

They tried to brighten his days by leaving slices of chocolate cake on his pillow but it was of little consolation in the light of what had happened. His mother had died alone. She had brought him up single handed. His father flying the nest when he was a little boy. Memories of his mother flooded back to him. During the day she had worked as a machinist in a clothes factory sewing industrial overalls and at night she had worked in a launderette. Two jobs to earn more money, to give him a chance in life. Now look at him. When she came home at night she was deadbeat but she never complained. As a treat she would bring him home a bag of chips. Tucked under his mother's arm they were the best chips in the world. If she had one dream in her life, it had been to travel the world. In her later years Jake would watch her dozing in her armchair, a picture of Venice or New York opened up in a magazine lying in her lap. Their front room was always cluttered with travel brochures but they were only pipe dreams as far as he could remember she never had a holiday in her life.

Lying on his bunk, Jake listened to the wind blowing across the roof of the prison. The night blacker than black. Nobody should die alone but most people do. When his mum really needed him where was he?

Then there was that leather case. The leather case that changed everything.

In the early hours of the morning a thunderstorm broke and acted as a wake-up call. Followed by a heavy downpour the temperature dropped when Jake heard his name being yelled out by an officer.

Throwing on a pullover Jake walked onto the landing and looked down through the well. A young officer on the ground floor was stretching his neck muscles looking up, a dubious expression across his face. "There's a package for you at reception."

Over the months Jake had learned to walk slower, do things slower, like showering, rearranging the little contents in his small cupboard by the side of the bunk. Time was drawn out, sometimes priceless. Jake had learnt to weigh up each option, but today in his excitement, he found himself quickening his pace. Intrigued as to what was waiting for him he felt like a kid anticipating Christmas day morning. Making his way down the iron staircase Jake emerged into the shafts of daylight that shone down from skylight. Passing the pay phones on the ground floor he was struck by the thought of ringing Carol. What did he have to say? Whose voices were they in the background? In hospital he had fought against ringing her every moment of every day. The 'I love you's' replaced by niggling paranoia that slowly crept up on every prisoner when they least expected it. Selfish, she would have wanted to talk about his mother and their baby that was growing inside her. But he couldn't let her see him like this. In time the cuts and bruises would heal. Then perhaps.

Glancing at the TV a race meeting was underway and a few prisoners had gathered around the set waiting for the horses to bolt out of the stalls. Money was replaced by cigarettes as to who was going to be first past the post.

The supercilious desk officer who had a face like he regularly read obituary columns, sighed loudly, before dropping a small, battered case onto the counter with a heavy thud. Sliding a document across the counter the officer clicked the top of his pen and handed it to Jake. "Put your monogram on the dotted line please Jacob." This officer's talk was limited, his tone always low, all things an effort. Leaving his signature on the requisite-form Jake picked up the case and was surprised as to how heavy it was. Making his way back to his cell he cradled the case in his arms as if he was carrying a ticking bomb. Looking down onto a white envelope which was sellotaped to the top of the case he read the address: *James Jacob, Brainforth Prison*, followed by his prison number. The handwriting was scripted in fountain pen and unfamiliar. Knowing all too well that the letter had been read and the case opened he felt like his privacy had once again been violated.

Inside his cell Jake found Conrad pulling the bars on the window. It was a weekly check the officers undertook themselves. In the past some prisoners had chiselled away at the concrete to loosen the bars. Three floors up, some prisoners were delusional, believing they could scale down the building, skip past the guard dogs then scale the thirty foot prison wall and escape to sunnier climates. But for some prisoners to pick away at some stone was just an act of simple boredom.

On hearing Jake enter the cell Conrad turned from the window, his voice following him like an undertaker's as he walked to the door. "Sorry to hear about your mother Jake."

Jake acknowledged Conrad with a nod but was deep in thought. Lingering, Conrad tried to engage Jake in polite conversation but realised Jake was evasive and left.

Staring down at the envelope a strange feeling passed through Jake's body, his hands started shaking, he felt claustrophobic and his chest wheezed and he struggled for air. Reaching through the bars he opened the window. Inside his cell he had the luxury of a window that opened slightly and the air which drifted across his face felt like silk. Regaining his breath, his attention returned to the letter and he picked it up. Running it under his nose he sniffed. It smelt of pipe smoke. Ripping open the envelope, he slid out a single sheet of white paper. Whoever had written the letter had struggled to hold a pen. The writing was shaky and broken.

Dear Jake,

Before your mother died she made me swear that I would somehow get this case to you. Apart from a few knick-knacks she left nothing else. All of which I have boxed- up and will keep for you. Up until her last days on earth she was very proud of you. She always said you were the best thing to happen to her; her boy; her Sonny Jim. She was a wonderful sister to me, and like you, I will miss her with every passing day.

Keep your chin up son.
Uncle Billy. x

Uncle Billy had been like a father to Jake, his tears everlasting.

The case resembled the size of a large shoe box. As a young boy Jake vaguely remembered it under his mother's bed and always wondered what was inside. As far as he could remember it had always been battered, its smell familiar, its brown, cracked hide holding a mystery with his childhood imagination. One of the two brass latches held it shut; just. The other latch was broken and clung on for dear life to the thick leather, a splatter of mould running across the surface. Worn, heavy frayed stitching barely kept the case from disintegrating but through all its dilapidated appearance it looked sturdy and held a proud history. Used as a child's seat it had been sat on over the years as a relief to tired young legs in bus stations, airports and railway stations. Its rawhide top was cracked and dipped in the middle and bore the embossed initials J.H.A. in faded gold.

Running the tips of his fingers across the initials Jake thought of his mother and his past. If there was a clue as to who the case had belonged to the initials meant nothing to him. Most of his childhood memories had long gone.

The case had sat at the end of the bunk for the rest of the day before Jake decided to open it. For some strange reason he felt apprehensive as to what was inside and what he might unearth. When his grandmother's sister died, they found a loaded gun in her bag. A Will? A love letter? Skeletons in the cupboard? Pandora's Box? Whatever was inside could open a can of worms and it wasn't to be taken lightly.

Sitting on the bottom bunk he nestled the case across his knees. Taking a glance at the open cell door he watched as a few prisoners passed by. Somewhere on the landing he heard the sound of a mop bucket and smelt disinfectant. Satisfied he wasn't being watched or wasn't going to be disturbed he flicked open the brass latch and lifted the lid of the case. Again it smelt earthy; musty; he became fearful, hesitant.

Inside the lid of the case was a blue, silky, lining. In the middle of the silk was a gold emblem of The Matterhorn. Underneath ran the words *'James of London, the finest of Swiss Chocolate.'* It triggered a memory, a salesman's case, once holding small trays of the best chocolate in the world. But what memory?

An assortment of papers, photographs and newspaper cuttings spilled from the case and he felt a cold tingle run down his spine. Before him lay his past and possibly his future. At first glance the majority of faded papers meant nothing. A few bills, empty envelops with exotic stamps from around the world but nothing else. Perusing the images from a by-gone era, a number of the photographs were sepia. Some colour, some black and white, a reminder of family keepsakes. Everything spoke of another time. Void of any daylight Jake imagined the case to have been hidden under his mother's bed without ever being opened for years. At first he was scared as to where to start; his hands were shaking as his mind raced. As his eyes danced from photograph to photograph he began sifting through the case. From one piece of paper to a black and white photograph then back to a newspaper cutting. His birth certificate, a school report, a class photograph, fragments from the past. Where to begin? *Relax, time is on my side, there's no need rush.*

Removing a few papers Jake came across a framed, black and white photograph. Instantly he recognised the photograph which had rested on his mother's dressing table for years. The size of a postcard, the ornate edge of the frame felt cold in his hands as he looked down at two young children wearing Hiawatha headdresses peering out from behind a large oak tree. The glass in the frame held dust, the glass cracked in the bottom right hand corner. Aged around six his mother was beautiful, a beaming smile splashed across her face; she was just a child. Uncle Billy was next to her; they looked happy; brother and sister, not a care in the world, their heads and hearts laid bare. Turning the frame in his hands he noticed a place and date scribbled in faded pencil on the back. *Frindley Woods, April 1930.*

Bewitched by the contents inside the case Jake came across a set of mixed photographs bound by an elastic band. Looking into the faces of the pictures, some were familiar, mostly family. All of them told a story of the past and he wondered what secrets they kept close to their hearts. One snap was one of himself, aged around eight or nine, he was holding onto his mother's hand at the fairground. In the background were the Super Dodgems Cars and The Dragon Ride and for one split second he could feel the warm sea air on his face and smell, doughnuts, candyfloss and toffee apples. At their feet were a picnic basket and a bottle of dandelion and burdock. An onion tear appeared in his eye. Running the knuckle of his right index finger under his bleary eye he prevented a tear from spilling onto his cheek.

Coming across a small book he turned it over in his hands to the front cover. Embossed on the front was the picture of a ragged sailing boat and an old man's, weather beaten, bearded face. 'The Old Man and the Sea' was written by Ernest Hemingway and he recalled reading the book and seeing the movie starring Spencer Tracy. Flicking through the pages a piece of paper slipped out of the pages and floated down resting at his feet. Picking up the paper he found it was a cutting from a newspaper, the story having been ripped away and removed from around the photograph of a bare-chested boxer. The boxer's eyes pierced the shot, his gloves trying to punch their way out of the newspaper. Disregarding it he placed it to one side and delved deeper into the box. Continuing to search he came across a prayer card and studied the front. It had a watercolour of a plant with striking orange leaves. Turning over the card Jake read the prayer on the back.

Beware of men who speak well of you.

Then at the bottom of the card in small letters were the words.

Amaryllises
South America

Puzzled, something felt peculiar. Tipping the contents of the case out onto the bed Jake picked out a strip of black and white snaps taken inside a photo booth. His face lit up. It was of him and his first girlfriend pulling grotesque faces into the hidden camera. Her name was Hilary and he could still hear her laugh which sounded like a hyenas. It was her endearing trademark. Both had just turned sixteen. Sweet sixteen. They had shared their first kiss which led to their first fumble on the back row of the Gaumont Picture House on a Saturday morning. They were in their own little world, oblivious to the usherette's torch and being surrounded by hundreds of screaming kids and the sounds of thundering hooves of horses and bullets flying as the cowboys tried to fight off the Indians. Everlasting strips and the smell of liquorice were replaced by a squirt of Hilary's mother's perfume, his first feel of a breast, which was followed by a loud slap. It was a summer of fun and kissing which eventually led to Jake losing his virginity in the sand dunes as the sun beat down on his bare backside. They were in love. Or so they thought at that age. Where did she go? What had she done with her life? Married? Divorced? Kids?

A certain photograph triggered another memory and helped pass the time, another second, another minute. Through the bars of the window the sun was trying to creep inside the cell. Over the months Jake had come to work out what time of day it was by the position of the sun. In a few minutes it would be around ten to three in the afternoon. His thoughts then drifted to Carol as it often did at this time of the day. He could see her throwing on her coat, checking her hair in the hallway mirror; hear the front door closing behind her, her laugh. How he longed to be with her now he was to become a father. But he wouldn't be there at the birth. Nor would he be able to feed his baby, change his baby, see his son walk for the first time; he would miss that first smile.

Snapping out of the gloom he looked down at the papers and photographs spread out on the cover of the bed. Coming across a thin book, the title read: 'The Origins of Qigong'.

Flicking through the pages he came across a number of pencil sketches. One was of a Chinese Warrior riding a horse. Both were covered in heavy armour. An icy shiver shot down his spine. Jake's hands started to tremble. Flicking through the pages he paused at the sketches when his voice returned inside his head. He could hear him telling the story as if he was turning the pages for Jake. One picture was of the Warrior holding a baby. The voice came to him again. Another sketch was of the Warrior lowering the baby into a well. Another page, another sketch, more words, frogs surrounding the baby in the bucket from the well. The smile on the Warrior's face. Jake's chest pounded. Dropping the book he sifted frantically through the papers on the bed and found the newspaper cutting of the boxer. At first glance he didn't have any recollection who the boxer was, but on looking closely, his eyes; the curl of his mouth seemed familiar. Mystified, his head throbbed. Agitated his thoughts and his voice swirled around inside his head – then the voice evaporated. Was it?

Picking up a pencil he drew a pair of glasses around the man's eyes.

Astonished Jake started circling the cell. It was him!

Sifting frantically through the papers and photographs, two words shot up at him like a bullet. Murderer. Hanging. They were faded words, words on the front page of an old newspaper. Spreading out the page in front of him he started reading the article. What he read was like a dagger through the heart.

Judge Boot had sat his normal passive self throughout the trial interjecting only once to quiet the packed public gallery's cries of murderer! After retiring the jury returned in just under an hour. Back into the cold courtroom a unanimous verdict of guilty was announced. The courtroom fell silent as an Usher placed the black cloth on Judge Boots head. Looking across at Jim Harold Abbott, Boot said that he had been found guilty for the callus murder of Heather Wilson and that he would be taken to a place of execution; Brainforth Prison where he would hanged by the neck until he was dead.

Jake crunched the newspaper article inside his fist. Springing to his feet Jake paced the cell, turning in circles his head was spinning. The photograph of the boxer; the words in the article went over and over again, impregnated into his mind. Murderer.

Hanging. Jim 'Harold' Abbott – J.H.A. – The initials on the case.

Finding himself on the landing Jake could feel the sweat running down his neck as he searched for Rose or Conrad. Across the well he noticed a couple of prisoners muttering to each other. *Think twice about it Jake, you're already on borrowed time.* It was the voice inside his head that made him take a step back. *Think, please God, help me think, please God help me. What should I do?* Finding a way for an officer to believe him wouldn't be easy; it would be impossible. Finding a way to convince anyone would be madness. It had been a while since the Ghost Boy. Jake suddenly running along the landings saying that he knew the identity of the ghost would get him certified.

Finding himself in a black cloud and irrespective of what had just happened Jake held his tongue.

What Jake wasn't expecting was that someone had heard that voice as well and was already plotting his downfall.

RUTH JACOB
AGED 72
ENGLISH
1977

CHAPTER EIGHTEEN

Gone but not forgotten.

Ruth Jacob's funeral was to take place the following Monday, on the last day of October. In the absence of Ruth Jacob's one and only son his trusted uncle had arranged the burial service. What Jake would have done without his Uncle Billy; to say he was a God-send was an understatement.

Billy was three years younger than his sister and Ruth Jacob's only brother. A retired fireman of forty years service he had been a hero and father figure to Jake. Awarded a medal from the Queen after he had rescued three children from a burning hotel room in the early sixties Jake's uncle had done what his father should have done, boys stuff. Football matches, swinging a cricket bat, fishing; wrestling in the back garden. Explaining how the birds and bees worked. Uncle Billy was always there, always available, always with a few words of wisdom.

The burial was to take place at St Mary's Roman Catholic Church which boarded Oxford City Centre. Set against a backdrop of tall pine trees it had been the family church which over the years had embraced weddings, funerals, christenings, smiles, tears and the odd confession.

Jake was given compassionate leave for the day and was to be escorted to the funeral by Rose and another officer called Parkinson who was sour-faced and had a reputation of being a soft touch; although Jake had never witnessed it. Given a grey suit that smelt of mothballs it was too long in the sleeves and too short in the legs. He didn't ask where it had come from and was past caring. It was the first time Jake had been outside the prison walls and he had mixed emotions. On the one hand he was dreading the funeral; there would be relatives whom he wouldn't have seen for years. The boy who had let his mother down; the bad apple of the family; like father like son. As for Carol he had pondered over sending her a letter for days. Eventually finding the right words he asked her not to attend. "It would be best for all concerned. Please respect my wishes." She never replied because he never sent the letter.

Handcuffed Jake sat in the back of the rumbling prison van. Through the black tinted windows he watched the world flash by. Trees rocked in the wind, their gold leafs dazzling. Outside the thunder of a pneumatic drill vibrated through the floor of the van and shuddered up through his legs as strips of sunshine bounced around the inside of the van and stung into his eyes. He heard cars and the roar of a motorbike which took him back to that particular day, that rainy day when it all had gone disastrously wrong, when Harris lay bleeding, dying. Since his mother's death Jake had found the mental strain and the nervous tension of what lay ahead hard to take. Unbuttoning his shirt collar he loosened his black tie. How would his relatives react on seeing him, his uncle in particular? Examining the scar tissue around his eye he winced. It still felt tender from the beating he had taken, although the swelling had reduced; the bruising remained. Jake was also scarred inside.

Stopping at traffic lights, Jake listened to the conversation between Rose and Parkinson. Hunched over the steering wheel and twitching for a nicotine hit, Parkinson's gravely voice held a twenty a day habit. Slightly overweight, his blond crew-cut was cut to perfection, his long fingers strumming the steering wheel as he waited for the lights to turn green. Something about last night's football match and a dodgy penalty decision, mixed with the forthcoming World Cup, rattled between the two officers as Parkinson threw the van into first gear and took off. Like always Rose was practically animated. Handcuffed to Jake his knees were crunched up around his chest and beads of sweat clung to his brow. Through the van window Jake noticed children playing in a swing park. A beautiful long haired girl riding a bicycle; the sun reflecting off the windows of buildings; his eyes meeting Rose's momentarily. Then the van suddenly swung to the right, then a sharp left. Following a small church wall the van pulled up outside by the gates of St Mary's Roman Catholic Church. Underneath the van's tyres crunched to a halt. Through the van window Jake caught a glimpse of a group of mourners milling around outside the church entrance. Some of the black figures noticed the van and he could see them nudging each other and also the turning of heads. Cigarette smoke drifted up from some faces which were drawn and grey, their eyes piercing the van.

"Here we go Jake, take a deep breath lad." There was a spring in Rose's voice which was inappropriate for the occasion, but that was Rose. Suddenly the back doors clanged open filling the van with glaring sunshine. Sliding across the back seat of the van Jake tried to focus his good eye on his surroundings. Stepping onto the pavement Jake felt Rose and Parkinson grip his upper arms. There had been showers that morning and the air was fresh and light. Taking a collected breath Jake and the officers stepped through the wooden gates of the church.

Mourners, red rimmed eyes, turned their eyes and glued them on Jake as he was escorted through the churchyard. A breeze ran through the bare branches of the trees making a sound as if they were crying. Shuffling between the two officers along the stone path Jake felt a leaf brush his face and he could smell the flowers which were scattered around the stone obelisks and engraved tombstones that spoke of the past. Then in the shadow of the church's bell tower Jake came face to face with the mourners and his mother's friends for the first time. Some were familiar. A few distant cousins. Mrs. Cleveland her next door neighbour of thirty years and Aunt Myrtle who was never a real aunt. On seeing his nephew Uncle Billy stepped out from the huddle of mourners, the hair of his grey temples ruffling in the breeze, his face lined with sadness. Feeling like he'd aged twenty years Jake could feel himself welling up inside as Billy struggled to walk towards him. Hugging Jake with the strength of a twenty year old the embrace took the wind from his lungs.

"Good to see you lad." Kissing Jake on the cheek Billy held his face in his hands and stared him directly in the eyes. "Be strong lad, your mum would have wanted you to be strong." Looking down at the cuffs then up at Rose, Billy spoke out the corner of his mouth. "Can't you take these bloody things off him?"

Parkinson butted in. "Sorry, rules. It's more than our jobs are worth." There wasn't an ounce of remorse in his voice.

Billy's eyes were wild and black as he stroked his hand affectionately down Jake's arm. "You'll be alright son."

His hands shook as he handed Jake a card. On the front was a picture of his smiling mother in her youth with the words: – A celebration of the life of Jean Jacob. Underneath the order of the service. Tears shot into Jake's eyes as an overwhelming sense of loss came over him. "She picked the hymn. 'All Things Bright and Beautiful', it was her favourite hymn. It reminded her of our mum and dad when we were kids." As Billy spoke he wore a strong but sad smile. "Do you want to say anything? A prayer? A reading? A poem?"

Finding his voice Jake said. "I would, but with these on?"

Holding up the cuffs, Rose contemplated the request with a prolonged sigh. "I'm sorry the Governor would have me on report if he found out."

Shoulder to shoulder the three men walked towards the group of mourners. As the pebbles crunched underfoot the church became an imposing sight. Built in the late forties; a modern day statue of The Madonna constructed out of twisted iron hung above the entrance to the grey stone building. Flashes of white ran up the edges of the cornerstones to the bell tower which cast a large shadow across the surrounding graveyard and trees. For a few seconds the tension was broken by the sound of starlings flying overhead and a woman who came up to Jake and said. "Sorry for your loss. Your mum was a great lady."

Inside the church the smell of damp and musty hymn books lingered in the silent air. Crackling through a couple of small speakers hanging precariously from two giant stone pillars was the voice of Frank Sinatra singing 'Come Fly With Me'. Heads turned, eyes focused, their stares burning a hole into Jake as he stepped out of the vestry. At the far end of the church in front of an imposing altar; Jake saw his mother's coffin for the first time. Lying under a large stained glass window depicting the Last Supper. A kaleidoscope of light poured down onto a bouquet of white lilies which sat on top of the coffin. As Jake was led down the aisle he noticed Carol on the front pew. She turned and caught Jake's gaze. Wearing a small black hat she smiled, her eyes telling another story.

"I want to pay my respects to my mother." Tautness spread through Jake's body as another wave of emotion welled up inside him. Rose and Parkinson reluctantly led him over to the coffin. Kissing the tips of his fingers Jake placed the palms of his hands on top of the coffin. Lost in thought another wave of emotion swept over him.

"Ok Jake." Rose tugged Jake's arm and directed him towards the pews. They had barely sat down when. "That's not very nice Mr. Rose, why don't you let him pay his respects properly. Sitting behind Carol was Vince.

"Go on remove his cuffs?" Grinning, he had lost an alarming amount of weight; his eyes were ringed in black circles; his teeth yellow. Staring straight ahead Rose held onto an uncomfortable smile.

Vince cupped his hands around his mouth and raised his voice. "Everyone wants you to take his cuffs off Mr. Rose." There was psychotic sternness in his voice which made everyone nervous.

Parkinson shot him a look over his shoulder, his voice low. "With all due respect, this has got nothing to do with you."

Flanked by the two officers Jake became aware of the altercation which was causing a stare from the undertakers who were standing at the side of altar. Jake felt Vince's stale breath on the side of his cheek.

"Where's the brotherly love gone Mr Rose? Go on remove his cuffs."

Ready to snap, Parkinson's eyes narrowed. "We can't do that and I would appreciate it if you didn't interfere."

"If you've forgotten, we're not inside Brainforth. Gone are the days when I take orders from a prick like you."

Parkinson glared towards the altar, if he had a reputation for being a soft touch he wasn't showing it.

Vince came forward with another response, tapping Rose on

the shoulder. "Hey Rosy, I wonder what Mrs Rose would say when she learns about you dropping your trousers last Thursday afternoon?"

"What are you talking about?"

"In The Bamboo Sauna, over the garages on Devin Street?" Rose's eyes widened, his face white.

Vince raised his eyebrows and grinned. "Dirty devil Rosy; un-cuff Jake for an hour and Mrs Rose will be none the wiser. You've got my word on it."

Beads of sweat had gathered across Rose's top lip. Parkinson glanced across Jake at Rose. A nerve had been struck. Conscience colliding with his guilt. Swinging his attention to Jake, Rose removed a set of keys which were attached to a chain inside his pocket. "One hour Jacob, one hour, we'll be outside."

"What are you doing?" Parkinson's voice echoed around the church causing more of a stir.

Unlocking the handcuffs Rose reiterated what he'd said.

"One hour Jake, one hour."

"What are you doing?" Parkinson growled back at Rose.

"I'm the senior officer here."

Parkinson shot his finger in Rose's direction. "I want it to go down on record that if things go tits-up this was not my decision." Rose stood up and strode off down the isle. Parkinson reluctantly followed; embarrassed by the sea of watching mourners.

Carol sat down next to Jake, took his hand and kissed him on the cheek. No words.

Noticing Vince couldn't keep still Jake looked at his waxy complexion streaming with sweat. He whispered. "Are you alright?"

"Yes, I'm cool, lucky break eh? By chance a mate of mine who had twenty four hours in Brainforth recognised Rose going into the sauna, dirty bastard. Vince stumbled out of the pew. "Sorry, I need some air."

A wiry priest cut them short as he shuffled out of a side door. Positioning himself by the side of the coffin he coughed before addressing the congregation with a prayer then introducing the brother of the deceased. Billy's voice quivered with affection. Reminiscing about his older sister and their upbringing, he recollected stories about the war and how they had played as kids on the bomb sites; her love of reading and doing crosswords; her patience was her virtue; the love of her son. "My son, my son", she would say.

As the priest blessed the coffin another song by Sinatra floated around the church. Stepping towards his mother's coffin Jake was conscious of the undertakers standing in the wings and spoke quietly. "I love you mum. I'm sorry, so, so sorry. Please forgive me."

Carol was at his side. "She loved you Jake." She held him.

At the back of the church Parkinson stood watching, waiting. To the right of him Rose looking agitated, a furrow etched across his brow.

Turning to Carol Jake was a broken man. "I have to go."

Tears welled her eyes. "All in good time." A smile as long as the day zipped across her face. "I want you to meet somebody." Taking hold of his hand she led him past the font and the confessional box. Through a side door they left the dark church and into the daylight. A number of steps led down to a thin memorial garden which ran the length of the church. Surrounded by a rusting wrought iron fence, a stone sundial stood in a circle of rose bushes. As they walked along the path Jake became stunned.

Sitting on a wooden bench was Carol's mother. On her lap was a baby whom he instantaneously recognised. Skipping a heartbeat it was the same baby he had seen sitting on the lawn of his back garden, the same baby he has seen when the lightning had illuminated his cell.

"Say hello to your son Jake." Carol picked up their son and passed him to Jake. Holding his son in his arms for the first time Jake started crying uncontrollably.

At the front of the church Vince lent on a headstone smoking. Shaking, he needed a fix. Grinning across at Parkinson and Rose he threw up two fingers. He enjoyed being in control and soaked up the anguish across the two officers faces.

Rose leaned into Parkinson. "He'll be back inside soon. Every dog has their day."

"You're a wanker Rose. If you've forgot, we've lost a prisoner."

The relief across Rose's faces was plain to see as Jake stepped out of the church holding his baby in his arms. Handing his son back to Carol, he looked around for Vince and caught the back of him staggering out of the churchyard. Hugging Billy as the cuffs were once again unceremoniously clamped onto each wrist, there was urgency in Jake's voice. "I need you to come and see me?"

"Sure son." Billy fought back the tears.

"Please, as soon as you can it's important." The urgency had turned into desperation in his voice.

"I will son, as soon as I can."

Throwing her arms around his neck Carol burst into tears and kissed Jake on the lips. The grip round each arm tightened as Jake was led away down the church path.

Jake shouted back at Billy. "Please come and see me as soon as you can, it's important!"

Two hands thudded into Jake's shoulder blades as he was shoved into the back of the prison van. Crashing onto the metal floor Jake threw his handcuffed hands out to cushion his fall. As the van doors slammed shut behind him he heard Parkinson instantly fly into a rage. Struggling to his knees Jake felt the vibrations of the argument taking place outside. Throwing his back onto the wall Jake momentarily went back to holding his son when something occurred to him. Wrapped in self pity he had never noticed that Carol hadn't been pregnant. He laughed to himself. It was absurd. Suddenly the van doors sprung open. Lurching inside Rose grabbed Jake around the throat. Splashed by Rose's spit Jake came eye to eye with Rose's glare. "Nobody takes the piss out of me Jacob, nobody. Do understand; nobody." Smashing the back of Jake's head against the wall of metal the daylight disappeared along with the fresh air; the loves of his life, and the memories of his mother.

BILLY JACOB
AGED 70
ENGLISH
1978

CHAPTER NINETEEN

One summer followed one winter.

That morning Jake rose with the sun. Skipping breakfast then lunch, the hours that dragged by were unpitying. Transfixed on the door at the far end of the room the prisoners waited in silence. It felt like he had run a marathon and was still running. Agitated all day about the uncertainty of the visit a sickness had laid at the bottom of his stomach like a block of concrete. Suddenly the silence was broken by the echo of a buzzer and the opening of a security gate. Then within seconds the door opened. Instantly the room came to life as a stampede of rain soaked mothers and children swept in. Then, through the crescendo of noise and chatter he spotted his uncle. Leaning on his stick he was the last person to enter the room and presented a frail figure. Spotting Jake's wave Billy hobbled on his walking stick through the line of tables. Greeting each other warmly, Billy's palm felt cold and clammy inside Jake's grip. Slumping into the seat opposite his nephew Billy blew out a sigh of pain and relief at the same time. "What a bloody rigmarole getting into this place. Do I look like I'm concealing explosives under my coat?"

Jake afforded a smile. "You look well Uncle Billy."

"Not too bad considering they want to take my right leg off!" An agonising smile flinched across his face. "I told the doctor that it was the leg I scored a hat trick with in the Fireman's Cup Final, he's got no chance." Sitting back in his chair he unbuttoned his rain splattered coat. Jake caught the whiff of cologne. Coughing into the palm of his hand Billy looked across at Jake with those wild, black eyes of his and spoke in a calming voice. "Feeding you well in here are they?"

"Not bad."

"You look well enough, considering."

"Thanks for coming to see me."

"We're family. I would have come sooner."

"I'm sorry."

Tilting his head to one side Billy smiled, the corner of his mouth dropping. "I never got the chance to thank you properly for what you've done for me."

"As you said, we're family."

"But you're in here because of me."

"It was my choice."

"But if I hadn't got into that stupid card game."

"As I said it was my choice. Don't beat yourself up about it. You can buy me a pint when I come out."

Both men fell into a deep silence.

"I saw Carol and Freddy last week."

"It's difficult to talk about them being in here."

"I can understand that but there is nothing worse in this world than being lonely son. It can get a grip of you without you knowing." A frown appeared, Billy knew there was something going on in Jake's mind but he didn't know what.

Another silence swept over the men before Billy spoke. "Go on then lad, we can't sit here all day not talking and my leg is playing me up. What' troubling you?"

Jake banished a smile; he had always loved his uncle's bluntness. "When mum died she left me a small leather case."

"I know, she asked me to make sure you got it. She was very insistent. You know what she was like."

"Do you know what was inside?"

Billy caught the air of concern in Jake's voice. "I can guess. I though that's why you wanted to see me." Diligent in his answer Billy's eyes sharpened as he perceived Jake's torment and self pity. Looking around at the officers Jake discreetly removed the newspaper cutting from the back of his jeans pocket. Unfolding the paper he laid it out on the table, ironing out the creases in the paper with the palm of his hand. Sliding it across under his uncle's gaze he waited for a response. A lump lodged at the back of his throat. Running his skeletal fingers through his grey temples Billy removed some black-framed glasses from inside the pocket of his raincoat and perched them on the end of his nose. Leaning forward he studied the cutting. In less than three seconds the hoods of his eyes lifted upwards and he met Jake's. There was concern in his voice. "I thought it might be this."

"Jim Abbott – was he my dad?"

Moving nervously in his seat Billy looked around the room and thought for a few seconds, and then his mood lifted. "Yes."

Thunderstruck, a look of astonishment swept across Jake's face. He gulped hard. "Did you know him?"

"Of course I bloody well knew him, he was married to my sister wasn't he, they had you didn't they."

"Why hasn't anyone told me about him before?"

"It's a long story."

"If it has gone over your head, I've got all the time in the world."

"Alright take it easy son."

"Taking it easy is not an option Uncle Billy."

"This is very difficult for me son, try and understand it was a long time ago. Some things in life you try and forget; erase from your mind."

"I've guessed my mum changed back to her maiden name after he was hanged."

Billy's chin dropped to his chest as he nodded remorsefully.

"What was he like?"

"I don't know where to start." Billy composed himself for a few seconds. "First of all, you look like him across the eyes, the colour of your hair a little, nothing else as I can remember. To me, you've always looked more like your mother.

Folding the newspaper cutting Jake slid it back into his jeans pocket. "In the newspaper article he claimed he was innocent."

Contemplating a response Billy thought for few seconds before answering. "Your dad wasn't a petty criminal as such, more of an opportunist. In those days they were known as Spivs, nowadays they are known as an entrepreneur. Your mother knew that when she started going out with him. Our old dad used to go mad at her. I remember one night he locked her in her bedroom. 'You're not going to see that scallywag again', he would say. It was a long time ago. Just after the war. The black-market was a dreamtime for a man like your dad. Chocolate, nylons, make-up, food, everything was at a premium." Billy gave Jake a look, a stern expression strewn across his lined face. "If you're asking me whether I think he did it – I have no idea."

Exasperation flooded through Jake.

"Let it be son, no good dragging up the past."

Of all the questions flying around in Jake's mind he voiced one. "You don't understand. I have to know what happened."

For the first time the two men became aware of the noise around them. A baby crying, a young girl laughing, a heated argument between husband and wife, an officer's warning, more rain against the windows. Moving his hand up to his face Billy brushed his fingers across his top lip, he looked nervous, on edge, shaky. In his eyes he still saw Jake as a young boy, desperate for that ice-cream; desperate to score the winning goal in the FA Cup Final, hit the winning runs at Lords, but now all he could see was a tortured figure. His nephew had changed.

Slipping his glasses back inside his coat Billy lowered his shoulders and came to terms with the trial that was taking place. "When your Dad was convicted your mother went to see him. She asked me to go with her so I tagged along as support. He was in this prison of all places. I never thought I would see the day when I came back in here. It was a dark place in those days. It had a nickname and was known as 'The Hanging Prison', if you came in here you never got out. Our Dad was beside himself, there were reporters hanging around outside our house. 'If you go to see him don't come back. You'll bring shame on the family.' His shouting followed us out of the front door, down the garden path to the gate to the end of the street. What a bloody commotion. It was on the radio and on the front page of every newspaper. We travelled from London by train and took a bus to the prison. When we arrived we were told that we only had half an hour with your dad. Half a bloody hour. They knew we had travelled all that way but they didn't give a damn. We were shown into this poky room and your dad was already sitting there. He looked good considering all the shit he'd been through. We even had a cup of tea made for us by one of the prison guards. Your Dad told us he was innocent and what had happened. We both believed him. He remained strong but I think it was for your mother sake. Unfortunately the jury didn't believe him and he was sent down. We appealed, but it wasn't like today with forensics and all this modern-day stuff. The evidence was stacked against him. Your Dad was a very intelligent man, self-educated; he read a lot, all the classics. We knew what he was up to, but they were different times, hard times. Everyone tried to scrape a living; he was generous to everyone. He was like a modern day Robin Hood in some ways and well known in the area, that's why your mother changed back to her maiden name and moved from London to here. When our mum and dad died I came to visit her and have stayed here ever since. I always liked the countryside." His mind ticked over for few seconds. "Do you know he's buried in here?"

Jake's face dropped, his heart missing a beat.

"He was the last man to be hanged here, inside Brainforth. It was a statement of some sort by the authorities but we could never get to the bottom of it. We could only think it was the nature of the crime. The anti-hanging group asked your mother not to collect his body; they wanted to embarrass the Government, make a statement of their own. Who knows whether it worked? I remember the day as if it was yesterday."

Billy could see Jake was engrossed but wary of what he was going to be told next. "Do you want me to go on?" Jake nodded, his mind spinning. "He was to be hanged at midday, which was unusual because the majority of hangings were done at dawn. Outside the gates there was a large crowd of protesters holding placards with slogans on them like, 'God forgive' and 'Abolish hanging' – across the road another group held up signs with the words on them like, 'An eye for an eye' and 'Murdering Animal'. It was a crazy scene. There was mixed news circulating amongst everyone that Parliament were about to reprieve him at the last minute. In the House of Lords at the time they were debating the abolition of the death penalty and wanted him pardoned, but it was as if they delayed the decision so that the execution could still go ahead. Apparently they adjourned for tea and listened to the news of the hanging on the radio. When twelve struck the crowd went silent. I can still hear your mother's sobbing inside my head. It still haunts me to this day. God bless her."

Finding his voice Jake spoke. "But my mum would never have his name mentioned in the house, I remember Auntie Lilly saying….

…."That was to protect you from having the stigma of growing up with everyone knowing your father was hanged for murder. That's why she changed back to her maiden name of Jacob and moved here. Nobody hated injustice more than your father."

Running his fingers through his hair Jake agonised. "On my first night inside I was put in a cell with this prisoner. The following day he disappeared. When I woke up he wasn't there. I asked the officers and cons and they all said I was alone in the cell. I think he was my dad; he was identical to one of the photographs of my dad that my Mum left me in the case, the one in the newspaper. It was one of him bare-chested holding up his fists. You might think I'm mad and at times I've questioned my own sanity."

Shrugging his shoulders Billy once again leant forward and lowered his voice. "I believe you son. Whether I believe in the afterlife, spirits, ghosts is irrelevant. What I do believe in is fate". They looked at each other for a short time without saying a word.

Looking for a positive response Jake's eyes widened, his voice breaking. "He told me a story about a Chinese warrior and that he practiced Qigong."

Billy looked amazed.

"What Billy? You know something, tell me please."

"Your Dad learnt that from a Chinese guy who was married to an English girl. They lived around the corner from where we lived. I remember seeing him doing it once, waving his arms around."

"That's right." Jake felt alive.

"He wasn't a bigot like some people who turned their noses up at an English girl marrying someone from China or Africa.

He embraced all cultures; everything; he was unique really. His head was like an encyclopaedia – are you sure you didn't read about these things or heard about them when you were a child and subconsciously you've remembered them through….

…."No!" The palm of Jake's hand came firmly down on the tabletop. "He told me to appeal." Billy lent forward encouraging Jake to lower his voice. For a few seconds silence gripped the two men.

Running his hand across his chin Jake shook his head and laughed. "I don't know what to do anymore. I really thought I was going mad."

Clawing for an answer Jake listened to Billy's words of wisdom, his eyes flitting from one listening officer to another. "You're not going mad son. But listen, don't wait till destiny comes to you, go and find your destiny before your life passes you by. You don't want to live every day of your life with regrets." Considering a reply Jake contemplated the advice. "Your father was a survivor." Billy laughed, his face full of reminiscence. "He had a wonderful sense of humour; he used to wet his finger and hold it up to the wind and predict that he could smell rain coming. Usually he was right" Billy recounted. "There were so many, so many tight corners he got out of." Then he became solemn. "Perhaps getting off with the death penalty was one tight corner too many." An avalanche of words stuck at the back of Jake's throat, he had so many questions but he was afraid to ask.

Suddenly a loud buzzer reverberated around the walls of the room.

"Visiting time over!" One of the senior officers stood by the door and watched the room burst into another wave of emotion. Expressionless, his voice boomed out riddled with impatience. "Please make your way through the door!"

Chairs scraped across the floor, mixed with hugs and tears

until the next time. Rising to his feet Jake walked round the table and helped Billy to his feet. Supporting himself by his stick. Billy threw one arm around Jake's neck and kissed him on the cheek. Tears pricked both men's eyes.

"Time thank you everyone!" Another short, aggressive officer with a voice like a Butlins Red Coat walked down the line of tables smiling at the visitors as if it were their last day at a holiday camp. Hovering around Jake the officer nodded for him to hurry 'the goodbyes.'

"You take care of yourself son and keep fighting." Leaving the support of Jake's arm Billy tottered away on is stick.

"I love you Uncle Billy."

"I love you too son."

Stopping at the door Billy slowly turned and waved back, then disappeared.

Jake would never see him again.

DETECTIVE ADAMSKI
AGED 64
POLISH
1978

CHAPTER TWENTY
Another day wore on
And another and another.

Tortured metaphorically about the identity of the killer and how the investigation would ever be solved Dariuz Kuszczak sat smoking at his desk. Deep in thought he had been up all night studying witness interviews. Had he missed something so obvious it was staring him in the face? Resting his cigarette on the edge of the overflowing ash tray he exhaled and watched as the blue smoke circulated around the open office. His consumption of cigarettes was exhausting. Picking up the morning edition of the Krakow Post; the paper felt warm, the ink still wet. Kuszczak grimaced as he read the headlines.

The Shepherd strikes again.
People of Krakow live in fear of a serial killer.
No faith in incompetent police.

The headlines ran true; the scathing article lambasted the incompetence of the police department over the recent murder; when once again The Shepherd had eluded the authorities.

Kuszcak could not restrain the press from continually reporting irresponsible, unconfirmed reports which only added to rumours and to the myth of the killer and giving him the nickname of 'The Shepherd'. So 'The Shepherd' thought.

One unsolved murder is bad enough but
now four bodies have been found.
What have the police been doing for the past three decades?
In fear of their lives; terrified people can not sleep safe in their
beds at nights because of 'The Shepherd'.
The police department is a disgrace!
The people of Krakow want answers, not excuses!

At times he felt like he had his head screwed on backwards.

Sliding open the bottom-drawer to his desk he removed a bottle of vodka and small glass. Pouring himself a shot he knocked it down in one, then poured himself another. And he wondered why he drank so much. At least twice a day the police would receive a hoax call from somebody proclaiming that they knew the identity of 'The Shepherd' as the killer was commonly now known. One newspaper had christened the murderer, 'The Krakow Killer', but for some strange reason it didn't stick. Usually the call would come from a tramp wanting a warm bed for the night, "Let me come into the station and I'll tell you who he is."

"Get off your fat pigs arses and find the killer!" Then the receiver would go dead until the next day. The voices were always familiar, another lunatic seeking self publicity.

Once Kuszcak was known for his vivacious smile and personality, now his ragged posture and a face swathed in stubble said it all. Devoting himself to the task had taken its toll.

Re-lighting his cigarette he lifted himself out of his chair, folded the newspaper and dropped it into the bin. Making his way across the office to the rain-soaked window, he rested his forehead on the cold glass and looked languidly across the rooftops of Krakow. In the distance St Mary's Basilica soared into the sky like a giant needle. It was the first day of spring and it had been raining incessantly for the past twenty four hours and it had been over two months since the student's body had been found in the River Wista. When the body had been discovered crime scene investigators including himself had scoured the riverbank looking evidence. They had erected searchlights and worked through the night into the next day. They found nothing and Kuszczak was lucky to evade frostbite in both his feet. During the autopsy the morgue had been its usual pragmatic self. Just like before and the time before that and the time before that, everything about the body on the pathologist's slab revealed nothing, not a single clue, zilch.

It was the worst thing about being a policeman, Kuszczak hated a particular moment, but somebody had to do it. It was a dirty job. Informing the parents that their son or daughter was dead, murdered, was heart wrenching. Before he met them he would try and disguise the drink on his breath. As they looked down on their son's body, the mother cried out, her voice cutting the air as well as her insides.

"What have they done to him. What have they done to my beautiful, beloved son?"

Weeping, the father looked up from his son's body and turned to the detective. "Promise me you'll catch who murdered my son?"

Thwart with lies with his reply; Kuszczak's promised response masked the gargantuan task.

Daydreaming, scatterbrained, Kuszczak peered down and fixed his eyes on the flooded pavements which reflected the street lamps of the deserted streets. He'd come to hate Krakow. For him it had become a dark city. On his day off he would get out of it as soon as he could; to regain some sort of sanity in his life. As a catholic he went to church regularly and believed that God would eventually bring the killer to justice, but God was taking his time and his patience was running thin, making him question his faith. Pulling on the cigarette, his eyes once again followed the blue smoke as it circulated upwards. For the past year he'd felt like he'd been treading water, finding himself on more than one occasion trapped in a mental labyrinth of nothingness. Everyone had theories which drifted towards a vanishing point.

It was three in the morning when the phone rang. It startled Kuszczak who was just about to nod of at his desk. In the past he would have rushed to answer the call in the hope that something had been unearthed, a glimmer of hope. Eventually Kuszczak picked up the receiver. Interpol.

It was like a bomb going off, Kuszczak almost levitated.

Two cases made of tin had been unearthed by a builder who had been excavating a tiny plot of land. It was a pure stroke of luck.

The detective from Interpol spoke with a voice of someone who smoked more cigarettes than Kuszczak relayed the discovery.

"It's conceivable that these two cases would never have been found. They were made of tin and were partially crushed by the digger. Everything inside says it is the killer. The Shepherd's life has been a dark shadow, not anymore, not anymore. What luck! What luck!"

Inside the boxes were time tables of trains in and out of Poland, faded postcards of Krakow dating back to 1956, street maps of Krakow, museum pamphlets, photographs of Auschwitz, newspaper cuttings of the three murdered women and one of the murdered male student. A small tin holding a few sticks of charcoal, nail scissors, needle and thread was the evidence of the tattooing into the victims arms and the sewing of the coloured triangles onto the striped cloth. Also a small woollen hat was later identified as belonging to Tracy Jankowski the American student. But a more gruesome discovery was in second of the cases. At first pathologists thought it was just stuffing for re-upholstering furniture but after being examination it was found to be human hair.

In the nick of time Kuszczak threw on a suit and tie and remembered to shave. He hadn't slept for forty eight hours. Flying to London he had been met by an Interpol officer at Scotland Yard. Through an interpreter he was shown the boxes. The evidence was insurmountable; it was the news that Krakow had longed for.

Strutting into the room he felt like he was walking on water as he lapped up the applause and barrage of flash bulbs from the Polish and World's Press. After facing an avalanche of questions at the press conference the Polish police force along with Chief of police Kuba Lewandowski were praised for their dedication to solving the case. "It was a relief for the whole of Poland now that the killer was off the streets." For the grieving families both on home soil in Poland and in America who had endured years of torment, finding the killer of their loved ones was some sort of closure. Flowing with beer and vodka the joyous day turned to night in Kuszczak's office as the police celebrated and slapped each others backs. Paralytic, Kuszczak was oblivious to what his peers thought of him, beleaguered, he was now overwhelmed with euphoria. Through the haze his thoughts then ran to Adamski.

Finding a quiet corner he picked up the phone. Consulting his notebook he rang Adamski's number. As the phone rang he conjured up all sorts of images about the killer. It was late, well after midnight but he was sure Adamski would have heard the news either on the radio or seen it on TV. Emptying the last drop of vodka from his glass he then lit a cigarette and waited. A minute or two passed before an elderly woman answered and introduced herself as the house keeper. Her voice was frail, sleepy.

"This is Detective Kuszczak from the Krakow Police Department. I apologise for ringing so late at night but is Mr. Adamski there?" Taking a pull on his cigarette he felt like a cat on hot bricks as he anticipated the conversation with his nemesis.

"Haven't you heard Mr. Adamski died two weeks ago?"

Kuszczak hung-up without saying goodbye.

Adamski's rowing boat had been found drifting in the middle of the lake. With his head slumped over the side of the boat his rod was gripped in his hand a fish tugging at the end of the line. He had apparently suffered a heart attack. The case had gnawed at his soul every minute of every day. The police were never notified of his death and nobody from the department was present at his funeral. Twenty years of service. Buried in a small plot which overlooked the lake where he loved to fish, the service was attended by his son and a few close friends.

Adamski never knew about the discovery of the cases and went to his grave never knowing who the killer was.

CHAPTER TWENTY ONE

It never crossed his mind, those things never do.
And then it's always too late.

On that rainy afternoon, Jake had no idea that he would never see his uncle again. The same night Jake had never felt so lonely. Part of him had died; his world had tilted and he was about to fall of its axis. Lost in the night; all he could hear was his uncle's voice. The revelations about his father that had been revealed to him went over and over in his mind. Continually churning and playing with his emotions he found himself staring for hours on end at the photograph of his father in the press cutting. On one occasion he stood on tiptoes and looked out of his cell window. Stretching his neck in an attempt to see his father's grave, a full moon reflected off the greenhouse roof but the grave was shadowed in blackness by the huge prison wall. Sadness of thoughts, more decisions. What to do? The urge to confide in somebody was overpowering. For the time being keeping quiet, had to be the best policy. Seeing ghosts then announcing to the world that his father was buried inside the prison could conceivably put him into a straitjacket. He wondered how he had come from this to this.

For long periods he tried to teach himself Qigong; practicing meditation and breathing exercises. It made him feel close to his father. And so it continued, as the long days merged into the bricks of Brainforth Prison. Throughout the tedious nights Jake wrestled not only with the past but what the future held. One thing continually wrenched at his insides and nagged at him like a bad tooth that needed to be pulled.

Picking the right moment, the right time, Jake picked out the right officer.

Proclaiming that he'd always had green fingers, Jake picked out Rose. Subtly mentioning the dirty sauna; a little reminder of what Vince had unearthed about him did the trick. "Don't try and blackmail me Jacob."

"Blackmail is a dirty word Mr Rose. Sort this out for me and I promise, I won't mention it again."

Within two days his request had been granted.

The allotment and garden was a speck of dust within the prison confines. A green house which inside was too big for one person and too small for two was wedged into the corner of the prison walls. With little sunlight, it was the worst place imaginable for any plants to grow and be cultivated, but miraculously they did. Geraniums, daffodils, roses, sweet peas, even an orchid flourished in the summer. Running up to the door of the greenhouse was a stretch of grass as flat as a bowling green which was lined either side with potatoes, carrots, lettuce, spring onions and rhubarb. All in a healthy condition, the vegetable patch reminded Jake of Mr McGregor's vegetable garden in Beatrix Potter's 'Peter Rabbit', an illustrated book he had read as a kid. Where a flower could bloom, a flower was planted and swinging in the breeze from both sides of the greenhouse were two hanging baskets full of pansies. Inside Brainforth it was an oasis of colour and life.

Rose had escorted Jake outside and was told to wait. "Now we're even Jacob."

Kicking his heels, Jake was drawn to the mound of earth at the side of the greenhouse. A covering of morning dew covered his father's unmarked grave.

Bouncing off the glass of the greenhouse roof last night's full moon had been replaced by bright, morning sunshine. It was mild, with a slight breeze and Jake could feel the warmth of the sun on his face and could smell the wet earth drifting upwards.

Suddenly fingers snapped in front of his face. "Hey!" Sam's verbal skills where like trains buffeting into each other.

"Mr Rose says I'm stuck with you for the day."

Sam was a prisoner with 'real' green fingers who had worked the allotment for over a decade. Glaring into Jake's vacant expression he thrust the wooden shaft of a rake into his hand

"Right, let's see what you're made of. This isn't an easy touch you know. Gardening's tough. If you don't pull your weight, you'll be back inside and sewing mail bags."

Sam spoke with a sharp, alluring, Irish accent. Crooked teeth looked out of place against his sun-splashed face which was lined like a walnut and a deep scar which curved upwards from the corner of his mouth to the top of his cheekbone gave him the appearance of a seasoned gangster. His arms and hands were muscular, thick, soil and dirt ingrained under his fingernails. Well over sixty his barrel chest bulged under his bib and brace overalls and he creaked as he walked. Everything about him told a thousand stories.

Turning the stem of a plant in his fingers his voice was

mixed with frustration and a rusty cough. "You can start by raking through the soil."

Pausing for a few seconds Jake shielded his eyes from the sun. "Ok, boss."

"Do you have a problem with me being the boss?"

"No."

"Do you have a problem with raking?"

"Why should I have a problem with raking?" Standing his ground Jake waited for a response but all he got was a huff and puff as Sam squatted down with a groan and started planting a line of bedding plants. Although the sun held little heat it felt good on his back as Jake worked the soil with the rake. Wiping the sweat from his brow Jake felt his eyes once again being drawn towards the grave. Close up, the grass covering the grave was manicured to perfection. Chiselled into the brickwork of the prison wall at the back of the grave was a serial number. 135689. No headstone. No name. No flowers. No visitors. On the day Jim Abbott was hanged he had been alone. Could he hear the priest's prayers; taste the hangman's breath? Hear the Governor's cough; the crowd outside; his neck snapping that split second before he dropped through the trap door? Overwhelmed by the moment Jake brought the knuckle of his index finger up under his eye to stop a tear from falling.

"Give me a hand up will you." Struggling to climb to his feet Sam's right arm stretched out looking for a sympathetic lift up. Helping him to his feet Sam's arm held a solid bicep, his face holding a grimace. "My right knee gets stuck sometimes, rheumatism."

"You should see a doctor."

"Doctors are useless, they would only put me on some pills and tell me to rest. Who would look after my garden?" Grunting, Sam put the palms of his hands onto the base of his back and stretched. Licking his lips, he wiped the sweat from his forehead leaving a smudge of soil. "You look like you could do with a cuppa?" Before Jake had time to reply Sam had disappeared inside the green house. Filtering over the prison wall Jake could hear the hum of the traffic from the real world outside.

"Sugar?"

"No thanks."

"Here you are then; I'm not your skivvy."

Walking over to the greenhouse Jake was handed a mug followed by another grunt. Glancing inside the greenhouse Jake could see Sam felt right at home. Along both sides of the glass walls shelves were stacked tight with small potting trays of flowers and herbs. An aroma of lavender and coriander hovered in the humidity and at the back of the greenhouse a foldaway table held a thermos flask, milk, sugar, a dented biscuit tin and a dog-eared book with the title, 'Small Gardens and Allotments.'

Sam passed Jake a shabby fold-up fisherman's chair. "Take a seat." Sitting on a wooden stool with his back to the table Sam sipped his tea out of a chipped mug with the words 'Best Dad in the World' printed on the side. Following the sip with a lick- of-the-lips an inquisitive expression came across his face. "So lad lets get my scar out of the way first." Taking another sip of tea his breathing was laboured. "I tell everyone in this shit-hole that it was done by one of the Krays; Reggie to be precise." Smiling slightly, the scar lifted and ran back under his eye. "I said it when I first came inside to give me a bit of kudos. I thought myself as a bit of a hard man back in those days." Turning he picked up a ginger biscuit, dunked it into his tea then slipped it into his mouth and munched. "I got this by being a smart arse when I was about sixteen. I tried to stand up on the saddle of a motor bike. I was trying to impress a girl at the time." Running his finger down his scar he smiled for the first time. "I found out later that she fancied a mate of mine all along. Finished up marrying him. They had two kids together. The last I heard they had emigrated to Australia years ago. Good luck to them. So lad, tell me why have you been put in the garden?"

"I like gardening."

Sam shrugged his shoulders and gave Jake a furtive look. "I've worked this patch for the past ten years. I've had four murderers, two armed robbers, a bent copper, a bent politician, one rapist and two prisoners who were inside here for fraud and larceny. All of them said they were innocent. None of them could lie very well, nor can you."

Sipping his tea Sam looked at Jake over the rim of his mug, his eyes vibrant green, piercing. "You see, if I'm to recommend you to Mr Rose I have to be sure I can trust you. There are too many sharp instruments around here, if you get my drift?"

"You can trust me."

Picking up the biscuit tin Sam removed a small black and white photograph, blew away the crumbs and handed it to Jake. "That was taken ten years ago." The photograph showed Sam, Conrad and two other prisoners standing by the greenhouse. They were smiling; it was a sunny day and they were leaning on rakes and shovels. Slightly visible to the right was the grave; the foreground bare of flower beds or vegetables. Sam reminisced with a sense of caution. "That was taken on the first day of the garden. Conrad helped us construct the greenhouse. See that prisoner on the far left?"

Jake nodded.

"He said I could trust him."

"What happened?"

Sam pulled his shirt out from the inside of his overalls. A deep scar was visible. "It look like I've had my appendix out doesn't it. It was done with a trowel." Scratching the top of his head Sam stretched out his leg and winced. "I know about you, Mr. Rose has filled me in."

"Did he tell you I was a loony?" Jake stuck his tongue out the side of his mouth and rolled his eyes.

"Anyone who takes on Dutch must be nuts."

Both men reflected before Sam spoke. "There are plenty of nutters in here. You don't look like a loony to me."

"What does a loony look like?"

"Someone who you imagine a loony to look like." Sam returned the look. Sharing a smile for the first time the two men sipped their tea and continued weighing each other up. It was going to be a long day but somewhere deep inside Jake thought he was going to enjoy it.

For the next couple of weeks Jake and Sam shared stories, tended to the allotment, the flowerbeds and sipped tea. His enthusiasm for gardening was infectious and it had a soothing effect. Losing track of time Jake opened up for the first time and talked of Carol, relating stories of how they had first met and the birth of Freddy. At the same time Sam pontificated about his time inside Brainforth and talked about the prison with great affection noting how it had changed over the years, some good; some bad. Sam had been caught by the police back in the late sixties on the Costa del Sol. He was one of the first criminals to skip the country before skipping the country to Spain became the trend, hence being nicknamed the Costa del Crime. Given thirty years for armed robbery he escaped the police by slipping out of the courtroom window. Going on the run he was eventually caught after ten years when a tourist recognised him drinking in a bar in Puerto Banus. Tipping off the police, she thought she would get a reward. Armed robbery was something the two men could relate to, something they had in common, but in Sam's case a Bank Manager had got in the way of a double barrelled shotgun.

During the days, rain or shine, Jake dodged Sam's gaze as

he tended to his father's grave. Or so he thought.

Then one day. "So are you going to tell me?"

Jake didn't answer. But it was impossible to lie. The two men had bonded. His eyes, his expression, told the true story. "My father is buried in this grave." Waiting for a response Jake stared down. "That dream I told you about, that vision, whatever you want to call it, a ghost, who knows, but the guy who I was put in with on my first night inside was my father. I didn't know at the time. It was only after my mother died that I found out. She sent me some photographs of him in a leather case. I never knew him or seen him as a kid. Then my uncle came to see me. He told me my father was the last man to be hanged inside Brainforth." Turning from the grave Jake looked at Sam's face. "So what do you think of the loony now?"

Shrugging his shoulders Sam's mouth turned down at the corners, his eyes wide, bright, like the yellow flash in a cat's eye. "I better make us both a cup of tea."

Philosophising, Sam put it in layman's terms. "If I get rid of you then I might get another loony. I talk to the plants what does that make me? Better the loon you know than the one you don't." There was a mischievous look on his face when he said it.

Sam had become a true friend.

A month later Sam was taken to hospital with a suspected heart attack. He was found collapsed in the greenhouse face down. Blood had congealed on the flagstones from a head wound. On his back was a scattering of soil. Lucky for Jake he was in his cell when it happened, Rose had a long memory. Jake tended to the garden while a replacement was found but slowly the flowers in the greenhouse and the garden died. Who could replace Sam? It was his garden. Over the following weeks Jake maintained the allotment and the grave as best he could. Over the weeks he discovered he enjoyed manual work and the fresh air helped him sleep, releasing him of the anxiety he had just before he closed his eyes at lights out. Although the hum of the traffic over the prison wall was a constant reminder of the life he had left behind. He picked up on the songs of birds which had a relaxing effect on him.

Then one afternoon the priest came by with a dish that was best served cold.

The earth under Jake's knees felt damp. There had been a heavy dew that morning and the flowers dripped and the green leaves of the vegetables streamed with water. Pushing through the clouds the sun felt warm on his back as his hands dug into the wet grass and soil around the grave.

At first his voice was soft. "How are you today Jake?"

Turning upwards Jake looked over his shoulder, his eyes squinting into the sun.

Dropping his trowel Jake put his hand across his eyes. "Fine, thank you father?"

"You're doing a great job there."

"I'm trying my best."

"It was sad about Sam; I believe you two had become good friends. Are you ok?"

"It's a case of having to be isn't it father. Is there any news on him?"

"He's had a bad stroke. It is possible he may never recover."

Turning back to the grave Jake continued to plough at the earth. For a minute or two the priest stood there watching Jake work. Occasionally looking around the prison took the time to wave at a passing officer or prisoner. Standing, Jake brushed his knees free of damp soil. A passive look swept across his face and for a few seconds he was totally oblivious to the priest's presence standing behind him.

"Flowers always remind me of my time in Portugal." Silhouetted against the setting sun the priest spoke with affection.

"Bougainvillea where always my favourite, vibrant pinks and purple they were amazing against the white-washed buildings. Oh, to be young again. As a youthful priest I visited The Church of Santa Anna which overlooked the whole of Albufeira. It suffered an earthquake in 1755 if I remember, a tidal wave hit it and only ruins survived. But it's a beautiful place. Would you like to say a prayer?"

Confused by the unexpected offer of prayer Jake flicked the trowel with his wrist and it shot into the ground. "I think we've had this conversation before father. If you remember I said I think I was past absolution."

Bowing his head the priest rested his chin on his chest. Staring down at the grave with a puzzled expression he closed his eyes and clasped his hands across his paunch. Feeling a warm breeze drifting around the graveside he opened his eyes and breathed the fresh air in through his nose and sighed. "I've prayed for us both." Jake noticed a port wine birthmark like splash of paint on the top of the priest's head. He had seen it before. Where?

Taking a single step away from the plot the priest paused momentarily as if he had absentmindedly remembered something. "I'm sorry. I should have said, let the weak inherit the earth."

Then Jake suddenly remembered and shot back. "And be aware of men who speak well of you."

The priest gave Jake an unnerving look. "Why did you say that?"

"How many years have you been 'passing the word' inside Brainforth father?" At the same time he asked the question a chill shot down his spine. In the black and white photograph which was in the Governor's office the priest who was stood by his father's side on the day of execution had his head bowed. At the time Jake thought the mark on the priest's head looked like smudge or a blemish in the print. The hairs sprang up on the back of his neck; wide eyed, his face was riveted on the back of the priest as he walked away. He wanted to sprint after him and berate him so loud that the whole of the prison could hear. He wanted to scream into his face. *You knew my father. You were there at his hanging!* But he held back his heart pounding. It was if some invisible force was burning inside him, holding him back, telling him to stop and become more calculated. Scanning the yard, the prison windows, he wanted to scream out about the pitiful lies which the priest had been hiding behind all these years. The defamation he had concealed behind his so called faith.

Touching his cheek Jake wiped away a heavy rain drop. Overhead two magpies looped against a blanket of thick, heavy, grey clouds. He felt he could reach out and touch them.

CHAPTER TWENTY TWO

Learning from his mistakes,
Jake had to become as sly as a fox, as wily as a wolf.

The voice inside his head came from a long way away. There were forces working against him that he couldn't control. Self pity would eventually kill him, so Jake came to the inescapable conclusion that the prognosis was to use mind over matter. Playing on the priest's religious conscience he was determined to break his spirit. When training a bird of prey its captor stays up with the bird throughout the night until the bird eventually falls asleep in front of him. When the bird awakes he realises he has come to no harm but his spirit has been broken and from that moment onwards he knows his master. The procedure or modus operandi can be a gruelling battle of resolve, willpower and fortitude between bird and master. Jake was preparing himself for the long haul. Appearing nondescript, absent, melodious but at the same time making a conscious decision he was determined that throughout he would remain true to himself. Every time he had an opportunity to burn his eyes into the priest he would. At confession he would stare so convincingly that his Holiness the

Pope would become traumatised. From the top of the landing looking down Jake would draw-in the priest's gaze from the ground floor. Every time he looked up, he'd know he would be there. He would be the priest's shadow. It was his only hope and he would have to push himself to the limit.

And so he went to work.

At mass and communion on a Sunday Jake would sit in the front row not singing; not praying; just staring wide eyed as if he was in some sort of translucent trance. At confession he would ask the same questions over and over again. "Please help me father, please help me, I have nobody to turn to. Will you help me, will God help me?" Snapping back the priest knew what questions were coming next and he would dwell on his answer, his voice becoming increasingly irritable with listening to the same, constant, heart rendering plea. Sometimes Jake would rephrase the question and it was becoming evident how nervous the priest was becoming in his presence. Sweat would appear across his forehead and then slide down his face, then neck and under his dog collar. "I was told father, as young boy, that if I didn't tell the truth it would eat at my insides and the devil would smother me in my sleep." Incessant pressure. Every day Jake would consume the priest with his pure enigmatic energy, at the same time appearing absent. Avoiding the risk of talking to other inmates Jake had to out-wit everyone, gather cobwebs and voice his opinions only to the priest. He wanted him to feel like his guts were being ripped out of his stomach; to play on the hollowness inside and unlock the vital answers to Jake's questions.

Then one day.

Tending to the garden Jake noticed the priest walking across the exercise yard. Quickly angling the back of his metal trowel towards the sun he reflected the light directly across the yard into the priest's eyes.

Shielding his eyes the priest dabbed his face with a handkerchief and searched for the source of the light. He looked like a little boy lost as he walked towards the garden; his eyes gaping.

There was sadness in his voice. "The next time you come to Mass we'll talk."

The previous venom and frustration in his voice had disappeared, the guilt finally becoming too heavy a burden.

It was Friday, two days before Mass. For those two days Jake thought about what revelations lay ahead. Each night he lay staring at the ceiling. His thoughts drifted everywhere; from riding his bike; to his son; to his family; to Carol's face which could grace the cover of any magazine. At times he could see her smile as she looked over her bare shoulder at twilight and sometimes he caught the wind from the washing as it floated in the breeze in his back garden. Freddy's face was always there, in the background, when he fell asleep, when he woke. His mind was crowded with memories and at times they made him vulnerable, a dangerous pastime.

Then as the meagre light came and went. Sunday the 21st of December arrived, the day of reckoning.

CONRAD MILLER
AGED 65
ENGLISH
DECEMBER 1981

CHAPTER TWENTY THREE

Outside it was snowing, the prison a scattering of white, an icy mist floating through the air. Inside the chapel it was colder still. Delivering the final prayers of the day the priest crossed himself and blessed the small gathering of prisoners as they left the chapel. Pulling Parkinson to one side, the priest spoke to him about Jake staying behind and taking confession. Parkinson agreed and left to supervise the TV room which was in the next room.

Alone, slowly the priest's eyes met Jake's. A vigorous shaft of sapphire burnt through the stained glass window cutting lines across the faces of the two men as they stood there transfixed. It was the moment of truth. Crossing himself the priest used the back of one of the chairs as support before slowly sitting down.

Taking a deep breath he gulped hard, carefully choosing his words. "Do you know who is buried in the yard?"

"Yes, my father"

Looking at Jake's face; it was dark, deathly, as if he were waiting to go to the gallows himself. "When I learnt of your surname I knew you were his son. The first time I saw you in the canteen. You look like your father, you have the same smile, he was a little smaller but you can tell you're his son."

Jake suddenly felt cold. "I know you were there at his hanging."

"Your father, the night before he was taken to the gallows asked to see a priest."

"And you have lived with this for the past thirty years. What sort of priest does that make you?"

"There isn't a day that passes when I haven't questioned my faith."

A scattering of pigeons on the slates of the prison roof echoed around the walls of the chapel. Staring up at the Crucifixion the priest continued. "I was a fool and it's been my greatest failing. I was naive, no stupid, still fresh faced so I thought, ready to save the world. All the talk in the newspapers was about whether hanging should be abolished and the day after your father was hanged it was. I was working from St Paul's and the Monsignor there had flu and was bedridden, so I came in his place. The thought of giving the last rites to a condemned man terrified me. There was stillness in the air that night which I can't explain; it was as if time had come to a standstill. When I walked into his cell I was surprised to find him in a relaxed mood, he was reading a book. Hemingway if I remember. It was only by accident that my new diocese was in the same neighbourhood. I had never visited Brainforth or been inside a prison. I was left alone with your father and he told me the whole story from start to finish of that night. How he was arrested and tried for the murder of the poor girl. In the time I had with him, I found him to be both intelligent and engaging. Not like your normal everyday criminal who I was later to visit. We shared a cup of cocoa together which the officer made for us and we even did a crossword out of the newspaper. He had no reason to lie or fabricate events. Why would he? Confessing he was a petty crook he told me how he dealt in most things which would sell on the black market. Don't forget this was two months after the War had finished and unemployment was then the scourge of the nation. Soldiers were coming home to find there was no work, times were hard. I'm not making any excuses for your father but he had a family to feed and I don't know whether you know but he was at Dunkirk before he was discharged for ill health?"

Standing the priest walked across the room and poured a glass of water from out of a jug. The priest's hand shook as he brought the glass up to his thin mouth and took a gulp. Holding onto every word Jake took in a deep breath as he rolled his shoulders at the chill in the room. His legs felt weak so he sat down. Facing the priest he was offered a glass of water. Shaking his head Jake watched as the priest took another drink and continued, his voice quiet, sorrowful, the glass continuing to shake nervously in his hand. "Down at the docks your dad got 'a sniff' I think he called it, of a number of warehouses storing cigarettes and whisky. The night-watchman agreed to go missing and turn a blind eye so your father could break in. Then he heard a yelp, like a puppy. He froze thinking it might be the police or the night watchman who had suddenly got cold-feet. Then he heard a slap which was followed by a girl crying. He crept towards the back office door. Peering through the gap in the door he saw a young girl being held down. Heather Wilson was her name." Crossing himself again, he continued. "Your father went in and dragged the man off the girl and a fight took place. The girl was hysterical; her summer dress had been ripped from her shoulders. She was just fifteen. Grabbing hold of the oil lamp the girl brought it above her head ready to bring it down and strike her attacker, but in doing so the oil spilt on her and went into her eyes. Blinded, she let go of the lamp which dropped, smashing onto her head and it ignited. You can't imagine what she went through that poor girl; it can only be described as horrific. Your father went to her aid and the other man took advantage of the situation and smashed your father across the back of the head with something, knocking him unconscious. The girl found herself crashing through the door and out onto the cobbled street. The locals from a notorious pub called 'The Blazing Stump' spilled out onto the street and one of them a retired seaman who was the night watchman tried to help her but it was too late. Knowing your father was unconscious in the warehouse the assailant concocted a story that he caught your father molesting the young girl. A fight had taken place and he had defended himself. When your father regained consciousness he saw the scene outside in the street, panicked and went home to gather his thoughts. He didn't know what to do. Then it was too late. Who was the court going to believe, your father, a renowned petty criminal, or the words of a young respected policeman?"

Furrowed lines creased Jake's forehead he felt numb as his heart pounded. "A policeman?"

"The man who murdered Heather Wilson was a policeman."

A policeman?

Taking another gulp of water the priest coughed into the fist of his right hand before continuing. "Your father resigned himself to the hangman's noose; he always proclaimed his innocence. But the jury was unanimous in their decision and the final deliberation to the packed court by the barrister was cutting and decisive. Your father was convicted and sentenced to death by a Judge called Boot who had the nickname, Black Cap."

Crestfallen Jake looked into the priest's sullen eyes. "Since that first night inside here I've dreamt of monsters. Some nights I had dreams that were more like flashbacks. It was in winter time but in reality it was autumn, that dream I had on my first night inside wasn't a dream was it, it was reality?" Then he unlocked the vital question. "It was my father, wasn't it?"

Wrestling with guilt the priest crossed himself then turned and faced Jake, his eyes wide. "There is only one apparition I believed in and that is Jesus coming back after the crucifixion. What I will say is that you might have seen him or if not your soul might have."

"Believe me I saw him and you know I did. I thought I was going mad. Nobody believed me and I understand why. You knew my father was innocent. You have to tell people the truth."

"And you think they would believe the words of an old priest?"

Contemplating what he had been told Jake leapt to his feet. Bounding around the chapel his fingers clawed through his hair. Trying to find his voice he opened the window and looked down onto the exercise yard and took in a deep breath. Recovering he turned back into the room. "How could you live with yourself knowing that an innocent man was sent to his death?"

"The guilt has impregnated my soul. I told you, there isn't one day that passes when I don't think of your father. Please Oh Lord forgive me." Crossing himself, his eyes filled with tears.

"Well you have a chance do something about it now."

"What can I do?"

"He's buried down there."

"I have one more thing to tell you." His voice broke. "I told you that a policeman murdered Heather Wilson?"

"Yes."

"Well the young policeman's name was Conrad Miller."

Taking a letter from out of the inside of his jacket the priest held it out in his bony fingers. "I have written everything down in this letter." On the envelope was written in shaky handwriting *Mr. Hall, The Governor, Brainforth Prison.* "It is my confession; the guilt I have been hiding for what seems a lifetime."

A jolt of disbelief shot though Jake's body like an electric shock. At last the jigsaw was complete. For a few seconds he tried to contemplate what he had just been told. At that precise moment Conrad walked into the Chapel. A deathly silence followed as the three men exchanged looks.

As cold as ice Conrad locked the Chapel door behind him then gave the priest and anguished stare.

"I have told him everything." Holding out the letter the priest raised his voice at last, reliving years of guilt. "Everything has been written down in this letter."

Conrad gave a superficial response, a smirk across his face. "What are you talking about?"

"In this letter I have told the truth."

"Let me see the letter."

Crunching the letter in his hand the priest waved it in front of his face. "I have lived with this for to long. You will have to face the truth like I have and confess what you have done."

"You're going senile father."

"He had a right to know." Crossing himself again, the priest was losing control.

Conrad swung his gaze at Jake. His eyes were wild and black. "Get out!"

Jake shook his head.

"I said get out!" Jake stood his ground.

Turning to the priest, Conrad held out his hand. "Give me the letter."

"No, I will tell them everything." The priest squeezed his eyes shut, a firmness coming into his voice. "Even if they think I'm mad, I will expose you for what you are. I should have spoken out years ago. You are evil, the Devil."

Grabbing the priest by his jacket lapels Conrad wrenched his frail body up onto his toes. "Give me the letter." Pulling him sideways with murderous intent he threw the frail priest to the ground. Bearing down on him his fist cracked around the room as it thumped into the priest's face. Blood spurted across the priest's face as his body lay crumpled and broken. Eyes full of rage, Conrad ripped the letter from the priest's grip. Drawing his arm backwards his fist tightened. Just as he was about to strike for a second time he found a tight arm around his neck. Gripping Conrad in a head-lock Jake swung him around sending him spinning and crashing into the altar table.

Holding his throat Conrad looked up at Jake, his face strewn with rage and hatred.

"Attacking a prison officer. You'll get another ten years for that Jacob." Nimble for his age Conrad climbed to his feet. "And killing a priest. You'll never see the light of day again." Seizing the heavy, brass cross from the table he stepped over the priest and with forced effort brought it back over his head. In an instant Jake lunged at Conrad. As the two men wrestled with the cross the priest rolled over onto his stomach and started crawling across the floor blood smeared across his face. Eyeball to eyeball, Conrad grunted sending a spray of spittle out of his mouth. Wrenching the cross out of Conrad's hands Jake fell backwards. Tripping, the weighty cross slipped from his grip. In an instant Conrad stepped forward and slung a right hook and missed. Kicking out blindly Jake caught Conrad in the gut. Staggering backwards like a drunk the back of Conrad's head thudded against the metal frame of the open widow with a violent crack. Shattered panes of stained glass flew across the floor as Conrad's legs buckled beneath him. As his body went limp, his arms dropped lifelessly to his sides. Glazing over his eyes rolled up inside his head. Tipping backwards the momentum of his body flipped his legs upwards as Conrad disappeared through the open window.

No sound just the wind. A haunting swish as Conrad's body plummeted. Then a vibrating thud as the ground shook. It was a noise that would live with Brainforth forever.

Looking out of the window Jake saw Conrad lying in the snow and shattered glass. Blood was oozing out from the back of his head like a river of treacle. His legs were spread-eagled. One snapped in two like a twig. Both arms twisted out above his head. Warm blood flowed down Jake's neck from the open scar under his right eye. His head felt woozy and he was unsteady on his feet. Although the alarm blared out around the prison he was oblivious to any sort of noise.

Taking off his cardigan Jake slipped it under the priest's head. Reaching upwards the priest's thin, cold fingers stroked the side of Jake's face. "I'm sorry." His eyes were watery. Suddenly the door was smashed-in. Thrown to the floor Jake found himself being pinned down by three officers. As his arms were wrenched behind his back his face was forced into the floor. He watched as boots gathered around the body of the priest. Shouting, confusion, an officer tried for a pulse. Handcuffed Jake recognised Rose's voice. "Conrad is dead."

"Jesus." Cried an officer; his hot breath bearing down on Jake's neck. Another officer holding one of his arms blasted down his ear. "You prick!"

Rose was attending to the priest. "Be quiet! He is trying to say something." The chapel crystallised and fell silent.

The priest's voice was weak. "Jacob is innocent. Conrad murdered Heather Wilson"

Rose shook his head, a confused expression across his face. "Who's Heather Wilson?"

That was to be the last breath in the priest's body and it saved Jake's life.

FATHER PATRICK NOLAN
AGED 68
IRISH 1981

CHAPTER TWENTY FOUR

The bible.

Father Patrick Nolan had been a priest for over 40 years. It was only by accident that on that sad night in December 1946 he was ordered to go to Brainforth Prison to take the confession of a condemned man. That night he listened to the heart rendering tale of Jim Abbott and it had become etched in his memory as well as his soul. The night quickly became dawn. Inside the four walls of a cell he became overwhelmed by the occasion. He believed Jim Abbott to be innocent.

At dawn the priest left the prison, jumped on his pushbike and peddled frantically through the deserted rain soaked streets of Oxford. Arriving at St Paul's Church he ran round the back of the church to the Monsignor's house and started ringing the bell and banging on the door at the same time. Bleary eyed, the Monsignor peered through the door in his night shirt. Holding a handkerchief up to his ruddy nose he found the animated priest on his doorstep panting for breath the words spilling incoherently from his mouth. Straw like, the Monsignor's grey hair was bedraggled; he wasn't happy, stopped the priest mid sentence and let out a volley of expletives about inexperience, naivety.

"Are you stupid; you're not a policeman or a judge; you are a priest and not a very good one; you are paid by the church and Lord almighty to listen, not be judgmental, of course a condemned man is going to plead his innocence to a priest, a stupid priest who would get me out of bed with influenza at this God forsaken hour?" He continued saying that Father Nolan should reconsider his position in the church and choose another occupation that he might be best suited rather than one of the cloth.

With the door slammed in his face Father Nolan found himself within ear shot of the Monsignor's blasphemy and castigation from behind the wooden door. Lucky not to be defrocked on the doorstep he crossed himself, counted his blessing and put it down to him being stupid after all. The church clock chimed six times and in six hours Jim Abbott would be swinging from a rope.

At eleven that morning the priest returned to Brainforth. Alone inside a cell, the sun streamed through the barred window onto both men who knelt opposite each other. Realising he had forgotten his bible the priest recited 'the last-rites' from memory. As the cell door swung open the priest helped the prisoner to his feet. Standing in the doorway the prison Governor said it was time. Two officers stepped inside the cell. Holding onto Abbott's arm the priest could see the prisoner shaking uncontrollably. Through the cell door the hangman waited, his face was unadorned his posture stiff, in his hand a hood dangled. Led into the adjoining room by the two officers Abbott's legs went from beneath him. Void of any natural light the room was bare and held a deathly silence. Positioned over the trap door Abbott started urinating. "I'm sorry, I'm sorry."

From somewhere near a church clock chimed twelve.

Years later when Father Nolan returned to Brainforth on a humanitarian visit, the unmarked grave inside the prison walls rekindled his memories. Abbott falling through that trap door had taken something of the priest with him. Asked to become the prison priest he accepted the position partially out of remorse. It had only become apparent to him that Conrad had been the young policeman and the real murderer of Heather Wilson when Jacob arrived inside Brainforth. Nonchalantly mentioning to Conrad how Jacob held a remarkable resemblance to a man named Abbot who went to the gallows and whom he believed to be innocent. Conrad slipped up. The priest remembered how Conrad had mentioned in his one and only confession about his upbringing in the East End of London and how as a young policeman he had patrolled the docks at night. Unnerved by Jacobs arrival inside Brainforth Conrad let his guard down and the priest found his behaviour unsettling. Investigating, the priest went to the local newspaper office and searched the library for photographs of the trial. One photograph had the young policeman coming out of court; it was Conrad and it was only a matter of time before his conscience got the better of him.

At midnight on the day of the hanging Father Nolan knelt at the altar of St Paul's Church clutching his bible. Crossing his chest; he kissed his thumb and pointed up to heaven. Praying for the innocent man who had just been executed, he asked forgiveness as well as the strength to live with his guilt.

CHAPTER TWENTY FIVE

Conrad Miller had murdered Heather Wilson in the warehouse fire in 1946. He had been a policeman for just under a year when by accident he spotted the family heirloom in the window of a pawn shop. Sitting amongst a number of dusty collectables was his mother's cherished mantle clock. That's when he saw her for the first time. Through the window he watched as she served behind the counter. He found her beauty overpowering as her flowery dress swayed around her shapely figure. Her father stood next to her. Aged around fifty, he wore a white apron and a tallit on his head. Within seconds he had became infatuated. The young Jewish girl was to be the first and his one and only murder on British soil.

But to understand Conrad you had to understand where he came from. Conrad grew up and lived with his mother and father William Miller in the East End of London. Unemployed. Desperate for money. William Miller reluctantly borrowed a small amount of money from a Jewish money lender. Unable to pay the loan back and from orders of the lender he was beaten-up. Not once but three times. Eventually finding a job on the docks William Miller eventually paid off his debts but his resentment for Jews became impregnated in his heart and mind. This was just the start.

Before Germany invaded Poland and Britain had become involved in the Second World War William Miller had become a Blackshirt and supporter of Oswald Mosley's fascist party. Conrad didn't need much persuading into hating Jews or any other minority which didn't fit into Hitler's blueprint or criteria of being one of his master race. Conrad's bedtime stories were replaced by talk of the evil that was sweeping England. Not by the Blackshirts but by Churchill he who described as the fat devil with the large cigar. Ridiculing Churchill's speeches William Miller compared them to Hitler's rally at Nuremburg.

"Look at the fat, stupid Englishman, what a pathetic sight and look at the Fuhrer, straight backed, he is someone special, a genius!"

On numerous occasions Conrad could smell the beer on his father's breath after he'd staggered home from a Blackshirt rally and the grease in his slicked down hair. He listened, wide eyed as his father sat on the end of the bed and waxed lyrical about Hitler and Heinrich Himmler's vision of the Nazis and The Third Reich. Painting a picture of the Nazis uniforms and the shine on their boots, he explained how they were everything people in England should aspire to. For a nine year old boy those lectures weren't just the odd night; they were every night. In awe of his father, Conrad yearned to wear his father's Blackshirt and one day the uniform of the SS. Leaving his son with a goodnight kiss on both cheeks, his father would recite the last verse of the fascist song.

The streets are still, the final struggle ended;
Flushed with the fight we proudly hail the dawn!
See, over all the streets the fascist banners waving.
Triumphant standards of our race reborn.

At night Conrad would practice the Nazi salute in the hallway mirror and try and click the back of his heels in unison. Just like his father had taught him. Respect for the SS.

After a Blackshirt rally at Olympia in London William Miller was injured in a minor riot outside with the Communists, resulting in him losing his right eye. That night Conrad was woken by his father. Drunk, with a blood stained bandage running across his right eye and around his head, he whispered as to not wake his sleeping wife in the next bedroom. Following his convictions he explained to his son that he had to travel to Hamburg in Germany. There was a SS rally and it was an opportunity not to be missed. There, he was going to join the 'British Free Corps' a fighting unit for Englishmen who were invited to join the Nazis. It was his chance to fight for the cause; God's cause. One day when the boy was older he would understand and they would be united in victory as father and son. That night William Miller hugged and kissed his son and left him a sketch pad, a tin of charcoals and copy of Mein Kampf on the bedside table.

Then he was gone.

William Miller's legacy had a lasting effect on Conrad as a boy; his words were burnt into his young son's soul.

But before leaving for the Fatherland he had score to settle. Coming out of his usual drinking-hole the Jewish money lender acknowledged William Miller who was stood in a shop doorway as if he was an old pal. "Ah, it's my dear friend Miller." The first blow was vicious, the second deadly. Knocked to the ground every kick in the lender's body was a reminder. One kick; two; three; four; five thudded into the body on the ground. "Take that my Jew friend." Seeing the lender's round horn-rimmed glasses on the pavement Miller crushed them under his boot and left the lender in a pool of blood.

After a couple of months working for the Foreign Ministry in Berlin William Miller joined the fledging British Free Corps and was now drinking beer shoulder to shoulder with German soldiers.

During the rest of the war Conrad's mother started drinking heavily. Faced with the stigma and scandal of having a husband who had ran out on her and who now fought for the enemy she started to despise Conrad who bore the good looks of his father and who reminded her every day of the dishonour and shame she felt. On one of the heaviest nights of bombing London had witnessed she sat alone at a bar drinking. Not for the first time Conrad found himself alone cowering down below on the platform of a tube station. Cold and frightened he found he had a flair for drawing and he would sketch the faces that huddled around him on the underground. It was his only joy and every line of somebody's face that he drew reminded him of his father's leaving gift. As London burned overhead he wondered where his mother was. After the sirens went up, his mother would stagger home, inebriated. Discovering a swastika had been daubed on her front door with white paint she took the humiliation out on her son.

"You little prick!"
"Please mother."
"You're a weasel just like your father!"
"I'm sorry mother."
"The shame he has left us with."

"I'm sorry."

"Sorry! I'm sorry, for having given birth to you. "

Pushing him up against the wall, the back of her hand whacked him across the face. Blood seeped from a split lip. It was to be the first of many thrashings. He was more frightened of his mother than of Hitler's bombs. Then within minutes of a beating she would find herself sitting on the bed crying, full of remorse and shame.

"What have I done, what have I done."

Suffering from gout in her toes, as soon as the rage inside her went it quickly returned, blaming her agony on God and her son. "God is taking his revenge out on me for what your father has done to us."

Some evenings, if she wasn't drinking, Rose Miller would sit in her chair listening to war reports on the radio. Staring at the boy who sat at her feet drawing pictures a certain bulletin or Lord Haw Haw's Nazi propaganda would trigger a surge of anger inside her. Conrad's eyes which now resembled his father's were a constant reminder. The verbal, mental and physical bullying was relentless.

One early morning on his way to school Conrad was met by the postman on the doorstep. He handed him a letter. "All the way from Germany lad. I bet you Winston Churchill himself has read that." Written in fountain pen the letter was addressed to Conrad Miller. It was the first letter he had ever received.

Ripping open the envelope Conrad read how his father was overwhelmed by the passion of the German people and that soon he would send for him. His small, neat hand writing matched his small neat appearance and Conrad created an image of his father sitting in his high ranking uniform of the Fatherland at Hitler's table with Goerbels and Himmler, drinking wine and eating from the trough.

Hiding the letter from his mother he read it over and over again but it was little comfort for a boy who missed his hero and was terrified each night when it was throwing out time.

But although the postman came there were no more letters. Five long years were to follow.

1946. A year after the war. Conrad had just turned eighteen. Resembling a twenty five year old, he was tall, broad shouldered, his face littered with stubble. Illegally cashing-in some of his mother's savings he also pawned the chiming mantle clock which were his parent's one and only wedding present. On the morning he left for Hamburg to track down his father he packed a small rucksack with enough clothes to travel light, his sketch pad and his tin of charcoals. Before leaving he went into his mother's bedroom and found her sleeping-off the effects of the night before. Although the curtains were drawn and the room was in blackness he could hear her groaning. Tugging open the curtains a haze of light cut across a pathetic sight. Her foot was propped up on a pillow, her toes purple and black. White as the sheets on the bed her body resembled a spirit. She had no idea that there was someone in her room and that her son was leaving. Conrad suspected she wouldn't have cared. For a few minutes he stood next to her bed and watched her snoring. Her pumice-stone face grimacing with the pain of the gout; dead to the world. Tears rolled down both cheeks at his mother who once had the looks that turned soldier's heads in the street. Now inside he wrestled and fought against the urge to smother her face with a pillow. He left no note and no forwarding address. At the back of his mind he thought there was good chance he would never set eyes on her again. His mother had told him once too often that he'd inherited his father's evil character. From his mother he had inherited how not to love.

It was the end of summer and Conrad travelled by train to Dover, then by ferry across the channel to Calais in France. It was the start of an arduous journey through Belgium to Germany and he had little money. Abject poverty bruised the surface of the land and in its people and inside the compartments of the trains he travelled in his eyes were opened to the countryside of war-torn Europe. Abandoned machinery, derelict buildings, scarecrows with no crops to defend. The war had left little mercy.

Sleeping rough in railway carriages or in station waiting rooms, he passed the time by sketching portraits of people in exchange for the odd cup of coffee, a loaf of bread or some slices of sausage. On some occasions he was given a bowl of hot soup or a cold meal consisting of ham and goat's cheese and once an old woman gave him some salted fish. He had become an accomplished artist. Time tables were non-existent but eventually, after two weeks of travelling, Conrad arrived in Hamburg. The city was a waste land and he could feel it bleeding in front of his eyes. A blanket of grey dust covered the dereliction, a solitary tree being the only sign of life. Conrad had heard how Hamburg had been flattened by the allied bombers but nothing could prepare him for the despair he was witnessing. Finding his father in this carnage would be a miracle.

Walking for over an hour, every second was stolen from him. Taking his father's dishevelled letter from his pocket he stopped an old toothless woman, showed her the address and asked her for directions. She spat in his face, emotions and the scars of the war were momentous and still on a knife edge.

Living in hope he continued to ask directions from people who shuffled like zombies, living corpses. Thousands of single shoes, smashed spectacles, shattered glass, a single red ribbon from a little girl's hair, the ground held no life.

Passing a desecrated church he smelt damp, charcoaled

wood and incense. A priest was sitting on the steps. Mumbling to himself, his hands were tearing at his face; his body rocking from side to side. Fragments of glass were scattered around his feet. Behind him was a blown-out window that stretched up to heaven. A stone cross hanging precariously from the bombed out roof. Hearing Conrad's boots crunch across the stained glass the priest slowly lifted his head and covered his face from the sun. Wearing a grubby smock with dried blood splashed across the front, his eyes were haunted, full of distress. Squinting grimly up at the stranger he placed his hands on his knees and scraped his fractured body to its feet. Showing him the address like he had done a dozen times before, Conrad looked across the ravaged land as the priest pointed to a dust cloud about a mile away. There was pain in the priest's voice. He smelt of burnt chemicals, his faith drained from his body but Conrad had found a saint who sent him on his way with a blessing.

Kissing the envelope Conrad walked away from the church leaving a trail of footprints in the dust.

The address was another ruin, another ruin that had devoured the dead.

Deflated, Conrad slumped down on the bricks and started crying, tears cutting lines down his chalky face. Exhausted, he felt the heat of the sun burning across his shoulders and it became evident that he had become weak from the laborious journey.

Taking some bread and cheese from out of his bag he felt dejected and despondent. His world and his father's dreams lay in ashes all around him. Chewing on the stale bread, he noticed some bright red material sticking out from under some shards of granite. Leaning down he tugged and released the cloth. It was the Nazis flag, bright red with the swastika in the centre of a white circle. Dusting it down he folded it carefully then slipped it inside his coat.

A summer sunset bled across his face as his eyes drifted across the debris of ruins towards an old grocer who was struggling to push a small stack of potatoes on a rickety, wooden cart.

Conscious of the lack of trust with the people Conrad caught up with the grocer and found his flesh hanging from his frail body, his fingers and lined face ground in dirt. Disguising his accent as if he was slightly dumb; he spoke tentatively hoping the old man would take pity on the lost soul. "Excuse me."

Stopping the weary grocer, he let go of the handles of the cart and looked at Conrad.

Trying to regain his breath, his eyes gaped, his drooping moustache hiding his frightened expression. "Mochten sie etwas kartoffeles kaufen? Leider wird es nicht billig sein!"

"I'm sorry, I don't speak German."

Gliding his index finger across his cracked bottom lip the grocer's voice trembled. "You're British?"

"Yes."

"Where from?"

"London."

"You are a long way from home. Do you want to buy some potatoes? They are not cheap."

"No."

"What do you want then? I have no money. You can search my pockets if you like." His hand came up to his petrified face as if he was expecting to be struck.

"Please – I don't want anything, the priest…."

…."The priest is mad! He thinks he has been punished like a witch by the Holy Inquisition. Poor soul, he might be better off being mad. Now at least he doesn't have to listen to peoples vows and wipe away their tears." Smelling of rotting earth, the grocer picked up the cart and began to move off.

"I am looking for William Miller."

"I'm hard of hearing. Who?"

"William Miller. He's my father."

The grocer could hear the desperation in the young man's voice and dropped the cart again. "So you do want something?

"Yes."

His eyes held the fires of war but surprisingly the grocer's broken-English was comprehensible, having learnt the language from Humphrey Bogart movies and from books. 'Great Expectations' by Dickens had been his favourite. Badly burnt down the right side of his neck and face, his right ear had been melted like candle wax. He evoked memories of the night his shop was flattened by RAF bombers and how he was buried in the rubble which left him deaf in one ear.

"I think my father lived at this address"

"Why?"

"He sent me letter from here. Did you know him?"

"The man who wore the eye patch of a pirate."

His father wearing an eye patch was a surprise at first but he recalled the last time he had seen him. A bloody bandage across his head and eye. It gave him hope that finding his father would be easier.

"His German was excellent, I would not have known he was English if he hadn't confided in me – you look like him."

Running his fingers through his thinning white hair, the grocer recalled William the Englishman, who spoke German like a Bavarian, describing his good looks, his patch and his pride in wearing the uniform of the Fatherland.

Recollecting a conversation with a German soldier the grocer told the story of how the Englishman escaped a bomb blast but sustained a shrapnel wound of metal fragments to his leg. He was captured by the Americans and as far as he could remember he was to be extradited back to England and tried as a traitor.

The sentence was death by hanging. Lighting a cigarette, the grocer's fingers trembled as he continued, his voice beaten into severity. "He should have stayed in Poland; perhaps he would not have been captured."

"Poland?"

"Sorry let me explain. My mind is getting old and it wanders as does my voice." Taking a suck on the cigarette Conrad noticed that the grocer had very few teeth. As the smoke streamed down his nostrils the grocer continued. "He spent most of the war in Poland, but just before war ended he returned back here and was captured. He was held in a prison compound just inside the city boundary. Then I heard that he had escaped with a group of prisoners and rumour has it that he had fled back to Poland."

As to why William Miller went back to Poland the grocer wasn't clear. The infrastructure in Europe was chaotic and travelling anywhere could have taken days, weeks, months. He would have been stopped at check-points and ordered to show his identity papers. At the time there were hundreds of Nazis on the run and the allies was vigilant in trying to capture war criminals. 1.8 million Germany troops had invaded Poland on September the 1st 1939 and they had intended to completely eliminate the Polish race along with the Jews by 1975. Fanatical for revenge, the hunt was on. Then, as the grocer related a story he'd heard of the Polish cavalry attacking German tanks, his mind rewound and he remembered that the Englishman had a wife. She was Polish and came from Krakow.

"Are you sure, you must be mistaken?"

There was a remorseful tone in the grocer's reply as the stench of stagnant water drifted through the air. "I'm sure. That much I remember clearly as if it were yesterday, because after his escape he came to my house in the middle of the night. I'm sorry, but he was in a poor state of health. His leg wasn't healing and he was limping heavily. I gave him a clean change of clothes and some food, only some slices of bread and a little ham and he left when it became dark. He was determined to return to Krakow to find his wife; he showed me a photograph of her. She was a nurse, a very striking woman if I remember."

It was another shock for Conrad. To learn that his father was a bigamist overwhelmed him but for some reason he wasn't convinced by the grocer's revelation.

As a parting gift he left the grocer with his charcoal portrait. It was a poor effort, his hand, like the grocer's had been shaking uncontrollably. Watching the old man push the cart away with his head disappearing into his hunched shoulders, Conrad felt leaden, his spirit drained. Standing alone in the waste land he considered the possibilities. Yes, he had to go on. It was the right thing to do, the only thing to do.

Behold the morning soil.

Weighed down with exhaustion Conrad gave into sleep and that night in the hands of Morpheus he slept for over ten hours in an abandoned railway carriage. The next day his eyes bid a callous farewell to Hamburg as his search for his father continued.

Sharing the train journey from Hamburg with an accordion player, people hung around their carriage and listened to the music as Conrad grabbed the opportunity and sketched their portraits for food and a little money. Jurgen had been a German prisoner of war in a camp in Wales and with a smile as wide as the English Channel he boasted about how he had escaped by tunnelling his way out of the camp with his comrades only to be eventually caught. A jovial personality, the accordion player wanted to learn about England and its customs and Conrad of Germany. Jurgen related the day the English guards had posted on the walls of their huts pictures of the death camps. His face tried to hide the guilt of his countrymen but his eyes told the harrowing truth.

After a fortnight of travelling together Jurgen hugged Conrad goodbye. Giving him a conciliatory slap on the back they parted as good friends. Jurgen was Conrad's one and only friend that he would ever have.

If only the accordion player had known at the time.

Reaching Krakow, Conrad found himself searching and delving through the records of the people that had been catalogued as missing on church notice boards and in government buildings. Re-tracing his steps over and over again he questioned librarians and priests about his father who wore a distinctive eye patch and of his wife who worked as a nurse. After three weeks of probing through piles of records and examining photographs of the dead and the living under a magnifying glass Conrad took the desperate decision and gave up looking for his father. He had always held him in his heart as invincible. He was wrong. After a period of mourning Conrad found himself to be no different from the thousands of Poles whose lives had been destroyed by the war. He'd found the spirit in the Krakow people inspiring and delightful. Their world had vanished, but they were proud of their monuments; their buildings and churches; the symbols of a persecuted civilisation. Krakow was far removed from his roots in the East End of London but both places shared a spirit.

Staying in a hovel of a room where you changed your own sheets and which smelt of the abattoir across the road, he decided to return home. Outstaying his welcome the landlord felt unsettled by his tenant and had started to ask questions as to what the Englishman was doing in Krakow. Aloof, Conrad detected that the landlord was a diehard German who resented the allies. Perhaps he hid a dark secret left over from the war. Either way Conrad paid-up and left the emaciated landlord who struggled with an agonising chesty-cough which would eventually kill him.

It was whilst he was sleeping rough and trying to work his passage back home by sketching and selling his portraits round the bars and cafes of the city that he was fortunate to meet a young British diplomat in a smoky bar.

"Sit, sit young man and draw my portrait. Make me as handsome as Clark Gable!" His laughter shook the glasses on the table. Gesturing for Conrad to sit down at his table he didn't offer to shake hands but stood up and shouted for another bottle of wine. Charles Hyde was an old Etonion and part of a British delegation visiting Auschwitz, the concentration camp. Baby faced, with red, toby-jug cheeks. The two men shared a bottle of wine and a pack of cigarettes. Sketching Hyde's sharp features Conrad watched as the diplomat slowly became drunk. Talking of a prostitute who waited for him in a room around the corner he unbuttoned his shirt collar; whispering of contraband he unloosened his tie; describing how he had witnessed a woman having her head shaved in public for fraternising with German soldiers his tweed jacket slipped from his shoulders; emptying themselves of their Englishness the vodka took over from the wine.

"Do you know my dear boy, that there is a whisper of Germany being split into two with and a huge wall being built across the whole of the country?"

Hyde was drawing eyes from dark corners.

Slowly, becoming morose, Hyde lowered his voice as he sipped and dribbled his vodka. "You want to see the death camps; it is indescribable what went on in there." He began to talk more in whispers, details becoming fragmented, but Conrad had become engrossed in the diplomat's macabre description of Auschwitz; he could only sit back and admire the Nazis organisation in transporting the Jews from all over Europe and as far as Scandinavia.

Before he left Poland Conrad had to visit the death camp.

Interrupting Conrad's train of thought, Hyde looked at his portrait through bleary eyes and laughed "You have done a marvellous job young man; you have indeed made me look like old big ears!" Reaching inside his jacket Hyde removed his wallet, his boisterousness overwhelming the café. Fumbling through a wad of Polish bank notes Hyde slid several across the table. It was more than enough. Slumping to the side, his paunch flopped out from under his waist coat, as his fingers searched for the inside pocket of his jacket. Slipping from his fingers, his wallet dropped to the floor under the table. It was Conrad's chance to steal the wallet and he took it. After all Hyde was assiduously an Englishman, one of the 'Churchill Youth' wasn't he?

The following day, heavy headed, but with a pocket full of Polish money burning a hole in his pocket courtesy of the drunken diplomat, Conrad travelled by bus to Auschwitz. It was to be a pilgrimage to William Millers love of the Fatherland and nothing else.

It was to be his first visit but not his last.

Stimulated, reborn. That night back in Krakow Conrad booked into a modest hotel and went to bed with the images of the visit to Auschwitz in his mind and the swastika flag under his pillow. The flag was like a comfort blanket and masturbating he tried to think of what it would feel like to kill. To hold the power in his hands that could murder millions of people if he so wanted. It would be like killing flies.

That following night he found his first victim.

Klaudia Matyjas was a waitress who had survived the horrors of Auschwitz. She was going to become the first victim of a serial killer.

ROSE MILLER
AGED 50
ENGLISH
APRIL 1946

CHAPTER TWENTY SIX

His hands bloodied, Conrad slept little on the gruelling journey back through Europe. Once again he passed the time by drawing peoples portraits and watching the land fly by; the hills peppered with the crosses of graves.

On the day that Queen Elizabeth once again walked through the blitzed streets of the East End of London Conrad found himself identifying his mother's body.

A grey sheet was pulled back over a grey face.

Conrad nodded.

No fears, no tears only lost years.

Within seconds, Conrad kissed his mother on the crown of her head and left the morgue.

Rose Miller had been found by the side of a railway line. Her body was covered in morning dew; blood congealed her features making her face unrecognisable. At the inquest the coroner came to the conclusion of 'death by misadventure'. The coroner's finding was that Rose Miller had fallen from a bridge and died from a severe head injury. A large amount of alcohol had been discovered in her blood stream.

At the burial Conrad shed tears, not just for his mother, but for his father as well. Now he was alone in the world. Their family home had been boarded up. Rose Miller had left him nothing. Apart from the landlord of the local public house there was nobody else at her funeral. His blood chilled.

As Conrad stood outside his house, lost, his only possession was the shirt on his back, his sketchbook and his tin of charcoals. Across the road something was being fumigated. Then as he watched an old man trying to salvage something from around the bomb site, his heart stopped. A young policeman was striding towards him with a purpose. For a few seconds his mind returned to the derelict building on the south bank of Krakow. It was unfathomable to think he would ever be caught but to his relief the policeman turned out to be an old school friend who had previously notified him of his mother's death. They talked for a while about old school friends and of the doodlebug which had landed at the end of the road on the last day of the war and demolished the row of terraced houses taking the family of Jones with it. As the enthusiastic policeman reminisced the conversation drifted to the benefits of him joining the police force. Convincing Conrad, he said he would put in a good-word with his uncle who was a desk sergeant at the local station.

Joining the police was an impulsive decision; at first Conrad felt suffocated. He felt as if the policeman's words were tantamount to blackmail but he had nowhere else to go. Work was scarce and the country still lived out of a ration book, so he was grateful to start earning money.

Wearing his police uniform for the first time he questioned his unknown future and then related it to the Blackshirt his father wore. Would he be proud of him? Only time would tell.

After the murder of Heather Wilson in the warehouse fire Conrad swore on the bible to 'tell the truth and nothing but the truth'. But he lied through his back teeth and convinced the Judge, the jury and the court to send an innocent man to the gallows. He may not have put the noose over Jim Abbott's head but he had released the trap door. In essence he had murdered again. The front page of every newspaper followed the trial meticulously. In the pubs and corner shops of the East End everyone became embroiled in the trial that lasted for three full days. Like a small village, everyone had there own opinions. "Let him hang!"

But some knew and believed him to be innocent.

The day after the trial Conrad was back in uniform and walking the beat. In some peoples eyes he was a hero; keeping law and order; a hero who had brought a murderer to trial, a thug who deservedly had been given the noose. What he didn't expect was the random questions by his fellow policemen as well as the ordinary man on the street.

"I knew Abbott. He could never have committed such a crime – are you sure it was Abbott?"

Questioning his integrity and honesty Conrad became the object of the odd jibe on the street.

"You can see a bent copper a mile off."

As the main witness in the murder of the young Jewish girl Conrad didn't anticipate the passion and loyalty of the East End to the man who was executed. Abbott was one of them; born and bred; one of their own.

Overnight Conrad became a liability to the police force. Offered a transfer to another constabulary, he declined. Mud stuck and under the pretence of his imminent failure of ever being promoted, and disillusioned with law enforcement as well as the police being disillusioned with him, he decided to join the prison service and moved to Oxford and Brainforth Prison. The place where Jim Abbott had been hanged.

Then in the winter of 1965 Conrad returned to Krakow. Reunited with the smells of the city; to walk its snowy pavements, to taste its beer and hear its people's accents Conrad felt as if he was returning home. And once again the draw of Auschwitz beckoned.

But it was at the camp of Birkenau close to Auschwitz that he found his next victim. Anna Van Reed was a tourist guide, pretty, intelligent, a slip of a girl who held Conrad's gaze on more than one occasion as she guided the group of tourists around the wooden huts which sat in lines opposite the electrified fences and watch towers.

"Life meant nothing to the Nazis; they didn't care how many millions of Jews they murdered." That's all she needed to say to convince Conrad that she would be next. In memory of his father.

When the tourist party arrived back in the centre of Krakow Conrad watched and waited, then followed the guide through the streets and across The Market Square. Watching her go into a smoky bar Conrad nonchalantly followed her inside. Unbuttoning his overcoat he sat himself on a barstool; lit a cigarette and in the reflection of the mirror behind the bar watched the woman as she chatted happily to a group of friends.

Leaving before the woman he skipped behind a passing tram across the street and hid in the doorway of a restaurant. It had started snowing again and when she came out of the bar he followed. Walking a few yards behind, he shadowed her for about half a mile, then seizing his chance in a deserted street, he pounced. Violently shoving her to one side she toppled down a flight of stone steps which led to a basement jazz bar. Crumpled at the bottom of the steps, she groaned. Conrad was quick, flying down the steps; he gripped the girl around the neck and covered her mouth with his glove. A twist and a snap. Within seconds she stopped wriggling. As the life drained from her body he glanced up and noticed the opening times on a sign on the door of the jazz club. He would have to be even quicker.

Hurrying through the streets of Krakow he climbed into his hire car and drove back to the scene of the crime. Expecting to see a group of people gathering at the top of the steps or the police cordoning off the area he blew a sigh of relief, the grey fog of his breath icy in the cold air. Jumping out of the car he checked right and left. Apart from a golden light coming from a shop which sold crockery the street held a blanket of unintelligible dreariness. Swathed in darkness a shroud of snow covered the woman's black overcoat as Conrad put both his hands under the woman's armpits and hoisted her up the steps one at a time. Bundling her body inside the boot of the car he knew he had taken a risk. A huge risk.

As he drove through Krakow towards the deserted factory his knuckles turned white. Gripping the steering wheel he was sweating profusely. Inside the car the window screen had steamed up and he struggled to see which direction he was going. Listening to the woman's body rocking and banging from side to side inside the boot he drove over the Wista.

The storeroom reeked of death.

Once again Conrad followed the same ritual as he had done five years previously. Binding the girl's wrists behind her back; she was stripped naked and hoisted up from the wooden post. Watching, he winced as both collarbones dislocated as her body jolted forward. After an hour and two cigarettes Conrad took down the body; shaved her head, tattooed her arm and disposed of the body into the icy flow of the river.

Picking up a copy of Time Magazine at the airport Conrad nonchalantly flicked through the pages and found himself staring at a headline.

The Shepherd will kill again.
American family leave their tears in Krakow.

Underneath the headlines was the photograph of a familiar face. Reading a full page interview with the parents of their daughter who had been murdered in Krakow. It made good copy for Conrad; distressing news for the reader. Over the years the Polish police had checked and double checked and surmised and discussed that the killer could have come from outside the country. Why wait so long between each killing was one of the biggest questions? They had checked hotels of guests coming and going. Whether a person abroad could be matched to being in the country at the time of the murders. But it was a hopeless task. Blaming the incompetent Krakow Police Department, the parents of the American student Tracy Jankowski, had resigned themselves to the fact that the killer would never be found.

Conrad smiled to himself he now had another pseudonym 'The Shepherd'. He liked it.

As Conrad's flight touched down in London Detective Adamski watched from the bank of the River Wista as the body of Anna Van Reed was cut from out of the ice.

GARRETT CIEPLY
POLISH
AGED 20
FEBRUARY 1976

CHAPTER TWENTY SEVEN

Red sky in the morning, sailor's warning.

For the last time in November 1976 Conrad took a short break to Krakow; the city that held his secret; the city close to his heart. It was to be his last trip, a sentimental visit, a sentimental murder; one more for the road.

Treating himself to an upmarket hotel Conrad checked-in in under his real name:-Conrad Miller. After previously coming into the country under various pseudonyms times had changed. His passport photograph held no resemblance to the young artist who came into Krakow all those years ago. A lifetime ago.

Blood of the unsolved murders still floated over the city.

Strolling through the streets he watched as the shop keepers and wholesalers opened their stores. After paying a visit to the open air market of 'Plac Targowy', he went to view Da Vinci's 'Lady with an Ermine' on display at the Czartoryski Museum. Taking in the smells and the sights of Krakow and after a coffee and a slice of strawberry cheese cake at a patisserie he made his way towards the river.

As the crisp air cut across the Wista it cleared his head and also gave him time to think; to plan.

Setting foot onto the south bank he passed two policemen standing by a patrol car. Their dark blue uniforms neat, threatening, their batons and holstered guns at the ready. Just in case. They were interrogating a man over the bonnet of the car who looked inebriated; they didn't give the Englishman a second look.

Swinging left down Piwna Conrad shadowed the familiar wall at the back of a run-down tenement block. At the corner he nodded politely to an old woman scattering bread crumbs to a carpet of pigeons which were pecking around her ankles. *Feed the bird's tuppence a bag.* Conrad smiled sadly himself. He had seen Pygmalion on stage with Julie Andrews in London many years ago but for some strange reason the song always reminded him of his mother. It wasn't a good memory.

Turning another corner Conrad stopped, stepped back and leant against the wall holding his breath. Like a shadow he stole a look at a group of elderly people standing outside an abandoned factory. Wearing black hats; their hands set deep inside the pockets of their overcoats. They were praying; their heads bowed in front of a tall, gaunt Rabbi who rocked on his heels as he recited. "Hear, O Israel. The Lord is our God. The Lord is one."

Running his thin fingers down his prayer shawl which was draped around his shoulders, the Rabbi then gestured to a spine-curved man to step forward. Placing a large wreath at the base of the ornate, iron gates of the building the man stepped back and bowed his head in salute; his foggy breath evident in the cold air. After a few minutes the group embraced each other before slowly moving off towards a dark sandstone tunnel leading down to the river.

Walking past the factory Conrad paused, crouched down

and looked at the large wreath, the flowers and ribbon fluttering in the breeze. Standing, Conrad peered through the dirty glass into the factory. Metal pots and pans that had once been used by the army were stacked in a corner. Focusing his eyes on an elongated sign propped against the far wall he made out the words embossed into the metal – Oskar Shindler's Factory.

Obsessed by the secrecy of the storehouse Conrad realised that the area was changing and that Shindler's factory was becoming a pilgrimage site for many Jews throughout the world. He came to a quick decision. This would be his swan song, like it or not, the backstreets that had once been inhabited by the odd wild dog were changing from dark to light. It was inevitable that his place of execution would be discovered and getting caught was not part of the master plan.

Turning left onto Nadwislanska he paused nonchalantly outside the derelict warehouse. Crouching down he pretended to tie his shoe lace at the same time glancing from right to left. Then as quick as a bullet out of a gun he moved. Putting his shoulder against the decaying wooden door he shoved it open and disappeared off the street.

Conscious of his heavy boots making a noise across the cobbled courtyard he cushioned his steps and looked upwards, the sky was grey; full of snow. In a couple of hours it would be dark.

Inside the storehouse he breathed a heavy sigh of relief. To his surprise everything was intact, undiscovered; apart from the smell of sewage seeping from a cracked drain, it was just how he'd left it. Rolling his shoulders with the cold Conrad felt the adrenalin kicking into his body and closing his eyes he recalled the faces of his victims. The waitress, the American girl, the Auschwitz guide. Only the girl who burnt to death had eluded his executions. An indescribable smell of death was at the end of his fingers. Removing a bundle of rope from inside his overcoat he threw it into the corner of the dark room and left.

Then the likelihood of him finding his next victim was presented to him on a plate.

Approaching dusk Krakow was becoming a smudge on the landscape. As he walked back over the bridge Conrad was stopped by a young student in his early twenties.

"Czy zechciatby Pan znobic mi zdjecie?"

Conrad worked out the request of the student as he was handed a camera. Conrad reluctantly agreed to take the photograph as the over-jolly, annoying student continued to chatter away to him in Polish. Wearing a scull cap; it clung with great difficulty to a mop of blond curly hair which flopped down over his forehead. Positioning himself against the fading light and the backdrop of the city, the student struck a smiling pose. Cupid faced, Conrad scrutinised him through the view-finder of the Pentax camera with his right eye. For a few seconds Conrad was drawn to a gold locket around the young man's neck. He was ideal.

"Just move to the right a little." Conrad's accent slipped.

"Are you English?"

"No." Gesturing for the student to move to his right, he followed him with the camera.

The student looked at Conrad with mild curiosity and raised his voice as if Conrad was hard of hearing. "Oh, you sound English."

Don't raise your voice to me you little shit.

Shuffling to the right the student lent to his left resting his hand on his hip. "Is this ok? Try to get Krakow in the background. Are you going to say cheese?" Trying to conceal his ambiguous stare Conrad didn't answer. For the first time in his life, apart from inside the four walls of Brainforth Conrad found himself in the company of a homosexual. Self conscious, uneasy, he could feel his every move being scrutinized. Feeling like a specimen under a microscope Conrad lined up a camera shot as an awkward silence rebounded between the lens and the student.

"Cheeeese!"

Taking the camera out of Conrad's hands the student gave him a questionable look. "Thank you, I thought all Englishman said 'cheese' when they took a photograph. I'm studying English at Warsaw University. I know an accent when I hear one. I hope to be an interpreter for the military when I leave. Where are you from?"

Conrad strode off; the seething easily read through his unconvincing expression and gritted teeth. Muttering something rude under his breath the student exhaled and shrugged his shoulders. Turning, he walked towards the south bank, pausing momentarily to take snaps of the river and of the Krakow skyline.

Inflamed with rage Conrad found himself becoming virtuous, as a hatred for homosexuals he never knew existed, boiled inside him.

"Like the Jews they have polluted bodies and minds." His father's words drifted back to him like the icy wind cutting across the river. Eating him up inside, Conrad started to sweat profusely. A slush splattered tram whistled past. Overhead sparks crackled from the power cable; the noise of the conductor's bell and the rattle of the tram's metal wheels on the tracks adding to the ever-increasing fury inside his head. Feeling nauseous he cleared his throat of phlegm and spat. Looking back he saw the student at the far end of the bridge, his shadow dragging behind him. It wasn't an option; Conrad's mind was set. Tracking back he paused at the slight hump in the bridge. Spotting the student silhouetted in the distance, he quickened his pace.

Turning left over the bridge back into Piwna, it was as if the student was being drawn to Shindler's factory by an uncontrollable force. Shortening the gap Conrad was only a few yards behind; his breath on the nape of the young man's neck. Pouncing like a beast, he threw his arm around the student's neck. Wrenching him upwards he barged backwards through the wooden gate. The student kicked out, the heels of his shoes dragging across the cobbles. Conrad tightened his grip around the throat. Fighting for his life the student's face had turned purple. Clawing at Conrad's arms the two men dropped to the ground. A twist then a yank, the sound of the neck snapping reverberated though Conrad's arm's and body.

Savouring the moment Conrad lay on his back with the student's warmth in his arms. Dragging the body across the yard Conrad tumbled it inside the storehouse and let go of the corpse. Bending forward he rested both his hands on his knees and panted heavily. The kill had taken his second wind. Filling his lungs with air he looked up through the hole in the roof at the blackness of the sky. Multiple identities had possessed his soul. Below the hole in the roof, the ground was covered in pigeon excrement. Somewhere he heard dripping water; a shutter banging in the wind.

Walking back to the main gate he dragged it shut and waited in the courtyard. No footsteps, no cries for help, clean as a whistle.

Stripping the student's body he scrutinized the gold locket hanging from a gold long chain around the student's neck. Admiring the locket he removed it and slipped it over his own head. Binding his thin wrists behind his back with rope he threaded one end of the rope through the metal ring on the post then wrapped the other end around both of his hands. Pausing for a few seconds he regained his breath. Gritting his teeth; all his strength went into his arms as he pulled the rope. Hoisting the body agonisingly off the ground; the body slowly became vertical. Then with a jerk of the rope the student's head slumped forward. Conrad watched as the skullcap flipped forward and hung by a single hair pin. It was if his halo was slipping. Pulling on the rope, the crack of the collarbones dislocating echoed around the brick walls. With one last effort Conrad secured the rope around the hook at the bottom of the post.

For a few minutes he stared at the ghastly sight as the body and face took on different forms of grotesque deformity. Reaching inside his overcoat he removed the small tin containing the charcoals that he used when he was a young innocent sketcher of portraits as an overwhelming sense of guilt brought tears to his eyes.

Memories of how he was when he was a young man swept through his body; a carefree attitude snatched away from him with his precious life. Vomiting Conrad wiped his mouth with the back of his hand; he could feel his body temperature lowering and had to act fast. Although his hands were shaking he removed the nib from a fountain pen out of the tin with which he had tattooed the polish waitress; the American student and the tour guide. Once again the tattoo bore the same letters. Nothing new. He left his mark, like a dog leaving his scent on a tree.

After an hour of watching the lifeless body dangle from the rope Conrad had completely recovered, the purgatory lifting from his body. At one time he wrestled with the idea that the student still had his milk teeth. He looked that young but it was only an ephemeral moment. Feeling hungry he was just about to finish the concluding touches when he realised something which challenged him. It was his obsessive knowledge of Auschwitz.

Untying the rope around the hook he lowered the ash skinned corpse slowly to the ground. Reaching into his back pocket he removed the blue and grey faded strip of cloth with the green triangle. Pink; he needed something pink. His mind raced as he thought about what he was wearing. Pink he needed something pink. Then he remembered the wreath outside the gates of Shindler's factory.

With slight trepidation he stepped out into the courtyard and suffered the blast of arctic air hitting him from every direction. The kill had taken its toll as Conrad afforded a smile to himself. He was getting too old for all this excitement. Nudging himself out of the front gate Conrad's eyes pierced the blackness. Heading back towards the factory he heard the monotonous rumbling of a dredger on the river. A rat the size of large cat scurried past.

At the factory Conrad struggled to see the image on the wreath in the dark. Straining his eyesight he crouched down and focusing on the ribbon on the wreath he saw what he was looking for, what he remembered. Removing the nib of the fountain pen from out of the tin he gripped it between his fingers, then cut into both ends of the ribbon, carefully using the nib as a knife. Making a small laceration into the ribbon he cut out a small triangular shape in the material. A dog barked from somewhere making him swing around. At the same time he stood and caught his reflection in the blackness of the glass and stared at a face that had abandoned him.

It was the face of a monster.

Kneeling down on the ground of the storeroom he could feel the cold eating into his knees. Snow dropped through the hole in the roof and onto the back of his neck. Shivering, he scored the small piece of triangular ribbon and then reached back inside the tin removing a small needle and thread and then sewed the pink triangle to the striped cloth. Pleased with his work he knotted the cloth tightly around the right bicep of the body. Once again everything was clean. Little fuss. Meticulous. The wreath had a ribbon; it was pink, a stroke of luck. In the small tin was a pair of nail scissors. Blowing into his hands he began. Cutting the hair was laboured and he could feel the inside of his thumb starting to blister. The ringlets of the student's hair dropped onto the ground and his mind went back to Auschwitz. The ritual became mirrored by the possibility that in a past life he'd been an SS officer in a concentration camp. Snipping away, the outside world didn't exist; he was bewitched with what he was doing and he fantasised about the hair being spun into matting or stuffing for upholstery.

He celebrated outside by urinating up against the wall whilst feeling the snow flakes on his face. His breath felt warm in the cold air, sending out clouds of grey smoke.

With some effort Conrad lifted up the naked, limp body and hoisted it over his shoulder. It was about four hundred metres to the tunnel which led down to the footpath alongside the river. It was now or never. On the other occasions he had used a wooden cart concealing the bodies with a tarpaulin, but the base had rotted and fallen through. It lay abandoned in the courtyard.

Setting off Conrad's heart pounded, his breath tightened, but he had to keep going.

Three hundred yards to go, a trip, stumbling, he recovered, just. As he trudged his body was becoming more and more bent-over as the weight became unbearable.

Two hundred yards. He could see the blackness inside the arched entrance to the tunnel. An unbearable weight; the burden of the load was agonizing. Out of one ear he heard the dog barking again. It was getting nearer. What would he do if he was discovered? Would he have to kill again?

Entering the tunnel he could see lights shimmering across the top of the river.

A hundred, fifty yards, every step took on a new meaning, intolerable weight. At first he thought they were lights from the other side of the river. He stepped back. The lights were the eyes of hundreds of rats. Limply kicking out the rats smelt flesh. Catching one with his boot, he then caught another sending it thudding against the wall. Screeches; the noise of the rats; deafening, echoing inside the tunnel. Stepping out of the tunnel he shook his leg trying to release a rat that had bitten into the leg of his trousers. One clung to his back scratching; biting. Dropping the body, he hit out. Scurrying off the rats disappeared back into the tunnel, the blackness. Slumped over and panting heavily Conrad could feel his body shaking. Looking both ways along the footpath, the relief was instant. Deserted. Straightening up he felt the base of his back with both hands and winced with pain. Hurry. Lifting the body he dragged it to the river's edge. Sliding the corpse into the slow moving icy current Conrad watched as it disappeared into the black, swirling water. Wiping his face clear of sweat Conrad saw at the far end of the footpath a man walking his dog. He tracked back; lucky for him and his dog.

As he walked along the riverbank he regained his breath and composure. Pulling up the collar of his overcoat he thought of his recurring dream. The blackness; the body over his shoulder, the rats. He had experienced his nemesis; he had just killed. Like Jack the Ripper.

That night Conrad lay in the hot bath of his hotel drinking a cold Zywiec beer. Humming along to 'The Messiah' by Handle on the hotel radio he went over the steps of his latest and final conquest in Poland. Chuckling to himself he took a large gulp of the beer. What he had just done was a miracle. Everyone back in Brainforth thought he was sunning himself in Greece. Fools. Idiots. Toasting himself 'a warrior' he thought of his father; how proud he would be of his son. Murdering a man for the first time had sent shock waves of excitement through him. A homosexual and a Jew. Who would have thought it? The polish police would be tied in knots. Lifting his glass he toasted himself again with a smug expression. Like a cat with nine lives, his were still intact.

Conrad had been efficient; leaving no clues. Disguising his voice he sometimes made it heavy, sometimes soft. Walking with a stick, he limped. Wearing glasses, his eye-sight was perfect. Sometimes he sported a hearing aid, or a false moustache. He was a master of disguises, covering his tracks impeccably. As for the pink triangle he had sewn onto the striped cloth, it was a master stroke. Cut from the ribbon tied to the wreath outside Shindler's factory; irony had come to his rescue.

He always left his mark.

Tattooed in Auschwitz the waitress was dead when her arm had been branded by Conrad in the drabness of her room. She had been the first but when the body was discovered in 1947 they never gave it a second glance. Many people had tattoos on their arms as a legacy of the thugs in the death camps. William Miller had left England in search of glory and to be a part of Hitler's vision for the World but it was Heinrich Himmler; the instigator of the concentration camps, who became his real inspiration.

The tattoo on the arms of Conrad's victims was simple and he wanted to leave a mark in memory of his father. The letters in HEINRICH HIMMLER added to fifteen, two more letters than that of his father's name WILLIAM MILLER. All Conrad did was mix up the two names; a letter from Himmler's name followed by a letter from William Miller's name.

WILLIAM MILLER
HEINRICH HIMMLER
HWEIILNLRIIACMH HMIIMLMLLEERR

It was a red herring; Conrad had a clear head, sending the Krakow police department on a wild goose chase had given him a sense of satisfaction and invincibility. To him everyone became a subversive and he related wholeheartedly to the Gestapo way of thinking.

Rectangular light filtered through the slight gap in the bathroom window and Conrad made out the silhouette of a gargoyle which hung over the cornerstone on the hotel roof. It was a comforting reminder of who he was, along with his new locket that hung around his neck.

In twelve hours time Conrad would be out of the country; it had been the most marvellous day of his life.

Returning back to Brainforth Conrad never envisaged that his world would be turned upside down. James Jacob's arrival would see to that. At first Jacob was just another prisoner; another waste of space, but then that bloody priest had poked his nose into something he had no right to do. Questioning his faith, he delved into Conrad's past and confronted him about his time as young policeman walking the beat back in the East End of London. Conrad was clever and they talked under the rules of the confessional. The priest was beholden to his faith and the rules of Catholicism. That bloody Priest. The threats to his conscience threatened his sanity. That bloody priest. Threatening him didn't work and it played on Conrad's mind day and night. It was the first time he had felt threatened.

A shadow engulfed him and some mornings he would wake at dawn covered in sweat and swear he could smell the hell of the storeroom back in Krakow. Another day turned into another day and they became longer and longer as a haunting shroud enveloped him. Having covered his tracks in Poland it was the

Ghost Boy and the priest who overwhelmed his burden. Slowly he withdrew from society. Plagued by the nightmares of Jack the Ripper and being known as 'The Shepherd' he would sit in the corner of his bedroom in the dark with his knees up around his chest and self mutilate. Using the nib from the fountain pen he was careful to cut himself where it wouldn't arouse suspicion. Across his chest and stomach he would sheave cuts; once streaming with blood, his torso resembled a side of beef on a butcher's slab. Feeling the world closing in around him he looked at his deadpan face in the mirror and saw how the grey hairs had crept up on him unnoticed. Forgetting he'd grown old and verging on retirement he was seized by childhood memories of his mother which had been buried for years.

At daybreak he found himself walking to the police station with self detest. Giving himself up would be a relief; the anguish of guilt had become unbearable. Outside the police station he was one step through the main entrance when he suddenly heard his father's voice. "Be strong. Stand tall, be proud like the SS." Suddenly realising what he was about to do he turned around and went home; his courage weakening. His only solace was going to the movies. He felt comfortable in the dark. There he would immerse himself in the Wild West and John Wayne. But it was while he was watching a war movie that his father's beliefs were once again rekindled. Portraying German soldiers as stupid and who had the vocabulary of only one word 'Achtung' it infuriated him. Sitting behind a couple who were more interested in putting their tongues down each others throats, he felt repulsion. That night he once again descended into hell and prowled the streets looking for revenge in the only way he knew how. He looked for the priest, but couldn't root him out. As luck had it, a young prostitute, who he had thought about visiting on more than one occasion but never did, escaped his clutches.

Walking the desolate streets he returned home in the early

hours of the morning and once again self mutilated. Blindness clouded the reality of the world he lived in and cutting a series of letters up his arm symbolised his hollow existence.

Then the following day when he woke, it was if nothing had happened. The daily guilt of feeling like a cockroach had disappeared. It was as if sunshine had replaced the ice in his veins.

Pacing the landings of Brainforth with his usual aura of coolness, confidence and professionalism, Conrad's psychotic behaviour never came under suspicion and why should it? Nobody, as far as he knew would ever pick up a Polish newspaper, never mind read one, and as for anyone discussing the Krakow murders, it was none existent. He'd taught himself to forget; blank it out of each working day. Self discipline was what SS soldiers were made of; his father's comforting words of advice were never far away. He was inseparable from his father's Nazi beliefs. In Brainforth his starched white shirt matched his starched persona. Coming across as a trustworthy character, inspiring confidence and even sharing in jokes with the other officers, he was an advocate of moral high ground. His level-headedness was to be admired. But in the back of his mind there was always that bloody priest. Something had to give.

As for Jacob's dream, Conrad found it unnerving. He tried to rebuke himself, but found the reprimanding hour after hour draining. So he had a quiet word in Dutch's ear. "Do the Ghost Boy". For getting rid of Jacob Dutch would receive perks and have a blind eye turned to most of his misdemeanours. He didn't need much encouragement.

With Jacob out of the way there would only be the uncertainty of the priest to contend with. One step at a time. That time came and it was finally to be his downfall.

SIMON LONG AND PAUL AUSTIN
ALIAS
KIT KAT AND FRUIT SHOT
AGED 28 AND 31
ENGLISH
JUNE 1980

CHAPTER TWENTY EIGHT

A double suicide inside Brainforth was never mentioned in the national press nor was it reported on radio or television. It was an embarrassment to the prison authorities and after Conrad's exposure as a serial killer there had to be a fall guy. Governor Hall was that fall guy and his job was pulled from beneath him. Becoming complacent, like the officers around him, his suit had grown tight. And so he was put out to pasture like a race horse which had gone lame.

Fruit Shot who was serving life for the murder of his abusive stepfather wouldn't see outside the prison walls for the next five years. As for Kit Kat, who had done fifteen years inside Brainforth, he was up for parole. Agonizing about the two of them splitting up and Kit Kat's impending release; the thought of being apart from each other became distressingly unbearable to Fruit Shot. Kit Kat had looked after him in more ways than one. Sometimes Fruit Shot took liberties and played on the protection of his lover with other inmates. Nobody will touch me whilst Kit Kat is here to protect me. But with Kit Kat gone there would be many waiting in line who would see Fruit Shot as easy prey, now that his protector was out of the equation.

On Christmas morning, as Bing Crosby's 'White Christmas' played along the landings, Rose discovered them both dead in their cell. Hanging from bed sheets their fingers had to be broken to prise their hands apart. As their bodies were carried out of their cell the prisoners packed the landings and clapped. The applause was deafening.

They had left a note. It read: *We request only one thing. That we be buried together.* The request was never granted.

Kit Kat and Fruit Shot were psychotic; maladjusted; dubious characters. Two peas in pod but Jake had a soft spot for both of them; they found time for him, adopted him and God knows what would have happened to him without them. Infatuated with each other the pattern of their relationship never changed. Kit Kat and Fruit Shot had a blind devotion to each other; their tragic demise and the memories of Brainforth would live on and pursue Jake forever.

CHAPTER TWENTY NINE

1982
At last, after five long years,
the gates of Brainforth would finally roll open.

James Jacob squinted through the darkness and into sparkling sunlight. Bringing his hand up to his forehead he shielded his eyes from the glare of the sun and took a large intake of breath. Already he felt drained. After a restless night which he had put down to the impending excitement of the day that lay before him, he had dressed at 5 a.m. that morning. It took him less than five minutes to pack, and what little possessions he acquired over the last fire years were slung over his shoulder in his kit bag. He tried Qigong but he couldn't concentrate so for the next four hours he found himself sitting on his bunk. All he left behind was a stack of law books that he had studied over the years. When starting off Jake was amazed at the amount of books specializing in Law. Taxation, Sport, Shipping, Road Traffic, Insurance, Energy, Agriculture, there were hundreds and hundreds. Starting off with The Oxford Book of Law for Students, he progressed to Criminal Law and the appeals process.

By luck he found another specialist book about the Criminal Appeal Act going back to 1907 and a section on mistaken identity. On his appeal he represented himself and stated a case some sixty years previous. His appeal was successful, but more enlightening was the fact that he had started to study again. He hoped that the books he left behind would one day help someone else like him.

At his feet was the small leather case his mother had left him. Lost in excitement he had forgotten to take a shower and had skipped breakfast. His hair was combed off his face and the new, loose fitting shirt and new chinos felt and smelt good against his skin. Looking down, his trainers seemed out of place. One of the first things he was going to do was buy a new pair of leather shoes.

Taking in another deep breath, his memory returned momentarily to his first night inside cell number 43 and his father's voice. It had become locked inside his head and now knowing the truth, he reminisced. Every second with him had been a priceless gift. Two minutes earlier he had been escorted across the exercise yard by an officer who didn't look a day over nineteen. Looking towards the large holding cells to where Sam's garden had once bloomed with colour. The small garden along with the green house had gone. His father's grave exhumed for a proper burial to come. In this grey world some things lived on. Where this father's grave had been he noticed two daisies. They were bright white, the only sign of life, and they swayed slightly in a breeze that cut along the ground. *In a few years from now nobody will remember you and nobody will remember me. All that will be left will be the daisies growing up from both our graves.*

Then the sound of the gate and Jake picked up the leather case.

But in less than an hour James Jacob would be dead.

JAMES JACOB
AGED 35
ENGLISH
JUNE 1982

CHAPTER THIRTY

Let there be light.

Jake's time in Brainforth had come to an end. As the gate rolled open he felt euphoric and he found himself whistling for the first time in years. It made him laugh.

A week before his release Jake learnt from Rose the truth about Conrad. With the help of Interpol and the Polish police they had uncovered a crime that had remained unsolved for what had seemed an eternity. In reality for the Krakow police and the victim's families it had been.

Rose found his excitement hard to contain. Bringing tea and cake into Jake's cell the day before his release, Rose related the story of Conrad's killings which had been tracked back by the police, and how Scotland Yard had been assigned to profile Conrad for future crimes involving serial killers. With overcrowding inside Brainforth they had demolished the small garden and greenhouse to make way for a holding unit. Unearthing two tin boxes under the slabs in the greenhouse; they discovered inside a number of items.

Inside one box was a thread worn swastika flag; black and white photographs; the book 'Mein Kampf; a girl's woollen hat; a small tin containing nail scissors and a needle and thread. Inside the other box was the grim discovery of human hair; the victim's hair. Conrad's macabre mementos.

But it was one photograph that completed the profile of Conrad Miller. Learning that he was driven by a 'father fixation' and with the assistance of a Jewish organisation hunting war criminals, they searched the archives had matched one particular photograph from Auschwitz to one found in the tin box.

In the wooden room where the Nazis held the watershed trials of the Polish prisoners William Miller stood straight backed holding court. Smug, he sat behind the wooden desk signing death warrants of the Polish prisoners. Unmistakably, the photograph was of William Miller. Proudly wearing the uniform of the Nazis he wore his trademark black patch over his eye.

Rose thought he knew the person he had been working with for the past decade. He was mistaken. Conrad had left his legacy.

"You're a free man Jacob." Rose offered an olive branch of a handshake. His words there the sweetest Jake had ever heard. The two men shook hands. "Good luck Jake. I doubt whether our paths will ever cross each other again."

"I hope not Mr. Rose."

After his appeal Jake was also being released for good behaviour, but not before he was questioned about what had happened in the prison chapel between Conrad and Father Nolan. He was called up as a witness at an in-depth enquiry. When the news broke of Jake's father being buried inside the prison he had to live for short time with more jibes, – 'Like father like son', he heard the whispers, but he was used to the prison walls talking back to him. If it wasn't for the dying words of the priest and the letter of confession Jake wondered if he would ever have seen daylight again. God knows what would have happened to him. He prayed for Father Nolan more than once.

As the seconds ticked away Jake spared a final thought for the prisoner who was spending his first night locked-up inside and who was surrounded by the walls of cell number 43. God help him.

Brainforth owed Jake nothing and for the first time he didn't want anything from Brainforth. His conscience was free. If only he could have bottled the joy inside him.

Everyone could feel it. It was like and eclectic pulse in the air.

As the world opened before him Jake took his first step to freedom. As a draft of cold wind kissed his cheek, he felt ecstatic. Feeling comfortable with himself and in control he advanced with a triumphant smile into a barrage of cameras and noise. Microphones and a scramble of questions hit him from every angle. Like a rugby scrum, a melee of reporters buffeted Jake, and trying to compose himself, he found his heart racing. Through the huddle of heads he searched for a familiar face. Where was Carol? Would she be there? Would she be with Freddy?

"What are your plans for the future?" Jake looked at a mole-faced reporter holding a dictaphone up to his mouth. Stringent eyes stood out on stalks; his face desperate for a story for tonight's news programme. "What are you going to do on your first night of freedom?"

"Use your imagination."

"Could you comment on the news that The Home Secretary is re-opening your father's case?"

"My father's soul rests with the truth – he will at last be

given a proper burial which he deserves, and I will not rest until his name is cleared of all wrong doing."

"Will you want an official pardon from the Home Secretary?"

"Yes, that's what he deserves. Everyone has the right to a proper burial and have their name engraved on a headstone. "

A cameraman stumbled; regaining his balance, another question came from the side of him. "I'm from the News of the World; my editor has a proposition for you regarding a series of articles."

Then another voice hidden behind another explosion of flash bulbs came at him. "I assume you'll be taking a long holiday somewhere"

"Don't assume anything."

It was a fastidious reply and Jake felt the answer scratch the back of his neck; he wondered where it had come from, how it would be construed. In the morning Jake would find himself on the front page of every daily newspaper. On every news programme that night. The highlight of every television debate. In every work place; in every living room; in every pub across the country.

"Is it true that you were present when the priest and the officer were killed? Can you describe to us what happened?"

Then before he could answer, he saw them.

Standing by the side of a black cab was Carol waving, a strand of hair brushed across her face, her eyes holding tears. Pushing his way through the circle of reporters and onlookers, death hovered towards him.

Then another face; a familiar face, tired, ringed eyes, murderous eyes, then the glint of a blade as it plunged into his chest. As the world turned red a woman screamed, words, venomous words spat from deep inside a man's throat. "I'm sorry. He made me do it. He said be careful of smelling a tulip, there might be a wasp inside. Jesus! What have I done?"

A gargle of blood; the thud of a forehead slamming onto the

cold concrete but he held onto the leather case.

There was horror across their faces and in their eyes as they peered down on him; Jake felt a hand behind his head and warm liquid seeping from his chest. Police sirens; fading milky blue sky; shapes moved out the corner of his eye; cameras flashing; a woman's scream. "Oh God. Please no God." Someone held his hand; eyes darting; cold; so cold; a hand compressing his chest; warm air blown into his mouth; blood on a woman's hands; the taste of blood; a white light; nothing; silence; blackness.

Vince had been recruited; easily recruited; junkies will do anything for a fix. Dutch's revenge was sweet and Vince was a way of showing how he could manipulate people like the devil incarnate. Jake had been the one who got away and he didn't like it. Nobody made a fool of The Dutchman, certainly not someone who had put him on the canvas and who was considered mad. Left with stigma he felt weak and paranoid. Newspaper cuttings of Jake's meteoric rise to fame through the tabloids covered the walls of his cell and the thought of prisoners inside his new prison and back at his old haunt in Brainforth laughing at him drove him to the edge. On hearing of the knifing he burst out laughing. But not for long. A few hours later a young upstart, one of his new recruits who fancied himself as the next number one thrust a blade into his gut. Not once, but sixteen times. Amazingly he survived.

There is a saying in Holland. 'Be careful of smelling a tulip, there might be a wasp inside'. It was his message.

Vince, high on heroin, disposed of the knife over the bridge into a river, the same river where he had committed a murder when he was a young boy. Once again that river played a part in his life; death in its bloody waters. He was later caught and would spend half his life behind bars.

People who have died and who have been brought back to life say that their life flashes before their eyes. They see themselves as young children, as teenagers, then adults. As for Jake he recognised his father and mother instantly. Their arms around him were blankets of comfort. They said something but Jake could not hear.

Jake watched them somehow; an out of body experience of sorts. A dream within a dream.

Then light and James Jacob came back.

Carol's face looked down on Jake and he felt her hand stroke his forehead. His chest was tight. Wired up to a cardiac machine. Not for the first time. He was told by his doctor that he had 'a good set of lungs and that his breathing had helped save him.' Taking up Qigong had saved his life. He thanked God and then thanked him again.

A week later Jake left hospital. Carol in his arms was the best feeling in the world. A feeling that he'd dreamt about for over five years. Five long years. A kiss; her lips on his; the sweetest, a kiss that would last forever.

Oblivious to the world around him Jake climbed gingerly into the back of a cab. Driving off to another blaze of flashing cameras and the shouts of the press Jake slumped into the back in the cab and looked at himself as a young boy.

"Say hello to you daddy Freddy."

"Hello son."

"Hello Daddy." His voice was quiet, confused, overcome by the moment.

Looking into Carol's eyes Jake took hold of her hand as the emotion welled up inside both of them.

"Who is that man mummy?"

"Which man?"

As the cab sped away from the hospital Freddy was kneeling on the seat and pointing out of the back window.

Carol looked. "I don't see anybody."

"He has been smiling and waving at me."

Jake turned and looked through the window. Standing by the side of a tree was his father. Wearing the same prison clothes and the same patched-up glasses. His smile was mute, kind and happy, as if he was holding back.

Carol searched for somebody and then took her eyes back to Jake. "I don't see anyone, do you?"

A smile of contentment shone across Jake's face. "Yes."

A tear rolled down his cheek as he held his father's gaze for a few seconds before he slowly vanished.

A mile along the main road the cab stopped at traffic lights. In the distance the giant walls of Brainforth bled into the sunset.

In Southeast Asia there is a snake that is called The Taipan. Anyone unfortunate to be bitten by one has minutes to live. A single bite sets the heart racing out of control and its venom can kill up to a hundred adults. Shooting through the blood stream, the venom attacks the autonomic nervous system, triggering an anaphylactic reaction which paralyses the brain and the body. Causing a meltdown of the nervous system, the heart stops for a number of minutes. In some recorded incidents, where a person has been bitten and survived after the swift administration of venom coursing through their veins patients are unable to speak with eyes wide open. They can see and acutely hear everything that goes on around them. Not unlike the living dead of stroke patients. Clinically in those recorded minutes when the heart stops they have been presumed dead.

There were many people who were directly or indirectly affected by 'The Shepherd'; families; the Krakow police; the hanging of Jim Abbott; an innocent man to name a few. On the morning Conrad died he had been hypnotically drawn into cell number 43.

Suddenly the cell door slammed shut behind him. "You're a failure. A useless good for nothing." It was his father's voice. Sitting on the bottom bunk was his drunken mother. "You little prick." Letters were branded onto her bare arm; the floor covered in his victim's hair. Lambasting him for being a failure in life and for not having the strength to change the world, which had been his duty to man-kind both his father's words and his mother's merged into a torrent of abuse.

Irrevocably, his last seconds on earth where as if he had been bitten by The Taipan Snake. Paralysed, unable to move or speak. Eyes bulging open, he saw the clouds moving above Brainforth. Irony has a strange way of coming back to haunt you. When hitting the ground both Conrad's shoulder blades shattered and dislocated. Around his neck was the gold pendant. Engraved on the back was the Star of David and the student's name Garrett. Inside the locket were two photographs of his grandparents. Both had died in Auschwitz and both had worked in Shindler's factory. Conrad's eyes then slowly closed as the world died around him. But before his evil spirit lifted from his body he watched as the coffin lid closed shut on him and he listened to it being screwed down. Blackness. Voiceless whispers. The roar of the furnace. Then he heard his voice. "What goes around comes around; welcome to hell 'Shepherd'. Your father is waiting."

Sometimes, more than most, as the way of the world, good news follows bad and vice versa. The years had taught Jake to acknowledge his crime and that serving his time was justified. There were times when he had thought he'd lost his mind. The thought of never holding Carol again or watching his son grow up, hear him laugh, watch him play, become a fine adult, get married and have children of his own would have killed him and for several minutes it did. As the paramedics fought frantically to save his life in the back of the ambulance he saw his mother and father together for the first time. Their love held no bounds and it gave his life meaning. Carol and Freddy were the sweetest of rewards. Fate has a funny way of showing it; if Jake hadn't been put in cell number 43 on his first night inside Brainforth he would never have found his Shangri-La, met his father or discovered spiritual enlightenment. Tragic circumstances had brought them together but his father was to become Jake's spiritual guide. After much deliberation and soul-searching Jake was convinced he was. Far fetched? Life knows things we don't, and the story will run on and on.

Jake would always carry his father in his heart and some days he swore he could hear his voice on the wind.

ACKNOWLEDGEMENTS
'The best thing you can give anyone is time'.

In writing this second novel I would like to thank certain friends and family who have made it possible. Sharon Fadden, Mike Fadden, John Hassall, Sam Gibson, Angela Hannah, Joe Gibson, Gary Davies, Elaine Saunders, Joshua Polkinghorne, Rachael Polkinghorne, Andy Jackson, Hannah Jackson, Peter Forest, Cushla Allison-Baker, Steve Price, David Thompson and to my two wonderful daughters Chloe and Molly.

Special thanks go to Cheryl Barber, Malcolm Barber, Steve Barber and Pete Horner for their enthusiasm in the publication of this book. To my dear sister Clare and to Paul and Hazel Gee who have been my sounding boards on more than one occasion; their belief in me is unfounded.

In researching this book I have had the support of two great friends. Brian Hughes who defined certain terminologies and text and to Keith Raybould whose expert background and knowledge in police investigation work has been invaluable.

In the winter of 2010 I visited Auschwitz on the outskirts of Krakow in Poland. It was partially my inspiration for writing this book and an experience that will live with me forever.

If you have enjoyed reading *Declaration of Guilt* you are now invited to read an extract from Marc Gee's third novel to be published in 2011 titled, *'Have you heard about Alex Sinner?'*

"Have you heard about Alex Sinner?"
"What about Alex Sinner?"
"He's been arrested for murder."
"You're joking."
"I never joke about murder?"

I was arrested for the murder of Tony Phillips at dawn. Am I innocent or guilty? Now there hangs the dilemma. In proclaiming my innocence to the police I have one major problem. I can't remember a single thing that happened last night.

By the way my name is Alex Sinner.

Apparently, I had sat drinking with Tony Phillips in a bar called Holland's for a couple of hours. Which is strange, considering he doesn't like me and I don't like him. We have a history. His body was found an hour after closing time on a winding footpath running alongside the canal. His skull had been caved in at the back of his head. So you can see my problem.

"How long have you known Tony Phillips?"
"Over thirty years."
"Why did you kill him?"
"I didn't."
"You said, and I quote. 'I can't remember a thing about last night'."
"I know I said that but you would remember killing somebody. Wouldn't you?"
"I don't know, you tell me."

As I said; you can see my problem.

And that's how much of the day has evolved. Told to strip, I was thrown a white overall whilst my clothes were sent off for forensic examination. And so I'm left here waiting for my solicitor to arrive. The only thing I have for company is a dog-eared magazine and lukewarm cup of tea with one spoon of sugar too many. As for the jungle drums in my home town I can imagine them going into overdrive. So, while I'm sitting here alone in a holding cell I may as well relate my story to you. After all it passes the time and I've got nothing better to do.

I was born and raised in Brainforth in Oxfordshire. They only thing that my town is famous for is Brainforth Prison which sits along the main High Street like a Victorian dinosaur. It's usually on the TV for all the wrong reasons. I'm a regular visitor there which I will come to later. It has never occurred to me that one day I might end up in there serving time; it never does I suppose until it's too late. We'll see.

Brainforth Town holds a population of around fifty thousand people. Everyone knows someone who knows somebody. Over the years I have attended the local primary and secondary school and played football for Brainforth FC, the local team. I have a son called Shaun, who is named after my father who originally came from Cork in Ireland. I won't tell you about the divorce just yet, this story is depressing enough already.

Anyway, everyone knows each other in Brainforth. If I need a plumber, I know one; if I need an electrician, I know one; if I need a mechanic, I know one and guess what, if they need a gas fitter they know me. They scratch my back and I scratch theirs and it's been like that for years. Good mates, people who you can rely on. I even went to school with my solicitor. He was always late and still is, some things never change. Get the drift?

At our football club we run five teams. Eleven players a team, plus a couple of subs if we're lucky, that's fifty to sixty players, plus the manager and a handful of fans and ex-players who bravely stand on the touchline in all sorts of weather, so say around a hundred people are associated with our club if my maths are correct. Notice I said 'our club'. At the end of the season party every player usually brings a partner with them. Double it, that's two hundred people, who I directly or indirectly know through just kicking a ball around. Then there are their kids and friends of friends. Not to mention the cricket club which I play for and who run three teams. Brainforth is a close community, incestuous at times. Like a spider's web of close friends, associates and business contacts. If anyone goes to work away or emigrates they always return like a bad penny. That's why everyone knows everyone in my small town of Brainforth. But not everyone likes everyone.

So let me take you back forty years ago. Alex Sinner, sixteen, school boy, horny. That was me. We've all been there. Acne, shaving for the first time, girlfriends and my first run-in with Tony Phillips. He was from a different school and was a Roman Catholic. He was bigger than me, better looking than me and basically superior in every way, than me. Was I jealous? Looking back you bet I was. But then there was Barbara Buckley. For some strange reason Barbara Buckley fancied me and not Tony Phillips and he couldn't come to terms with it. His ego had been nudged in the wrong direction by this little shit who was useless at everything and he didn't like it one bit.

That's when the first of many punches were thrown between Alex Sinner and Tony Phillips.

AUTUMN KILL

Marc Gee

To order online please go to www.troubador.co.uk

PRAISE FOR *AUTUMN KILL*

"I love it when you start reading a book and you don't know where it's going to take you and the more you read the more intrigued you get. This certainly happened with *Autumn Kill* and I wasn't disappointed."
Nickie Mackay, BBC Radio Merseyside.

"A gripping first novel, taut with the body count rising from the first chapter."
Dr C Allison Baker, Criminal Profiler.

"I read a lot of books. Wow! I read it over the weekend, the kids never got fed and the housework was put on hold. Could not put Autumn Kill down."
Maria Byrne, Leasowe Library Manager.

Recommended in Waterstone's top summer reads for 2010.